THE SECOND MARY

Cassandra Bohne

Tribulation Publishing
CYPRESS, TEXAS

Cassandra Bohne/Tribulation Publishing
P.O. Box 1457
Cypress, Texas 77410+1457
www.tribulationpublishing.com
info@tribulationpublishing.com

Publisher's Note: This is a work of fiction. Names, characters, places, and incidents are a product of the author's imagination. Locales and public names are sometimes used for atmospheric purposes. Any resemblance to actual people, living or dead, or to businesses, companies, events, institutions, or locales is completely coincidental.

Book Layout ©2013 BookDesignTemplates.com

Scripture quotations marked (NKJV) are taken from the New King James Version®. Copyright © 1982 by Thomas Nelson. Used by permission. All rights reserved

Scripture quotations marked (NIV) are taken from THE HOLY BIBLE, NEW INTERNATIONAL VERSION®, NIV® Copyright © 1973, 1978, 1984, 2011 by Biblica, Inc.® Used by permission. All rights reserved worldwide.

Ordering Information:
Quantity sales. Special discounts are available on quantity purchases by corporations, associations, and others. For details, contact the "Special Sales Department" at the email address above.

The Second Mary/ Cassandra Bohne. -- 1st ed.
ISBN 978-0-9983140-0-6

To Mica – for your love and protection, then and now, I thank you.

Are you ready for His return?

—CASSANDRA BOHNE

CHAPTER ONE

The First Vision

I couldn't have been more than seven years of age when everything began.

It was a bright and crisp, picture-perfect summer day. The clouds were on extended holiday as the perfectly blue, velvety soft sky gave way to an expansive, blank slate. As far as I was concerned, all was right in the world.

My best friend, Lisa, and I were playing in and around my next door neighbor's classic pick-up truck, as we typically did for light entertainment on those wonderful, worry-free days of summer fun and shenanigans. Lisa and I habitually chased each other around the top of the bed of Mr. Cunningham's truck and jumped off frantically when things got a little too close for comfort. I usually hopped off from the back of the truck onto the hard, hot pavement of the driveway or from the right side onto the plush, green lawn. The latter, of course, was my preferred method of escaping. On this particular day, in this specific instance, I chose to take a dive onto the comfortable, well-kept lawn.

As I began my routine trajectory off of the pick-up truck bed, my eyes travelled down to the yard below and, instead of soaring off of the vehicle, I came to an immediate stop. I gripped and secured my foothold and balance and glued myself to the truck to keep from plummeting into the very depths of the hair-raising hell that had literally been unearthed before my very eyes. The casing of my body froze solid as my blood curdled and fears skyrocketed.

In one fleeting second, the beautiful, perfectly kept grass had vanished, as if the top layer of the earth had been meticulously peeled away so that I could personally bear witness to the horror of what lie lurking underneath. Standing just shy of four feet tall, I stood before a spine-tingling view of the earth's dark and cavernous interior that appeared to reach the depths of a few hundred feet below the ground.

An intense heat emanated from the rocky grounds to the cave walls and tunnels; the entire subterranean cavity was covered with a deep orange glow. Patches of dancing flames were also scattered throughout the entire cavern. The flames and radiant heat were the only light sources in what would have been an otherwise pitch black abyss.

A string of withered and shriveled zombie-like men and women were slavishly chained to one another. Laboriously, they walked in a sluggish procession as though they were being led to an ill-fated destination against their will. Their faces screamed silently with unimaginable torment and fatigue; their dilapidated bodies could barely muster up the strength to move. Their damned souls yearned for a death that would never greet them.

Several well disseminated ladders connected the strata. All but one of the ladders remained well beneath the surface of the earth. However, one of the ladders reached high enough to where the lawn should have been. Well within my reach, I could have climbed down on it quite effortlessly if I had desired to do so but I was paralyzed by extreme fright.

Chief, authoritative figures marched throughout the region and monitored each of the tunnels and working areas. They seemed to have more stamina than the chained slaves but the same stench of dread and death encased each of the factions, generals and prisoners alike. It was fairly difficult to discern the task at hand or what they were trying to accomplish, but it seemed as though they could have been refining the walls and unstable elements.

I looked up to discover that the brilliant, blue sky I had just frolicked under had morphed into complete darkness. Thick obscurity permeated the air surrounding me. My best friend had disappeared and there was no one else in sight. I didn't understand what had just happened. I was alone in this bleak and threatening realm. And although the summer sun had just been blazing and inebriating heat sprung from the hell below, an incredible icy chill suddenly fell upon me.

Atrocious thoughts crept through the thousands of tiny crevices in my mind as I peered into the frightening province of the hell revealed to me just below the surface of my neighbor's front yard. For one fleeting moment, I wondered whether the tall, lanky ladder within my reach was meant for me to climb down on. I trembled as I imagined someone or, even worse, *something*, climb up out of the deep, fiery chasm. I even pondered the unthinkable notion of death, my own death.

Had I just died? Was this the sunken route to the consuming pits of hell? Did this monstrous gorge open its buried doors for the sole purpose of devouring my tiny, insignificant body? Was this noxious catacomb meant to serve as my final resting place?

The torrent of petrifying possibilities left me hopeless and terrified. Despondent and alone, I desperately desired to set my eyes upon the beautiful world I had inhabited only seconds before.

Would I ever return to it? Would I ever see my family and friends again?

I shut my desolate and frightened eyes as these shocking thoughts and questions paraded through my frazzled mind. I just couldn't bear the grisly sight any longer. Then, just as quickly as it had appeared, with one single blink, the vision of hell vanished. The lavish green lawn returned and was entirely intact. I looked up at the kind, comforting sky and felt the greatest sense of relief as the warm sun beat down on my still cold, shivering skin.

And that was the end of it.

Needless to say, I was traumatized and disturbed for many months, maybe even years. My bewildered brain attempted to process what had happened to me at such an early age, but more importantly why it had happened. My efforts proved to be fruitless.

I considered whether other people had inexplicable experiences such as mine. Could others out there have had similar appalling visions as clear and convincing as my own? Even though my curiosity had reached its peak, I couldn't dare reach out or even mention the forbidden subject to anyone I knew. I was left in oblivion, with no answers. I had nothing to go on but my own haunted memories.

As difficult as it was, I struggled obstinately to erase these horrific images from my mind and foolishly pretended that the vision never transpired. I tried to assure myself that the curious, paranormal episode was actually a freakishly realistic nightmare or a meaningless hallucination.

Despite my concerted energies, I could not convince myself of such nonsense. The unspeakable event was just as real as I was. For some unknown reason the gates of hell were opened to me when I was just learning to live and function in a world much larger than I could have possibly dreamt of!

Needless to say, I could never bring myself to step foot inside Mr. Cunningham's truck again.

I didn't dare speak of this appalling experience to a single soul, although I was troubled by it for most of my early life. I didn't know then that this traumatic event marked the first milestone in a lifelong voyage of self-discovery. This was the first of many enigmatic, supernatural encounters that would later come my way. Of course, I was only a small child then so I couldn't begin to understand or fathom the grand plans God had in store for my life. But what mortal being ever could?

CHAPTER TWO

Childhood

Growing up, primarily due to the ever increasing stresses with my immediate family, I chose to spend the majority of my weekends, summers and school holidays with my grandparents. I likened my grandparents' humble abode to my safe haven, my sanctuary. Throughout every phase of my life I carried many beautiful and fond memories of my kind and compassionate grandparents; my love and care for them ran deeply. In many ways, the love they generously poured out on me nourished me and more than made up for the lack of affection I felt at my own home.

My grandfather was a loving, kindhearted man and without question, served as the spiritual leader of the family. He was especially stern and uncompromising when it came to what was allowed to sneak in or infiltrate his family's vulnerable eyes and ears. As a result, our everyday activities were very different than most folks. We often rotated through different pastors on the television set instead of settling for the obscenities that most families opted for. At bedtime, we routinely fell asleep listening to sermons that my grandfather had recorded on his trusty cassette tapes. He had a vast collection.

My grandfather also encouraged me to read the Bible for at least one hour each and every day I came to visit, which ultimately resulted in many hours of scrupulous, dedicated biblical study. I didn't begrudge my reading sessions nor did I particularly care for them; I simply did as I was told. In no time at all, I grew so accustomed to the Bible sittings that surveying His word became second nature. I familiarized myself with each of the Bible characters and their incredible, unbelievable stories. His word astounded me. I took everything I read as complete truth. After all, this holy manuscript represented a physical manifestation of the word of the Eternal God. How could any of it not be true?

My grandmother was a simple, uneducated woman who, in any circumstance, carried with her a tremendous faith in Jesus Christ. This resolute conviction was her greatest source of strength and managed to see her through the toughest of times. My grandmother was exceptionally spiritual and not at all religious. In fact, most of her Pentecostal family shunned her repeatedly for straying from their strict dogmatic doctrines. But my diligent grandmother paid no attention to their blatant indignation; she stood firmly on God's word and her concrete foundation could not be shaken.

I, too, was a strong, unqualified Christian but I was much too young, both physically and spiritually, to truly appreciate an unshakeable faith of the magnitude my grandmother exuded. I admired my devout grandmother and her unwavering Christian beliefs. Her fundamental character was uncontaminated and pure; she lived every day of her modest life with the indestructible faith of a child of the Most High God.

There was never any doubt that I was my grandmother's favorite grandchild. Similar to the obvious envy liberally bestowed upon me by my brothers and cousins, my aunts even displayed acts of jealousy and resentment towards me; they knew I could do no wrong in my grandmother's eyes.

Although we shared a very lovely bond and a spectacular array of cherished moments, there were some other not so bright recollections of our relationship that I could never break free of. My grandmother was used to conveying arcane messages to me that I was never able to come to grips with at such an early age. The emphatic echoes of her dismal communications afflicted me for many years.

Throughout my childhood, my grandmother repeatedly emphasized, quite nonchalantly and with great conviction, that the devil had been pursuing me, though she never explained why. In all likelihood, she may not have actually known his motives. There were no hidden undertones in her message, no anger or any type of malicious intent to frighten me. Her frequent admonitions were rather sincere and very matter of fact.

Never in my life had I heard of such bold or outrageous allegations, so I naturally tried to rationalize the preposterous claims. Initially, I took this "nonsense" to be my grandmother's naivety or superstitious, cultural influences shining through. For the most part, I ignored her brazen assertions. But, as time progressed, I began to notice that she never mentioned these ridiculous notions to any of my brothers, aunts or cousins; she only directed these very precise and disturbing words towards me. My persuasive grandmother expressed this stern belief so often that there was a defining moment in my life when the bizarre admonition began to sink in, take root and sprout.

I often mulled over whether this sly devil my grandmother regularly referred to could really have been after me. It didn't make any sense at all. What could I have possibly done to catch his eye or upset him? My thoughts later morphed into, "Why is the devil after me?" Soon my question solidified into, "Why isn't he after anyone else?" In a world full of billions, why was I on his radar? Why was I singled out? After all, I was just a young, innocent child.

Or was I?

When I was about 8 years old my mother drove my grandmother to visit a family friend. I happened to tag along, as I often did when my mother played the distinguished role of my grandmother's chauffer. This particular family friend happened to dabble in some of what I referred to as the "dark arts," though I can't recall which specific "art" she practiced. I could never forget the look of absolute astonishment on the woman's pale face when she opened the door to find little old me standing motionless on the steps of her meek and overcrowded porch.

Her eyes lit up and sparkled as she marveled in amazement. The woman looked at me in an intriguing, inquisitive manner and then immediately redirected her gaze approximately three to four feet directly above my head. Her countenance beamed liked the blazing stars in the heavens as she stared seemingly into mid-air, obviously overcome by something incredible. I looked up and found exactly what I had expected, nothing.

As the mystic scrutinized the space just above me, she told my grandmother that I had a guardian angel towering over me, protecting me. The woman knelt down to my level and repeated herself, as though I didn't hear her the first time she made her announcement. Softly, she whispered that my angel loved me very much and casually recommended that I wear some kind of angel pendant or ring to show my acknowledgment and gratitude.

Specific details regarding the angel's appearance or sex were not revealed. Regretfully, I didn't bother to ask any questions. I may have been too enthralled by the fascinating concept that I overlooked the particulars. I didn't know whether angels were even categorized by gender type but I let my imagination run wild; I envisioned my guardian to be a powerful, soaring male.

I didn't know what to make of this woman. Might she have been mad? I seriously doubted that she was crazy but I knew, without a doubt, that she most certainly was not a normal human being. She possessed a very rare gift whereby she could see beyond our physical world into the supernatural or nonphysical realm. She was convinced of my towering, protective angel and my grandmother and mother did not hesitate to adhere to her claims.

I didn't affirm the unusual, albeit inspiring, observation nor did I show any hint of excitement. Although I projected a sense of reticence, the truth was that I was filled with joy. I had always sensed that there was some sort of enigmatic, defensive spiritual force surrounding me; I just didn't know how to rationalize or explain it. I could never bring myself to make such bold or outrageous proclamations.

Despite my outward indifference to these angelic assertions, deep inside, my soul soared with a delightful confirmation. I jumped up and down with excitement, comforted to know that my angel was there with me, just like I believed he had been all along. The difference was that this time someone else besides me knew it as well.

Against my instruction, I didn't rush out to buy any specific trinket representative of my belief in angelic beings. I didn't believe in this form of hollow tokenism. I was certain that my noble protector recognized my deep appreciation; I didn't need a memento or relic to demonstrate my fervent esteem.

It wasn't very long after this eye-opening and uplifting incident that my mother, grandmother and I attended a very memorable Sunday evening church service. As I covertly disregarded the sermon and delved into my own imaginary world, I was soon greeted by a portly gentleman with short, dark wavy hair. The stranger smiled at me, from the row directly behind me, with friendly, welcoming gestures. He looked as though he had just about as much interest in the sermon as I did, which happened to be about slim to none. My intuition told me that he would have liked to keep me company in my fantasy world rather than heed the monotonous message crying out to his deaf ears.

My newfound "friend" and I exchanged innocent pleasantries throughout the evening but as the closing comments were underway I looked back and found nothing but a vacant seat. My buddy was nowhere to be found. I thought he had gone without saying goodbye but, sadly, I was mistaken. We were reunited in the desolate parking lot where he impatiently waited while pacing outside of his run-down, navy blue compact car.

Like a ton of bricks caving in and crushing me, it suddenly became very clear to me that this man was not at all friendly; my new "friend" actually wanted to harm me. My heart pounded as I realized that his mission was to kidnap me and take me away from my family. My mother and grandmother must have noticed his charismatic trickeries in the church auditorium because the very moment they saw him, they too began to panic.

Where had all the churchgoers run off to? There was no one in the barren parking lot that we could yell out to for help. Cell phones were somewhat of a rarity then so we weren't left with many options. We couldn't call the police or reach out to anyone in the family. This was one of those classic fight or flight moments that I had recently learned about in school; without a moment's hesitation the three of us naturally chose flight!

Frantically, we leaped inside our car and my mother drove off faster than Danny Zuko's iconic take-off in Grease. Instead of taking the usual route home, my supercharged mom zigzagged rapidly through one of the nearby subdivisions. With some sensational methodical maneuvering, we eventually lost the depraved animal that, only minutes before, was just a few feet away from capturing his young, trusting prey.

I was astonished and incredibly grateful for my mother's remarkably impressive NASCAR-like racing skills. I believed adamantly that the path of protection laid out for us and our ultimate safety was meticulously orchestrated by my guardian angel. I thanked God and His loyal messenger for saving my life.

Naturally, this terribly scarring event plagued me for many years. And although this tragedy was one of my first encounters with the enemy, it was far from the last.

I had my firsthand invitation to the sinister world of the occult during my early middle school years. For the most part, I was relatively naïve and ignorant with regards to their customary practices and beliefs. I could not comprehend that people, let alone children, would actually make a decision to worship the devil. Why would anyone want to be on Satan's ghoulish team? How could someone freely choose to dedicate their life and surrender their soul to supreme darkness and depravity? This concept, so foreign to me, was actually quite rampant. I was shown, very early on, just how much of an overwhelming stronghold Satan had on our society. The devil had a voracious appetite and his preoccupation didn't stop with adults only; the formidable practice of witchcraft was a reality prevalent even among middle school aged children.

The faction that I was first introduced to happened to be an all-girls club who, for some reason, had their evil eyes fixed on me. Most days, the pre-teen delinquents wore all black clothing with dark, crimson red lipstick. Their rigid attire and makeup were reminiscent of the heavy metal bands that my stealthy aunt would watch on MTV, when my grandparents weren't around, of course.

For about six months, this sinful clique actively tried to recruit me into their wicked organization. At first, they befriended me, quite subtly. Then they began to open up and share some of their dark and dire hobbies with me in hopes of enticing and luring me in. Most of their questionable rituals were performed during the school lunch hour and Physical Education out on the playing grounds. Thin branches and sticks were used to draw arcane symbols in the dirt; the only one that was clear to me was the infamous pentagram. Each of the girls carried cryptic tokens and relics with writing and symbols completely foreign to me. They used their cherished Ouija board to communicate with spirits from the other side. The band of loyal followers constantly prayed to their leader, Satan.

My connection with their association was purely educational. My curiosity was peaked and I was slightly interested in knowing what they did, although I could never comprehend why they did it. Neither the girls themselves nor any of their peculiar activities frightened or intimidated me in any way. They were just another up and coming ensemble eagerly trying to expand their inadequate presence. They soon found their rigorous labors were wasted as I had no thoughts of joining their immoral assembly. Eventually they gave up their recruiting efforts but made it very clear that the door would always be open for me if I were to ever have a change of heart.

It didn't take long for me to appreciate that evil was heavily disseminated and more widespread in this world than I had ever imagined. The wholesome place that I once believed to be unadulterated had suddenly and permanently ceased to exist. The ravenous devil had his far-reaching hands in our innocent school systems. His cunning clutches had even infiltrated our sacred churches. What disturbed and intrigued me even more than my stark awakening was that I was beginning to recognize that the devil had been burning to get his filthy hands on me!

CHAPTER THREE

Gifts From Above

In my junior year of college God presented me with a very rare, precious gift that I would come to treasure for the rest of my life. There was no telling how valuable His generous endowment would later prove to be or how it would be intricately linked to my destiny. How could I have ever fathomed that this gift would one day function as a vital instrument in God's divine plan, a plan literally designed of biblical proportions!

For personal reasons primarily related to family, I attended a local university and lived with my parents during my college years. One solemn afternoon I sat quietly in my bedroom reflecting on my life and the drifting, aimless direction it was apparently headed in. I happened to be caught in a concentrated, philosophical meditation when a powerful concept came over me like a stubborn winter wind. I suddenly had a persuasive notion to pick up oil painting as a brand new hobby. The thought of lifting a paintbrush had never before entered my mind nor did I have any noticeable interest in the arts themselves. But this idea was more than a fleeting whim; it felt more like an instruction. The strange thing was that the very strong directive wasn't at all self-imposed. The overwhelming ordinance originated from somewhere far outside of me; it came from above.

13

Without a speck of schooling or "Painting for Dummies" guidance, I didn't give the silly notion a second thought. Filled with enthusiasm, I got dressed and presumptuously set out to the nearest art supply shop. Like a toddler on a university campus, I wandered around the innovative and unfamiliar territory in oblivion and grabbed what I believed to be the fundamental tools necessary to activate this new, exciting voyage. I picked up a few canvases, some tubes of paint, a couple of bristle brushes and a small, unassuming wooden easel.

When I got back home I set up all of the equipment in my bedroom as best as I knew how. I sat in my cozy new "art studio" in stupefaction. I sat and sat for what seemed like an eternity. Dumbfounded, I had no idea what to do or where to begin. As I struggled to trigger this new initiative I decided to pour myself a soothing and relaxing glass of rich, red wine. As the delicious libation settled in, I began to squeeze some of the thick paint out of the tubes. Without thought or any apparent awareness, my paintbrush magically swirled its way onto the blank, beckoning canvas.

Before I knew it, my first piece was done. It was a playful, colorful abstract resembling a few planets bursting their way through the universe. Or it could have been microscopic organisms magnified to full zoom. I really didn't know what it was. The curious painting had basically created itself while I obediently held the brush and watched as it sprang to life.

The compulsion to paint came from a force that stemmed from somewhere deep inside of my soul, well beyond my consciousness or understanding. Somehow, I was unconsciously driven to pick up the paint brush and get to work. Initially, I was stumped and mystified. I later discovered the extraordinary truth behind the mystery; the impulse came directly from God or the Holy Spirit. His commanding spirit overcame me and spontaneously compelled me to paint at His will; I had no choice in the matter.

In essence, I was God's medium as He painted through me. The experience was almost ceremonial. Each time "we" painted, I drank a glass of red wine; sometimes I even indulged with two. I played tranquil, uplifting music in the background; classic oldies, a Billie Holiday collection, romantic medleys or an inspirational Christian mix seemed to work quite well. I had no earthly idea what I was doing or what I was creating. I was oblivious to any form of technique or talent. I simply surrendered my compliant and cooperative hand to Him and He graciously took complete control.

It didn't take me long to realize that I could not paint of my own volition. On several occasions I endeavored to take on this daunting task without His divine nudging, but I inevitably failed, quite miserably, with each attempt. I was so humiliated by my paltry efforts that I immediately disposed of the canvases before anyone could witness the shameful mess I had made. The few times that I endeavored to paint without the wine also proved to be disastrous and disgraceful.

Was I trying to prove to myself that God's spirit was indeed working through me? Maybe I was trying to see whether or not I had any ability of my own; it quickly became rather evident that I did not. Because the precipitous urge to paint came so unexpectedly, I may have been trying to alleviate any underlying doubts and gain some level of understanding. I quickly learned that in order to paint successfully, I needed both the divine inspiration and a measure of red wine on the side. There seemed to be a special, intangible quality trapped deep inside the DNA of this heavenly elixir.

As the years passed, I came to cherish this unique, supernatural rendezvous that I alone shared with my heavenly Father. Each private session was beyond beautiful and incredibly intimate. None of His paintings appeared to be associated with one another; each one had a very unique style and technique. I never questioned what each distinctive piece represented. I never even considered why He chose to paint through me. None of this mattered at the time. I was incredibly blessed to have this glorious, surreal relationship with God. And although He didn't call on me to paint very often, I was always ready when He did. I felt like a curious, impatient child, anxiously eager to see what work of art He would create next.

It was also during my college years that I became cognizant of another one of His priceless gifts. I was twenty years old when I knew with absolute certainty that I could sense the presence of evil. God had graciously granted me the astounding ability to discern spirits.

I could have possessed this protective trait earlier in my youth but without being fully conscious of it. One of my stronger recollections of this awareness occurred early one morning while shopping at the grocery store. Capriciously, I walked down an aisle and passed by a gentleman who was carefully considering the products on the shelf. No eye contact was made between us. He didn't once look in my direction; he stood there statue-like, carefully examining his buying options. Just as I passed him by, my spiritual antenna rose to high alert status. I sensed a strong supernatural influence informing me that this man was up to no good, he had evil spirits dwelling inside of his soul. I was confused and staggered by the awareness and communication travelling from my spirit to my mortal mind. Although stunned by this compelling, intuitive voice, I wasn't accustomed to receiving these arcane messages so I simply ignored the beacon and carried on with my shopping.

Just a few minutes later, I sensed the ominous admonition and heard my spiritual voice warning me that evil was nearby. I stopped dead in my tracks, turned around and discreetly surveyed my surroundings. Interestingly enough, the same man was just down near the end of the aisle. Still empty handed, he prudently examined the shelves in the same manner as he had done before. He slyly glanced in my direction, but instantly turned away when he found me staring right back at him. Unlike the time before, this time I opted to heed the warning God had spiritually communicated to me. As I continued with my shopping I kept my newly discovered antennae raised. I found that this stranger and I just "happened to be" in the same aisles several more times. It became fairly obvious that I was being pursued. Although I didn't know his exact intentions, I recognized that his plans were nothing short of malevolent. In the end I stealthily evaded him, left my cart of groceries behind and made a speedy getaway.

As I became further mindful of my capabilities, it seemed that my God-given gift strengthened and developed.

One Sunday afternoon as I headed to a nearby ATM, my spiritual radar buzzed with a great tenacity. I wasn't cognizant of the fact that there was a vehicle in close proximity until my spirit informed me of a nearby evil presence. Without even looking at my surroundings, I sensed imminent danger. The second I peered into my rear view mirror, I immediately recognized that that was where the unwholesome entity originated from. I had to figure out a way to outmaneuver my pursuer. Without a moment's hesitation, I turned into the bank parking lot.

The bank was closed; there were no parked cars anywhere in sight and the ATM line was deserted. The main road even appeared to be abnormally barren. I decided to hide along the back side of the building instead of going straight through to the ATM. The classic, black Trans Am grazed slowly through the parking lot. I glanced inconspicuously at the driver as he cruised by, but his window tint was pitch-black and I couldn't make out a clear identity. In fact, I couldn't make out anything at all.

He zoomed by, but instead of stopping at the ATM, he went straight through it and raced out of the parking lot.

With time, I realized that I could rely on my "sixth sense" without question, even in heavily crowded areas.

Early one morning, as I walked into a congested grocery store entrance, I immediately detected evil. There were people coming and going when the advantageous warning sounded off. I inspected my surrounding area in hopes of locating the guilty perpetrator. As soon as I laid my eyes on him, I knew, without a doubt, that this man was the culprit. Like the Terminator, I felt as though I was preprogrammed with the villain's specific profile and data file; as soon as he was in my sight, I fiercely locked onto my target. The charlatan was innocently looking at the newspaper stand as I subtly examined his appearance and took a mental snapshot of his unpleasant features. I then wandered off into the store.

Cautiously, I scanned my environment as I strolled through the aisles. For the duration of my visit, the perilous figure was nowhere to be seen. I thought he had gone. However, as I exited the store, I spotted the lurking predator parked in the front row of the parking lot. His beat up, navy blue pick-up truck was parked so that it faced the direction of the store entrance. The truck ignition sprung to life the moment our eyes connected. I immediately went back inside the store to find a security guard. The guard escorted me outside and the malefactor sped away as soon as he saw that I had protection by my side.

Since the first notable and memorable occurrence, I subsequently experienced a myriad of other eerie incidences where an evil presence was either nearby or intended to harm me. I never stopped to question why, suddenly, I was bestowed with the priceless gift of recognizing evil and mal-intent. I never wondered if these events were uniquely mine or if experiences such as these were common or perhaps even universal. Nor did I stop to ponder why the devil and his ruthless and relentless army appeared to be after me. I didn't consider the outrageous notion that I was distinctive or exceptional in any manner; I merely became more conscious of the rampant evil that existed in our world.

Did I, unsuspectingly, have these exceptional abilities all of my life? Did I simply lack the acumen to unlock them to their full capacity? Did the discernment of spirits truly spark to life in the church parking lot all those years ago when I instantly knew that my new church friend was actually my enemy in disguise?

My special gifts were well beyond my understanding but I believed, wholeheartedly, that they somehow transcended the gates of our physical world. However, I kept my capabilities closely guarded; I never boasted or flaunted my abilities. I could never even bring myself to mention my idiosyncrasies to my closest friends or family. The paranormal events that I experienced became an integral part of my existence, yet I didn't stop to question their role or significance. I simply and humbly appreciated my uniqueness and strove to live my life in a normal fashion.

If these distinctive competencies weren't enough to be thankful for, I was also greatly appreciative of my supernatural gift of prophecy. Through dreams, visions or a type of spiritual perception or communication I was able to predict or "see" events and activities that related to me or someone especially close to me. My husband and children were the first to witness this particular aptitude on a regular basis. They quickly began to distinguish me from most of the people they knew. They recognized that I was not ordinary; I was someone very "extra-ordinary."

CHAPTER FOUR

Marriage, Children, Grandmother

I never had fancy notions of a grand, lavish wedding. I could never even come to grips with the universally accepted institution of marriage. And I most certainly was never fooled by the concept of a knight in shining armor that would magically turn my life into a fairytale world of unimaginable bliss. Furthermore, under no circumstances whatsoever, did I dare consider the prospect of motherhood.

The idea of being anchored down by anyone or anything was absolutely unspeakable and went against my highly spirited and independent nature. Besides my fundamental, innate character traits, my anti-marriage stance was also heavily influenced by the amount of depravity and corruption prevalent in the world. I was left jaded at an early age.

Utilizing my paranormal perceptions, I frequently felt as though one of the devil's faithful foot soldiers was in close proximity. Even more upsetting was the fact that wickedness seemed to flourish and multiply in every facet of society; immoral practices were progressively becoming widespread and commonly accepted as the norm. Each day, the bridge between good and evil was increasing exponentially. Black and white was becoming more obscure as the acceptable gray scale mounted and triumphed.

Was there any goodness or chivalry left in our degenerate world? Why should I bother to marry? Even more importantly, why on earth would I want to bring innocent, helpless children into a shattered world governed by darkness and debauchery?

Despite my stubbornness and stern views, in due course I eventually relinquished my beliefs and said the words I never thought I would dare speak; I said "I do" to my husband Phillip. Phillip was a kind young man with a genuine and sincere heart. It was his gentle heart that won me over in the end. Although he had a considerable amount of growing up to do, I could clearly see the great man inside of him just waiting to sprout and develop.

What happened to the old Cassandra? What happened to my "single for life," anti-marriage rhetoric? My staunch, former views had flown out of the window, never to be heard from again. Just like that, my life had changed and my former dogmas had disappeared into the still and silent winds of the past. Mysteriously, the old me was vanquished and became ghostlike, like a foggy, distant memory of an old, long-lost friend. I couldn't quite fully grasp my sudden and unforeseen transformation but I accepted it, nonetheless.

Then, in no time at all, I found myself to be pregnant.

The alarming news of the pregnancy spread like wildfire and massively shocked anyone who ever knew me. This was a 9.9 on the Richter scale! There was no way I could possibly give birth or mother a child. Having children went against everything I once piercingly proclaimed and solidly stood for. But somehow, my once predominant reservations of bringing children into this cruel and unforgiving world had abruptly said goodbye and departed my psyche. The new Cassandra cordially greeted motherhood as incredibly pure and miraculous. My heart and eyes were opened as I realized that a child was the most beautiful gift of the highest form of love. In spite of the wicked, threatening world they would be born into, I vowed to love, treasure and protect my children at all costs.

Thoughts of my desolate childhood crept in and greatly vexed me. As a child, I longed to feel a semblance of maternal love but instead I was always left feeling discarded and disenchanted. My arms never embraced the warmth of a tender hug. Not once did my heart sway to the soothing symphony of a sincere "I love you."

I assumed that my mother's heart must have been deeply wounded and scarred and ultimately incapable of the amorous affections that any child would naturally crave and require. I could not bear the thought of my children ever having to experience the loneliness and uncertainties that I often struggled with. I passionately desired for my children to feel sanctuary in me and my incessant love every moment of their existence.

I knew I couldn't accomplish this on my own. What could I do but turn to God for help?

I prayed that God would give me a kind of supernatural love for my children, one that this world had never known. I sincerely requested that they would always, every second of their lives, know with absolutely certainty that my heart belonged to them.

God answered my prayers.

The moment my daughter Allison was born, radiant fireworks of immeasurable love burst in the air and flooded the entire operating room as I held her snugly in my sheltering arms. The fireworks never stopped exploding.

Just six months later, I had another colossal surprise; this one was a "double whammy." During my annual checkup, my doctor hit me with the joyous news of another pregnancy. This time I was blessed with twins, a boy and a girl!

My grandmother was a twin and stubbornly believed that one day, before she left this forsaken world, she would be the proud, glowing great grandmother of my precious twins. She spoke to me of this "fantasy" many times throughout my teenage and young adult years. My response, of course, was that I would never have children and therefore, logically could never have twins. She knew what she knew and didn't bother wasting time arguing with me or attempting to persuade me; she simply grinned modestly like the Mona Lisa. This was my grandmother's delicate way of letting you know who was right and who was wrong.

Needless to say, my grandmother was beyond ecstatic when she heard the news of the twins. I obviously shared in her enthusiasm but I had some natural concerns as well. The doctors and nurses taunted me with very upsetting statistics regarding twin pregnancies and their associated risks. Once again I turned to God. I asked Him to give me faith, to help me cast my worldly fears aside. My primary supplications were to have a healthy boy and girl with strong birth weights. I must have asked for this at least three times a day during my pregnancy but I didn't think that my compassionate Father would mind.

Similar to my first pregnancy, the second one also turned out to be a walk in the park. With just four more weeks to reach full term, Alexandria and Alexander were born just one minute apart in near perfect health. They weighed in at 6lbs 3oz and 6lbs 2oz, respectively. God had answered my prayers; the twins were born in good health with birth weights more robust than even some full-term, single pregnancy births. God was sharing His glorious goodness with me in a most beautiful way. No mother could have been more grateful.

Given the nature and adjacent timing of my pregnancies, it felt as though I was the mother of triplets. But instead of pulling out each of the hairs on my head every night, the first few years of motherhood proved to be heavenly and curiously unruffled. Never before had I felt such a strong protective bond and closeness with another human being as I did with each of my darling children. They were truly a part of me; they were miniature living, breathing extensions of my very soul and being. With the birth of my children also came a life-changing epiphany

– my children weren't just gifts from the Lord; they were extensions of God Himself.

I was very thankful that my grandmother was still living when my children were brought into this world. Although she only knew them for a couple of short years, she was able to build substantial and enduring relationships with each of them.

Allison was the first great grandchild of the family. The exceptional bond she shared with her great grandmother was evident from the very beginning. The first time Allison looked into my grandmother's eyes there was already a strong sense of familiarity. It was as if she had somehow remembered or recognized those eyes from another time or place. She and my grandmother appeared to communicate without words, on a purely spiritual level; it was an incredibly precious and profound union.

My grandmother's connection with the twins was also wholesome and powerful. When they were together there was an unequivocal amount of joy and laughter, very reminiscent of the merry days of my own childhood spent with my grandparents. These simple, non-pretentious times of togetherness were unforgettable snapshots of how life was meant to be lived. These were the caliber of memories that would always be there to desperately cling to in times of need or despair.

My grandmother died of cancer in March of 2009, just one month before her 75th birthday. Fortunately, the family had been given ample warning of her inevitable demise so I took advantage and made every attempt to visit her as much as I physically could. I was a working mother with 3 toddlers at home and spare time was a rare commodity. Juggling work, family and my grandmother proved to be much more difficult than I had originally anticipated. But it didn't matter how long or frequent my visits were; each moment with my grandmother was meaningful and cherished. Although we sometimes partook in memorable dialogue, most of our time was spent sitting silently, enjoying each other's physical and spiritual company. Sometimes she slept serenely while I sat quietly watching over her. As she slept, I mused over the multitude of dreams that her spirit could have been taking her off into.

While my grandmother rested, I often daydreamed and reminisced about the lifetime of treasured memories we were blessed with. I knew that she was somehow aware of and could perceive my presence. She felt my love from the deep seas of her slumber; I was certain of it. My love was an overwhelming love that transcended our world and made its way straight to my grandmother's angelic heart.

One morning, after many months of agonizing suffering, my feeble grandmother drew me in close to her emaciated, pale face and whispered to me in a very soft voice. She held me close and confessed that her battle was simply too arduous and she was tired of fighting. I looked deep into my grandmother's exhausted eyes and heard her unspoken words. Without a moment's hesitation, I simply told her that she could rest without guilt. I assured her that everything would be fine. With a great sigh of relief she gave me one of her gentle, affirming smiles. We understood each other.

The courageous woman that had cared for me all of my life was ready to let go. She just needed someone to tell her that everything was going to be all right. She needed some kind of assurance and sense of release so that she could freely and easily move on from this physical world. Just a few short days later, my lifelong love entered the glorious kingdom of God.

I had never lost anyone closer to me than my beloved grandmother. Her death was a blow to my system and shook every facet of my world. Her passing was extremely difficult to deal with. But God reminded me that my grandmother's spirit was awakened and given new birth, it was really just her mortal body that had moved on.

For a few excruciatingly painful days of nonstop, gushing rivers of continuously flowing tears, I struggled with the fact that my grandmother's bodily form no longer existed in this world. I could no longer watch her thin lips transform into a beautiful smile or gaze into her deep, intense eyes. I couldn't call her on the telephone just to hear the sound of her pacifying, tender voice or contagious laughter. I couldn't touch her soft skin or run my fingers through her freshly curled and colored red auburn hair. Every aspect of my grandmother's physical existence was suddenly eradicated from my life. My life was shattered, my heart broken.

Fortunately and rather quickly, the Lord helped me come to grips with my new reality, which sadly happened to be completely void of my grandmother. With God's wisdom and influence, I experienced a drastic transformation. I realized that my grandmother's corporal absence was OK; her spirit had taken over and was reigning gloriously. I began to sense my grandmother's presence in a way that my mind couldn't possibly comprehend or even describe. I felt closer to her than ever before. My grandmother was with me, but in a completely spiritual fashion. She surrounded me like the atmosphere that enveloped and protected its sacred earth. Her divine spirit covered me like a warm, cozy blanket on a cold winter's day.

This unexpected insight and awareness gave rise to a massive amount of comfort and peace inside of my soul. I was encouraged and enlightened with the knowledge that my grandmother was not dead; she was more alive than those of us she left behind.

CHAPTER FIVE

Vision of Heaven

O n an ordinary summer day in July of 2009, I had one of the most extraordinary experiences of my early life. It was then that God took me to the most magnificent place that I had ever laid my earthly eyes on.

Although it was decidedly early, I opted to call it a night right after tucking the kids into bed. I wasn't necessarily sleepy but I did feel that both my body and mind could use some much needed rest and relaxation.

For quite some time, I lied motionless on my back, with nostalgic memories of my grandmother repeatedly playing on the big, black screen inside of my head. After reliving a countless number of comforting moments spent with her, my wondering thoughts began to dwindle down to nothing as my mind began to go blank. Mindless and unenthusiastically, I stared at the dull ceiling, as I typically did when I wasn't ready for bed. I closed my eyes and I was taken to another world or realm. Heaven was revealed to me the very second my eyes sealed shut.

The instant I closed my eyes, a modest but luxurious looking lavender garment appeared out of nowhere. It didn't take long for me to realize that the frock was actually someone's robe. The silky smooth looking robe was physically so close to me that it took up most of my visible viewing area. I regret not reaching out to touch it, although this may not have been possible had I even tried. I quickly moved away from the velvety robe so that I could get a better view of my surroundings. Or did it move away from me? I couldn't tell. The precise mechanics of what was going on were very hazy.

The lavender robe greatly resembled a massive theater curtain that gently opened to reveal an extravagant and masterfully set stage. As the distance between the robe and I slowly increased, I saw the man to which it belonged; it was the Lord Jesus Christ!

Jesus was lovely and mesmerizing, like a stunning, unforgettable sunset. His full-length robe gently embraced the ground and hid the Lord's feet from my sight. His movements were so delicate that I couldn't easily determine whether He was gliding, floating or walking. But the bends and movements in his legs and knees quickly answered my question – our Savior was indeed walking. As He strolled along, Jesus, with His long, graceful strides, maintained a very calm, collected composure.

Jesus had shoulder length, wavy black hair that glistened as though saturated with some type of oil. It was slick back and perfectly intact; not a strand was out of place. His eyes were dark brown or black and not a single wrinkle or blemish resided on his smooth, fair complexion. Jesus' face and lips were narrow and a thin layer of black facial hair sheltered his well-defined cheek bones.

The moment I gazed upon Him, I felt the magnitude of His impeccable purity. There was nothing in this world that I could liken it to. I experienced, firsthand, the embodiment of total serenity and uncontaminated love. Like a magnet, my eyes were fixed upon the glory and power of the Lord. It took a considerable amount of effort to look beyond His Majesty at what else had been revealed to me.

I immediately understood that I was a spectator in this divine new world. Based on everything I perceived and witnessed, I seemed to be hovering or flying around inconspicuously. As I flew further away from Jesus, I saw a little girl that couldn't have been more than 10 years old. She was approximately 50 feet behind Jesus. She had long, light brown hair that went mid-way down her back; half of her hair was pulled back and perfectly cut bangs covered her forehead. She wore a light blue dress that resembled Dorothy's from the Wizard of Oz. She was playing casually in an opulent, ornate garden; the grandiose scenery was unlike any I had seen on earth.

It was only when the girl and glorious landscape were revealed to me that I realized just how massive Jesus was. Like a skyscraper, He towered above the girl at least 50 stories high. The girl was enraptured by her spellbinding surroundings as she curiously wandered about and explored the fascinating gardens, completely unaware of Jesus' existence. My first thought was that she didn't notice her companion because of how elevated and colossal He was. I later wondered whether she was fully aware of His presence but had simply grown accustomed to His company. Knowing that Jesus was always in her vicinity could have given her a comfort that allowed her to carry on in her own world, in her own merry way.

Throughout the vision, the young girl remained thoroughly absorbed by her surreal environment. The heavenly garden was adorned with vibrant colors and brilliant splendor. There were an infinite number of yellow, blue, lavender, pink, purple, orange and white flowers of all varieties and sizes. Small trees and bushes covered the plush, grassy meadow. The sky was a soothing, almost pastel blue. It was bright and sunny, though the sun was nowhere to be seen. In the center of the garden was a small, clear brook that sung a sweet hypnotic melody as the water danced its way across the tiny pebbles it housed and showcased.

I was under the impression that this was the girl's first visit to this wonderful new world. She seemed overwhelmed by the beautiful blossoms as she stopped to smell and truly take in each bloom, as though for the very first time. She crossed the brook over a classic looking, small wooden bridge. She took her time wandering through the gardens, though there were times when she skipped cheerfully as she played with a furry, snow white bunny that timidly, but loyally, followed her in close proximity.

All the while, the little girl was enthralled by the majestic garden, but never seemed to notice Jesus, who was also always there with her. He always maintained a good distance ahead of the girl, as though guiding her but without her knowledge. She seemed completely oblivious to the fact that she was trailing in His path, following in the precious footsteps of Jesus Christ.

I suffered with a deep, intrinsic desire to stay in this enchanted realm. I wished to take the girl's petite hand in mine and skip freely with her. If given the choice, I would have chosen to leave behind all of my worldly cares and concerns. My heart yearned to stay in Jesus's heart-warming and nourishing presence. Strangely, I had no longing to speak to Him; our spiritual connection was so pure and powerful that words were not at all necessary. Jesus consumed me and His presence captivated me; I felt hypnotized or spellbound.

Unfortunately, something triggered my eyes to open and the resplendent vision was suddenly gone. Though all of me ached to return to the heavenly garden, I felt the security and serenity of Jesus' essence carry over from the garden into my bedroom. Though I had only experienced a microscopic piece of His celestial world it was more than enough to sustain me for a lifetime.

As I thanked Him and exalted His great name, God shared some inspirational news with me. He informed me that I was the little girl and Jesus was always by my side. He was there protecting, guiding and leading me at all times, through every phase of my life. With a huge smile on my face and a heart filled with gratitude, I contemplated whether Jesus literally saw me as a young and innocent little girl. I knew the answer. Everything in His extravagant garden was fresh and unsoiled and so was I. God confirmed my thoughts and reiterated that I was His child, blameless and pure. His unconditional and prodigious love for me was so pronounced that He didn't notice any of my many imperfections or faults. Jesus had died for me and through His sacrifice I was made perfect in God's eyes.

I was entranced by the tenacity and wholesomeness of His endless love and grace. I thanked Him for the supreme sacrifice He made for me - undeserving, reprehensible me! Still smiling, tears rolled down my eyes as I marveled in His greatness and mercy.

I didn't question why the Lord God manifested Himself to me in this spectacular manner or why He chose to take me to this breathtaking place and share His poignant, cherished message with me. The one thing I knew with absolute certainty was that, after my grandmother's passing, I became progressively closer to God. I felt His pervasive, hallowed presence on a regular basis. The relationship I shared with my Father had significantly morphed into an intimate and substantial one.

The Almighty God had been with me for all of my days but I hadn't fully grasped and appreciated this cosmic concept in its entirety. But, in all of His kindness and compassion, He began to refine my thinking and temper my heart. The Creator of the Universe also began to reveal Himself to me in entirely innovative and astonishing ways. His imaginative revelations were beyond belief and well beyond anything I or this world had ever seen.

God's mind-boggling interventions in my life swept me away and left me entirely dumbfounded. His wondrous Hand came down from heaven, touched me and changed the course of my very existence!

CHAPTER SIX

After Grandmother's Death – More of Him

For at least two unusually demanding and exhausting weeks, I had put off the stimulating sensation that moves me to get out the canvas and paintbrush. The never-ending trail of obligations and stresses associated with work, family and activities related to the children ultimately led me to put aside each of the many commanding compulsions I had to paint. Though I begrudged each instance of my disobedience, time was becoming a rare and precious commodity that seemed to be lacking on all fronts. I just couldn't find the perfect window to dedicate to His glorious pastime. However, regardless of how crammed my life seemed to be, the Holy Spirit wasn't prepared to give up on me that quickly.

One evening, just moments after committing to a relaxing movie night with the kids, I sensed a dynamic spiritual energy take over me. The vehement force was so intense that I was rendered defenseless and obedient. I did not have the strength to resist the authoritative instruction and was immediately compelled to grab the essential supplies. There was work to be done.

Unfortunately, my children had to wait. With great sincerity, I apologized to my disappointed children, poured myself a glass of rich, red wine and surrendered myself to God's mandate.

The Holy Spirit had completely overtaken my body and was eager to expel its creative juices. Not a single second was spared; I was upstairs no more than 30 minutes and then it was all over. Without any rhyme or reason that I could consciously perceive, I splashed various shades of blues, yellows, greens, and reds onto my color plate. The promising colors then magically made their way to the canvas.

I distinctly remember thinking that the painting was complete but then, without knowledge as to why, I picked up the paintbrush and dipped one of its corners into a yellowish paint. I surveyed the unique work of art, took a small step towards the painting and quickly brushed over a small section of the lower right side of the painting. It was only then that I "knew" that the final stroke had been laid.

God's creation was complete; I sighed with an immense sense of accomplishment. I experienced great relief and satisfaction and I sensed that the Holy Spirit was pleased with the final product. A huge burden had been lifted off of me though I couldn't understand how or why.

I stepped back, keenly examined the painting and somehow recognized that it represented His Holiness, the Supreme God. It was a spiritual knowledge fed to me by God Himself; I wouldn't have known this otherwise. His large, prominent eyes were the central focus of the canvas; they were dark green and dramatically fierce. I didn't see or sense anything else obvious in the painting but I felt a tremendous, inexplicable power emanating from it. God's overwhelming, invincible presence inundated me.

Over time, I developed a strong "reverent fear" of the painting that I began to refer to as the "Face of God." I couldn't place my finger on what exactly drove my fear but it was incredibly pronounced.

On some long, drawn-out nights, I even experienced great difficulties sleeping because the cryptic painting haunted my thoughts.

Phillip had hung the painting on a living room wall that was clearly visible from where I slept in our bedroom. I often closed my eyes and tried to fall into slumber but my paltry efforts were thwarted by His perpetual gaze. I could not successfully ignore the influence of His mysteriously penetrating work of art.

I felt a vigorous, living presence originating from the painting at all times, energy unlike anything I could comprehend. We kept the painting on this wall for just a few short months until I finally worked up the courage to admit that its deep secrets invaded and engaged my thoughts almost every night. My husband subsequently relocated the persuasive piece of art. Its new residence was not much of a concern so long as it was not visible from the bedroom. As expected, my sleeping radically improved.

I never shook the "reverent fear" I had acquired for the painting; in fact the angst grew more resilient as the years passed. I gazed into God's fiery, dramatic eyes quite often, consumed by bewilderment and awe each and every time. I couldn't help but wonder what He was staring at with such an intense wrath. What angered Him so? My spirit knew that this gripping painting was extraordinary and distinctive; my mortal mind struggled to piece it all together.

But He didn't just leave His footprints on the walls of my home; God manifested Himself to me at work as well. Evil and depravity were dominant forces wandering about each and every nook and cranny of the work environment; never before had I sensed more of the devil's wicked influences than I had during the nine or so hours of each draining and demanding workday. I endeavored to steer clear of the office politics and shenanigans. I made every effort to lay low but my attempts continuously failed. I was befriended and sought after by many of my coworkers but I steadily remained very selective in my office interactions.

In time, I developed a very endearing friendship with a woman named Martha. She was twenty years older than me and in many simple, subtle ways reminded me of my grandmother. Martha and I went out for lunch regularly. We never tired of discussing the woes of work or the joys of home. We shared many common interests but our favorite pastime was fashion; on many occasions we splurged on extravagant but unnecessary shopping sprees. And without fail, each morning we greeted each other with our much famed "tea time."

One morning while brewing a cup of tea, I overheard Martha and another coworker, Mark, talking in a very surreptitious manner. In a very faint voice, Mark told Martha that his job was to protect me from evil. Martha grinned and said that her mission was the same as his. I was stunned and perplexed. Though incredibly intrigued by what I overheard, I could never bring myself to mention this covert and rather unusual conversation to either of them.

Of course I knew that evil pursued me, but how were they privy to this undisclosed information? I wondered if they could be part of God's army of angels abiding on earth. As incredulous and absurd as that sounded, what if it were true? And if it just happened to be true why would He send them to protect me? Who was I and what did I need protection from?

I felt very comfortable and relaxed with Martha and after three years of friendship we built a much cherished camaraderie. But despite our close bond, there were some subjects we never brought up. We never engaged in conversations involving religion and spirituality. I was naturally very guarded and never divulged too much of myself or my beliefs with anyone, including Martha. She knew me well enough to respect me and the boundaries I had established.

But during one unforgettable luncheon, much to my amazement, Martha brought up the name of Jesus. She then delved deep into her distant childhood and shared some of her most personal spiritual experiences with me.

Martha's father was a preacher and evangelist; his primary purpose in life was to save lost souls by bringing them to salvation through Jesus

Christ. Martha had seen and experienced so many incredible and inexplicable events as a child of a missionary. She was an exceedingly faithful woman and her intimate relationship with Christ was more than admirable.

As I sat listening attentively to Martha reflect and relinquish her inspiring stories and beliefs with me, I couldn't help but wonder why she suddenly elected to bring up religion after three years of casual, non-threatening conversations. But my answer was quickly brought to light. Martha shared her personal history with me so that I could understand her upbringing and appreciate her robust relationship with God. She gave me the background and context that would ultimately lead to the point of the entire conversation. My dear friend Martha had a divine message for me.

She boldly announced that God had an exceptionally special, epic purpose for my life; whatever it was she was certain that it was going to be huge. Martha didn't have the details of my life's blueprints but she shone with excitement as she pondered over the various possibilities. There was one stipulation; before I could begin on my journey, I first had to surrender all of my fears. These fears had a stronghold on me so great that I couldn't even begin to step in or gain ground on the path that was laid out for me. In order for me to fulfill His destiny for my life I needed to abandon the heavy-duty apprehensions that were clinging onto me and holding me back. The rusty shackles of bondage had to be broken.

Martha apologized for plunging into this distant space that we had previously avoided or skirted around. She stressed that she needed to heed God and obey His command. I thanked Martha for her courage and quietly sat in a concentrated disorientation. Baffled, I didn't have the slightest indication of what His will for my life could be. I didn't even understand what fears were in dire need of annihilation.

For the next few days I reflected on the compelling communication God had sent me through his faithful servant Martha. My mind immediately took me to a conversation that my husband and I had just had a couple of weeks prior. Phillip had a vision of me preaching to a devoted congregation of thousands. He didn't know the subject of my address but he knew that people were flocking from all over the world eager to hear whatever it was I had to say.

I dismissed Phillip's vision in a heartbeat but he could not cast it aside. He knew God had great plans for me. I, on the other hand, knew, with absolute certainty, that I would never preach to thousands. Extremely reserved, I guarded my beliefs so tightly that the thought of preaching to even one person was unnerving.

In the span of a just a few short weeks, God had given Martha a message and Phillip a vision. He was actively trying to communicate with me through various channels but my reception was weak. Something was holding me back. Slowly but surely, I began to recognize that doubts and fears were indeed drowning and hindering me but I was not yet ready to believe in my destiny.

Just one week after delivering this consecrated communication to me, a very healthy Martha passed away unexpectedly. After an extensive autopsy, the doctors were unable to determine the cause of her untimely death.

CHAPTER SEVEN

Everyday Life

The feel of the office environment drastically changed after Martha's unfortunate passing. Though there were many familiar and consoling faces surrounding me, the ambiance became taciturn and barren. Going into work every day morphed into an exhausting and strenuous exercise for which I had zero enthusiasm. The mounting stresses at work combined with a strained, disintegrating marriage were becoming unbearable.

I had been suffering in the marriage for quite some time but Phillip ignored my voluminous cries. He lived in a fantasy world filled with false hope; he was completely oblivious to the somber state of our marriage. Phillip could not understand and therefore could not accept that I was in a miserable state of mind, spiraling into isolation. He was in denial. Sadly, it was this denial that pushed me further and further away from him.

In the area of companionship, I was utterly alone and hollow. My nourishment and solace was found in my darling children. I had no confidence that our marriage would ever improve or recuperate but I remained quarantined for the sake of the kids.

As most parents would probably say, I knew my children were special from very early on. They exuded a raw and genuine form of love and happiness in every way imaginable. Their bright, inquisitive eyes sparkled like the stars in the heavens. They were celestial creations governed by their God given spirits; the flesh and bones were simply necessary for them to abide with me on earth as physical beings. Regardless of what we did or how we spent our precious time, when we were together, all was right in the world. My children and I identified with one another on a very deep level. Our spirits communicated freely and in very distinctive manners.

Alexandria was cognizant of my unique attributes before Alexander or Allison sensed anything out of the ordinary. One evening, all of the children were playing rambunctiously upstairs; they were laughing and carrying on loudly for hours on end but then silence suddenly stung the atmosphere. I grew concerned as my motherly intuition kicked in. Suspiciously, I called for them so that I could visibly see that they were safe and intact. I peered into Alexandria's eyes and was able to perceive the children's clandestine activities. With complete confidence, I simply said to all of them, "Please don't get inside the toy box anymore. It could fall apart and you could get hurt."

Alexandria's already curious eyes grew with astonishment. She asked me how I knew they were hiding and playing inside the toy box. They had never before attempted this feat nor was there ever any prior discussion of it. Alexandria was in such disbelief that she began to ask me if there were hidden cameras in their bedrooms. Her young mind could not understand how it was that I could have possibly known what they were up to! I told her I just "knew" it. I later explained to her, quite simply, that there were times when God revealed certain things to me and when He did I did not doubt or question Him. With her lips curled up, she looked at me in complete awe, as though I were one of the greatest mysteries of all time. That was a critical turning point for Alexandria; she never looked at me in the same light again.

As time passed, the children witnessed many more instances of my special God-given endowments. They were amazed by their mother's curious abilities. I was also astounded as I felt my "powers" strengthening and substantially developing. I decided to test the limits. I honed in on other hidden senses that I felt were readily accessible but not yet tapped into.

On several occasions, I found myself having a thought that Alexandria would somehow recognize and comment on. This happened enough times for me to realize that these occurrences were not mere coincidences. I toyed with the idea of telepathy and ran with it. I began communicating with Alexandria without words; I looked into her receiving eyes and spoke to her using nothing but thoughts. We were both fascinated that she actually "heard" me in her mind! Neither of us could explain how this was possible but we both experienced it firsthand. We had a unique clairvoyant connection well beyond our human understanding.

Allison and I shared a very special connection as well. She was the only person who could somehow eradicate my thunderstorms and hurricanes and turn them into a sweet world of sunshine and rainbows. With a loving look, a gentle touch or one kind word, Allison could tap into the core of my heart and pump it full of love and compassion in a matter of mere seconds. I believed that my beautiful daughter was solidly infused with God and He used her to help me lift me up when I needed it most. Even at my worst and most regrettable moments, she could reach in with her small angelic hand and cleanse me of all malice. Without fail, she would always find a way to replenish me with God's goodness and grace.

Allison was, by far, the biggest fan of my artwork. She admired me and aspired to be just like me. Unsurprisingly, she asked me if I could teach her how to paint. As a mother, I was naturally overjoyed that she held me in such high regard. But there was one major problem – I didn't know how to paint. Allison didn't know the truth about how my paintings came to life. She had no clue that God was the true artist in the family, not her esteemed mother.

I supported Allison's request by buying her a special set of art supplies. I desperately longed to fulfill my aspiring protégé's grand wish even though I didn't have the slightest indication of how I would go about accomplishing this impossible task. I tried to give her painting lessons but, as expected, the sessions proved to be fruitless and ineffective.

I bought Allison her very own painting instructional so that she could submerse herself in the subject and educate herself. My hope was that she would learn some specific tools and techniques that could help her progress. But this didn't work out either; Allison wanted to learn from the greatest artist she had ever known – her mother. I had to tell Allison the truth, but this proved to be problematic. She saw the final products hanging in almost every room of our museum-like home. Each of the pieces she cherished carried my insignia. So what did I mean when I said I didn't know how to paint? My little angel was baffled.

As difficult as it was for her to comprehend, Allison eventually came to a level of clarity and understanding. This enlightenment only came with a touch of God's divine intervention.

One day, God chose to create a remarkably distinctive painting of what appeared to be an assortment of blue and gray decaying, unproductive tree branches. There was just one striking flower in full bloom on one of the dilapidated twigs. The one small blossom was a beautiful depiction of life and faith; it represented hope in the midst of darkness and death.

The children were fascinated by the painting and its obvious meaning, but were even more astonished by what came shortly after.

A small, fragile cherry tree resided in the center of our lawn. The recent, brutal winter had taken its toll on my treasured friend and rendered it comatose. Its branches were dry, brittle and apparently lifeless. There was clear evidence of death but I held on to the faith that my obstinate tree still carried some life. Phillip, on the other hand, was ready to uproot the tree and discard it.

Just one week after God and I painted His lovely representation of life, before the painting had even dried, one single, prominent flower appeared on our cherry tree. Just as I had firmly believed, our resilient tree was alive and thriving! For days to come, the children and I eagerly anticipated an opulent tree covered with hundreds of small cherry blossoms. But, much to our surprise, no other flowers came. We were simply presented with the one "blossom of life" just as God had shown us through His recent painting. The branches and the one solitary bloom were almost identical to the oil painting still drying in our game room. We were all stunned by the supernatural chain of events.

This was the first prophetic painting that God had revealed to us. This was the painting He used to help bring understanding to the children.

Ultimately, Allison recognized that God's spirit had been painting through her "special" mother all along; all of the paintings that hung on our walls were actually His personal creations. She was mesmerized by His astounding gifts and displayed an even greater appreciation for the pieces.

The children were in love with me in a beautifully captivating way. Despite my unwelcomed disciplinary actions and in spite of the times I lost my temper, their unending love glistened like beaming rays of sunlight sharply cutting through gray, copious clouds. On numerous occasions their generous affections left me in complete bewilderment. I never before appreciated how children could demonstrate such a deep and concentrated form of love.

With all their hearts, my children sincerely believed that I was an angel sent down from heaven; they had no hesitation in sharing their devout beliefs and they did so quite frequently. The children explained that they had to keep me happy because that's what God wanted them to do; this was one of His directives. They proved their efforts time and time again. With any suggestion of anger or sadness in my demeanor, the children magically popped up with the one singular purpose of restoring my joy.

Each of my children claimed that I was the best mother in the world, even greater than Mary, the mother of Jesus. They alleged that I was special because God and Jesus dwelled inside of me. The first couple of times they made their unusual and profound comments, I was stunned and perplexed. I didn't understand how my children could love me in such an unconditional, Godly fashion. But, with time, I grew accustomed to their loving yet very peculiar statements.

I was incredibly blessed and thankful that God answered my many prayers regarding my children and motherhood. I may not have been the greatest mother in the world but I was, undeniably, the most loved.

As much as my children loved and cared for me, I loved them a thousand times more. I admired their unshakable, enduring faith. They had the true, blind faith that Jesus referred to throughout the pages of the New Testament. They learned, very early on, that every good gift came from our Father in heaven. As a result, it gave me an even greater amount of pleasure to share my heavenly gifts and secrets with them. On the other hand, there were many things I could not share with them. I sheltered them from the inexorable darkness that relentlessly tormented me.

One evening, Phillip and I were having a heated discussion about our decaying relationship. Based on recent patterns and events, I predicted that we were rapidly headed towards a sweltering earthquake. Instead of standing my ground and having the last word, as was very typical of me, I forced myself to take the high road and passively walked away. Phillip, insistent on an argument, kept provoking me. But I didn't cave; I removed myself from the situation and went to the living room to put some much needed distance between us. I had to cool down.

Standing motionless in the center of the living room, I sighed, delighted to have actually prevented a hostile escalation. This was a major breakthrough for me.

My delight immediately transformed into solid fright as the air in the room turned icy cold. I was all alone, consumed by terror, as I heard the appalling echoes of a demon's growls. The ghastly rumblings were bloodcurdling and could not be likened to any known animal on earth. I honed in on various types of dueling, overlapping roars and snarls. I questioned whether there could have been multiple demons dispersed throughout the house but my spirit knew that the unnatural growls were all coming from one multidimensional, nonphysical entity.

The vulgar demon was so deafening that it should have been heard throughout the entire house, maybe even by some of the neighbors. The intensity and clarity of the volume was similar to that of a surround-sound theater system; the concentrated roaring seemed to attack me from every direction with refined clarity. Even though the reverberations completely surrounded me and penetrated the entire area of the house, the source of the piercing growls felt excruciatingly close to me; I could almost feel the beast's stony breath on my face. I was horrified.

This gruesome episode lasted about one minute, but the minute seemed to go on without end. When it was all over, I found my body shivering and draped with goose bumps. I was frozen, like a statue. I feared that I would hear the demon's clamors again or even worse, that the menacing entity would appear right before my terribly frightened eyes. Warped by petrification, I could do nothing but wait there in the center of the living room, feeling completely helpless and alone.

It took me a few solid minutes to regain my composure. When I finally collected myself, I shouted out to Phillip and the kids; I asked them if they had heard anything strange but my question was obviously rhetorical. Of course they hadn't heard the ear-piercing growls. If they had experienced the horror, they would have been mortified and already made their way towards me.

This foul and unforgettable offensiveness was meant for my ears alone. I had just been exposed to an audible glimpse of the spiritual realm. For some reason, unbeknownst to me, the Lord God wanted me to know that this vociferous demon was there with me.

I struggled to eradicate this spine-tingling experience, as well as many other similar ones, from my mind and from my life. I never spoke of what I went through; I believed that keeping these ghostly events to myself would help me persevere and move on. Perhaps I was in denial, but despite everything that I had gone through, I dared to believe that I was a normal human being. Inevitably, reality would prevail when another supernatural incident would present itself. The dreaded memories that I buried deep inside of me could never be exterminated; somehow or another they would magically resurface and resurrect.

Some experiences were just too haunting and bone-chilling that attempting to forget them was a wasted initiative. One terribly haunting recollection that could never be suppressed occurred during a family visit to my parent's house. It was there that I captured a photograph of a repulsive demon sitting coolly at my parent's kitchen table.

My father and I had a great relationship; we both enjoyed a good, hearty laugh. My laughs, however, tended to be at his expense. He seemed to enjoy being the butt of his children's joke so I was always on the lookout for opportunities to make him feel extra special. During this particular visit, I happened to catch my dad sitting in a rather awkward position on the living room chaise. His arms were spread out, one leg was high up in the air against the wall and his body was slouched low. I took advantage of the situation and thought this would be a great "pose" to send to my brothers.

I took a total of five photos with my cell phone, hoping that one would be worthy enough to distribute to the clan. I chuckled as I scrolled through each of the first four photos but then my heart immediately pounded with trepidation; a gruesome, evil entity had revealed itself in the very last picture!

My mother's cluttered kitchen table was clearly visible through an open door that parted the living room and kitchen, directly behind where my father sat. In the first four photos the table was unoccupied with four empty chairs, identical to the way it existed in the physical world. But in the very last shot, the demonic apparition presented itself sitting collectedly on one of the four chairs.

The specter's bulbous head was a deep, radiant orange that appeared to be burning from the inside out. The intensity of the glowing heat reminded me of magma and the fiery cave walls from my childhood vision of hell. The wraith's face was not clear or distinctive; his facial features were obscured and just slightly visible. His pumpkin-like head sat on top of a thick, black shadowy body with its black arms hanging stiff on either side of its boxlike torso.

Fear trickled down my spine and penetrated down to my very core. Filled with terror, I forced myself to turn my head and slowly glanced over at the kitchen table. As expected, there were no traces of the sweltering monster. Nothing was out of place or out of the ordinary, but I knew that the repugnant demon was there in another spiritual dimension, sitting quite comfortably in my parents' home.

I immediately thought of the children and began to panic; I didn't want them anywhere near this evil presence. I packed up the kids and let everyone know that we needed to head home. I didn't explain the sudden rush to leave. I deleted the tainted photo from my files and never mentioned it to anyone. I desperately sought to erase the dreaded file from own personal memory bank as well, but this proved to be impossible. It took at least six months to build the courage and strength I needed to step foot into my parent's home again.

The scorching image was permanently seared in my mind. Incredibly shaken by this appalling episode, I couldn't fathom or process what was going on. This was the kind of outrageous fiction in horror movies or science fiction films, not real life. Not my life!

I was puzzled. Was this manifestation God's doing or was it Satan's? I had always believed that God was in control of everything and it was only by His authorization that the devil could even operate. I didn't understand why God would allow me to witness the atrocity of this repulsive demonic spirit? Why did I need to go through this horror?

Despite all of my qualms and uncertainties, I forced myself to believe that God owned the keys to the spiritual dimension that co-existed with our physical world. For reasons beyond my comprehension, He opened the metaphysical gateway to the other side so that I could bear personal witness. He had a higher purpose in allowing me to experience each and every disturbing occurrence, along with the beautiful ones as well. I found some solace in my firm conviction.

My mind raced and played back the many other isolated, inexplicable incidences that I had suffered through from such an early age. None of it made any sense. I couldn't piece together this cryptic and paranormal puzzle that seemed to be finely interwoven with my life. God had given me glimpses into other spiritual realms since I was a child, but the question of why remained a complete mystery.

CHAPTER EIGHT

A New Love

My laborious life was morphing into what felt like a downward spiraling pit of bleakness and despair. I was in dire need of some critical, renovating life changes; I had to devise a strategy to better manage the distressing events and situations that caved in and bombarded me from every direction. I decided to make some changes. It was time for some serious action.

There were obvious circumstances that were out of my jurisdiction and control. For example, I couldn't control or eliminate the random evil manifestations that I encountered and aggressively suppressed and bottled up tightly inside. I couldn't bring my grandmother or Martha back to life. I also believed that my decision to remain sequestered in my marriage for the sake of my children was an inflexible one.

On the other hand, on a much more positive note, there were some aspects of my life that I did have full reign over. I had to take control. I started with updating my resume and was soon on a quest for another job. I needed to say goodbye to the piercing, daily reminders that Martha's vacant, ghostly cubicle brought to my deeply troubled heart. My dejected existence was in urgent need of therapeutic healing and rigorous restoration; I was in desperate need of resurgence.

My new job came in no time at all. I found my new office environment to be relatively comfortable and stress-free. I had an ideal boss, the perfect work life balance, and a very challenging yet fulfilling position. As novel as it seemed, I was only allowed to enjoy this new, short-lived opportunity for two fleeting months before God tactfully intervened and swiftly carried me away under his magnificent wings. He had other plans in store for my life, a comprehensive crusade greater than anything I could have ever imagined.

A position at another company spontaneously and effortlessly landed on my lap. Any ounce of logic and judgment should have urged me to decline the offer. I knew I shouldn't have even considered the role, but in the end I was compelled to accept. The Holy Spirit influenced me and insisted that I make the unexpected and apparently irrational transition. It was then that, unknowingly, the course of my life would begin to drastically change and shift gears. God was in the driver's seat and I was merely a blind, compliant passenger coasting along for the unforeseen and surprisingly bumpy ride.

David Connor was the head of the department that I had just joined; he was my boss's superior. The first time he and I met was during the interview process where he was rather reticent and subdued. Playing more of the assessor role, he kept his questions to a minimum. The bulk of the interrogating was left in the hands of David's chatty sidekick, my soon to be boss.

David kept a very professional demeanor throughout the course of the meeting except for the sudden, ephemeral smile. He gave off a very timid grin when I mentioned that wine tasting was one of my preferred hobbies; his eyes twinkled with a small suggestion of excitement. In that fleeting moment, I thought that he must have been a wine lover himself or maybe he even had a brief notion of drinking a glass of wine with me. That was an unassuming, transient thought that invaded my mind as quickly as it departed; I didn't think of it any further.

My concluding opinion of David was quite high; I found him to be very accomplished and refined. I was under the strong impression that he was a rather distinguished member of the organization. David was an average looking older gentleman. My best guess was that he was in his mid-50s.

The first couple of months on the new job went rather smoothly. I had minimal contact with David and my sole thoughts of him were strictly professional in nature.

Only a few short months had passed when I noticed some incredibly intense sensations stirring up and igniting inside of me; there was an emotional revival coming to life within my spirit. I began to experience a forceful attraction and magnetism towards a rather inconspicuous David; it was beyond all of my reason and understanding. I couldn't comprehend why or even how this was possible. I didn't find David physically attractive and we had little to no interaction in the office. I barely knew anything about this nearly complete stranger's personal life except that he was married with three daughters that he lovingly adored. To top things off and add further complexity, I was in David's direct reporting line. This one tiny, but monumental, detail paved the way for an awkward office environment that could have potentially given rise to personal as well as professional complications.

Despite the ongoing and increasing obstacles that Phillip and I endured, straying from my marriage never crossed my mind. I never once suspected that I could be one of those unfaithful wives that I shunned and detested. I didn't understand why I was attracted to David and my lingering thoughts of him began to trouble me. But what frightened me most about this distinctive situation was the fact that I was treading on unfamiliar territory. My sentiments were far from ordinary; they were forceful and unconventional. My heightened emotions bypassed the physical and originated from deep inside of my soul or maybe even beyond my soul, if that were possible. I had an overriding impression that there was something or someone else involved. An obscure, ubiquitous spiritual mastermind was at work; the primary goal was to unite me with David.

I couldn't surrender myself to these dynamic and dominant feelings; I was convinced that would have been the worst decision I could have made for both my personal life and career. I somehow had to take full control of the situation and harness the emotions that rapidly seemed to be taking charge and controlling me.

Distance was my primary tactic. I strove to stay as far away from David as I possibly could without causing suspicions or impediments to my overall job performance. I was certain that my cautious and well-engineered strategy would work. After all, we were separated by a layer of management so there was very little need for communication between the two of us.

Only a few short weeks after I implemented my premeditated plan, I learned that David and I would soon cross paths on the same corporate voyage. Although we had entirely different business purposes and itineraries, we would nonetheless travel to the same destination. My rampant thoughts went haywire. It was highly likely that there would be a team dinner or lunch penciled somewhere in the calendar. My heart soared at the thought of engaging with David in a more informal setting but I immediately composed myself. I was determined to stick to my guns and stay the course. This business trip would serve as the perfect platform to test out my tactical approach as well as my resolve.

As suspected, a team dinner was scheduled and my nerves were more than ruffled. The moment I equally desired and dreaded had finally arrived. There were just four of us present – David and his former boss Craig, my co-worker Jane, and myself. We ordered a nice bottle of wine for the table, but I was determined not to fall victim to its disastrous effects and influences. I couldn't give David the slightest indication that I had any interest in him. Albeit crass and unbecoming of me, I chose to ignore David for the entire evening. I felt that I had no other choice.

I deliberately routed all of my focus to Craig, who was perfectly suited to accept my interactions. He openly solicited my attention and took great pleasure and amusement in humoring me. I figured David and Jane wouldn't mind so much since they could easily delight themselves in office related topics and casually ignore my blatant rudeness. As long as my interest in David was masked it really didn't matter what anyone inferred from my communication with Craig. It was the perfect decoy.

My scheme worked like a charm. Unfortunately, it may have worked too well. By the middle of dinner, David did a complete one-eighty; he radically morphed from a state of relaxation to complete discontentment. Disengaged from the group, his dialogue with Jane had become nearly obsolete. As I laughed and continued my discussions with Craig, I occasionally glanced in David's direction only to find that his countenance was either an offended or saddened one. Regardless of the exact sentiments David felt, I knew I was at fault and my guilt-ridden heart began to sink. I couldn't bear to see the distress written all over David's face. I shouldn't have shunned and rejected him the way I did. But, in the heat of the moment, I staunchly believed that there was no other suitable alternative.

On the way to the hotel, I tried to make up for my insensitive actions with an attempt to resurrect David's spirits. Or maybe I expected to boost my own mood and rid myself of the plate of remorse I had left over from dinner. Either way, I longed to see a smile on David's wounded face. We laughed and joked as Jane drove us to the hotel. When we said goodbye I felt a great sense of relief. I sighed and hoped that I would never again have to put on an Oscar-winning performance like the one I showcased at dinner. It was incredibly exhausting.

My spiritual intuition and sixth sense informed me early on that my conscientious efforts were futile; regardless of my diligent efforts, my mission would ultimately fail. I predicted the exact event that would lead to the beginning of my "non-working" relationship with David. My unshakeable premonition taunted me for weeks. I was distraught. How could I possibly allow anything physical to happen between David and me?

For two long and drawn out weeks, I seriously contemplated avoiding the specific work affair that would kick things off between us. By doing so, I believed that I could prevent the fulfillment of my premonition. After all, I was still under the naïve impression that I had some form of control over my own fate and destiny.

I quickly recognized that my absence from this professional engagement could adversely affect my career. Against my better judgment, I attended the event and, as predicted, immediately found that there was no turning back. That night marked the beginning of the passionate, dreamlike journey that I knew David and I would inevitably embark upon.

For our first date, David and I decided to meet at a romantic wine bar conveniently located just down the street from our office complex. When I arrived, he had already made himself at home. David was settled comfortably on a small cozy couch that was suitable for a party of two.

I was apprehensive and trembling inside. Pangs of conscience and thoughts of regret invaded and consumed my mortified mind. I was a complete fool! I was a married woman for goodness sake! This was my boss! What on earth was I thinking? What was I doing there and more importantly, was it too late to turn around and leave? After all, I was exceptionally great at making up arbitrary yet convincing excuses. But David didn't deserve that type of treatment. He was probably just as nervous as I was. How could I just walk out on him and leave him abandoned?

I elected to stay, but only for a short while. I silently vowed that I would never meet with him again. As I stood at the entryway of the bar, staring at David and debating with myself, I regained my composure as best as I could and slowly strolled towards the increasingly daunting loveseat.

As soon as I positioned myself next to David, every ounce of anxiety and dread vanished in one single heartbeat. In fact, it was my beating heart that instantly crushed every one of my concerns. The first moment I looked at David's profile I knew there was nowhere else in the world I should have been but sitting there closely nestled beside him. All of my trepidations disappeared and I was completely at ease. From that point on, I had no reservations and broke the oath that I had just made to myself. Inexplicably, I felt that I had already known David and on a very profound level.

I couldn't explain what had just transpired, nor did I care to try. In a mere matter of minutes, I had made a complete transition from the nervous, remorseful me that had barely managed to step foot in the door to the fearless, besotted me that didn't dare think of moving from the most comfortable couch I had ever sat on. The unusual transformation was entirely surreal.

It was on that first date that David and I enjoyed our first bottle of red wine. I was immediately taken back to my interview when I professed my love of wine and David attempted to conceal his very unforgettable, bashful smile. The wine was satisfying and smooth and it certainly helped to alleviate some of David's tensions and inhibitions. After a few sips, he gained enough courage and confidence to put his big, strong hand just above my knee. He gently stroked my leg for a couple of seconds and then abruptly withdrew. He nervously apologized and asked me if his actions were ok. What he didn't know was that the moment he touched me, I knew that his hands were made exclusively for me; his hands were the only ones in the world that were meant to touch and hold me. I felt some kind of intoxicating energy dancing excitedly between the two of us; my body tingled in a way I had never before experienced or even dreamed of. Reassuringly, I smiled at David and boldly placed his hand back where it belonged.

David and I merrily ate, drank and laughed like a couple of old, lifelong friends recently reunited. We even discussed the prospect of a future trip together. This was our first date! I couldn't comprehend how two strangers could interact this way or connect as seamlessly as we did. Our relationship had just been born and was only beginning to blossom. But, strangely, it felt as though it had already taken off like an F-22 Raptor.

As we sat there enjoying each other's company, David and I embraced in our first kiss. And we kissed and we kissed and we kissed! The wine bar must have been illuminated from the inside and out; I felt thousands upon thousands of tiny sparks and beams of light flowing between us. I never knew kisses could feel as passionate and glorious as those David and I shared; I savored each and every impeccable one. Our lips were created and designed for one another's.

After that remarkable night, no force on earth could keep me and David apart. We had such a uniquely powerful bond that even we could not understand it or its origins.

We began to see each other quite frequently and before we knew it, we were a concrete couple with hopes of one shared, luminous future. Our time together was treasured but scarce; we cherished every moment we were fortunate enough to have and spend in each other's presence. Our robust feelings for one another grew exponentially; it was unlike anything either of us had experienced. It was fairytale like and well beyond our comprehension.

But as enchanted as our story was, reality starred in and played a central, leading role in our epic saga. I had learned, on that first divined night that David had also been suffering from a deteriorating marriage. But unlike the stagnant situation I was in with Phillip, David and his wife had already parted ways and were well advanced in their divorce proceedings. Despite his separation and impending divorce, he found it exceptionally difficult to be so emotionally involved with me while technically still a married man. And to add to his already guilt-ridden state I was still a married woman, albeit unhappily.

As David came head to head with his compromised values and principles, I also dealt with my own debilitating demons. Each day there was an obstinate, lingering battle firmly holding its ground on the shores of my mind and soul. I was tormented day and night. How could I carry on with David while still married? How could I execute this hideous act of betrayal on my husband? Regardless of our problems and the frail state of our marriage, Phillip did not warrant this unfaithfulness. No one deserved this form of treachery.

How could I continue with this covert affair knowing the impact my insidious actions would have on my innocent, God given children? They would never understand; they would never forgive their immoral mother.

I carried a hefty burden of guilt and remorse with me at all times. The straining stronghold was like my inexorable shadow, relentlessly neighboring me from one direction or another no matter where I turned. I couldn't break free from my uncompromising encumbrance. I tried to come to terms with my infidelity but there was no valid earthly justification that could lighten the heavy load of my ever-mounting affliction.

Despite my ongoing internal warfare, I could not bring myself to part ways with and say goodbye to my relationship with David. I needed David in my life like I needed oxygen to breathe and live; he was a vital part of my sustenance. I cared for him intensely, on a dimension previously unknown to either of us. Although fully conscious of my deep sentiment for David, I could never understand why I felt so strongly for someone I hardly even knew.

David and I agonized frantically over the various complications surrounding our respective marriages. But our marriages and families weren't the only danger zones that we were forced to navigate and hurdle through; we couldn't neglect or evade the unavoidable and ubiquitous barriers that we encountered in the office nearly every day.

David held a well-regarded, reputable position in the organization. He was the vice president of our department and I was in his direct reporting line. If the sensational news of our relationship leaked out, both of our jobs would be in jeopardy. David and I had to remain on strict, constant guard in order to avoid suspicions from the team and possible exposure. We acknowledged the perilous hazards and risks we faced but we accepted the consequences and carried on. David and I put our relationship and each other above all of the challenges and interferences that stood in our way. That was the only viable solution for a bond as unbreakable as ours; the only way we could move forward was together.

As time progressed so did David and I. We found ourselves spending a considerable amount of time together at work, despite all of the inescapable dangers and risks of getting caught. David understood that I had obvious time constraints and limitations with Phillip and the kids on the home front so to make up for the obvious time restrictions, we had to actively generate, as well as maximize, any and all moments of togetherness. Fortunately, the office served as the perfect platform.

The decisions we made were not entirely scrupulous ones, but in the grand scheme of things it really didn't matter to either of us. David and I suffered a deep desire and hunger to be with each other as often as we possibly could. We seized every opportunity that presented itself. We scheduled private meetings in conference rooms and snuck off for coffee and tea breaks in one of our many romantic, secluded nooks. We met for lunch daily and occasionally took loving strolls throughout some of the city's handsomely adorned grounds and gardens. We were in love and the consequences of our love essentially became inconsequential.

Quite regularly, David and I openly discussed our respective concerns and pressures, but with time we found that our apprehensions became insignificant and irrelevant. In spite of our sprawling complications and tormenting guilt, we somehow understood and accepted that we were eternally bound to one another. We had a profound, unworldly connection that we were only beginning to recognize and explore. Our cosmic union was immeasurable. We shared a love, unlike any other told of in the greatest of love stories. Ours was a divine love that was unconditional and timeless.

The emotions and sentiments I felt for David completely overtook every facet of my existence. After only a couple of months, I felt a driving, intrinsic desire to bear his child. Was I a mad woman? How could I possibly long to have a child with someone I had only known for such a short while? The truth was that it felt as though I had known David for hundreds, if not thousands of years; our union of love was immaculate and eternal. It almost felt odd and unnatural not to raise a family together.

I was a bit anxious about confessing my ambitious hopes of one day having a child together. David was twenty years older than me, had three grown daughters of his own and was most likely not interested in going through the tribulations of early fatherhood again. And of course, we were both still married, but not yet to each other!

In spite of each of my doubts and hesitations, I knew I had to divulge my maternal wishes to David even though I didn't quite know how to approach the delicate subject. I stopped all of my fretting and decided to offer my confession. I thought it best to take the direct, blunt approach. But before I could disclose my secret longing, much to my surprise, David took the initiative and brought up the subject of family; he shared, quite timidly, that he had a budding desire to bring our very own child into this world.

My heart sang as he spoke.

How could this deep seeded need suddenly sprout and come to life within us both? Where was this aspiration coming from? David and I were both reasonable and rational individuals and we recognized that this was a completely irrational declaration. But our hope of a child was beyond all sense and logic; it was beyond this world. It was evident that our minds were not involved; this pure and sacred yearning stemmed directly from our hearts.

David and I tried earnestly to rationalize and explain the immediate evolution of our relationship and the magnitude of our great love and passion. I never believed in the concept of reincarnation but David and I dared to consider the possibility that we could have been past lovers reunited in our present time and era. This idea was only one plausible explanation that our brains concocted to help us understand and substantiate our fated union. There had to be another element involved; the spiritual dimension was somehow at play but neither of us could possibly comprehend or appreciate how.

David and I discussed the illogical notion that the two of us shared one, unified spirit. Could it have been possible that it was actually this solitary spiritual entity that brought our two carnal bodies together in the physical world? As preposterous as these theories may have sounded to the vast majority of the population, for David and I the realm of possibilities was never-ending. Furthermore, each option we deliberated was entirely conceivable. We knew our love and bond was incredibly extraordinary and unheard of. We couldn't help but speculate as to how and why we could be so fortunate.

During one of our speculative and theoretical starry-eyed conversations, David facetiously suggested that we plan a visit to a palm reader or psychic. Perhaps we would find some form of enlightenment that would help us understand the origins of our relationship. We joked lightheartedly about it many times but I never gave it any serious consideration, as I didn't approve of this form of recreation. Then one night, after a late dinner, we happened to drive by a random palm reading establishment conveniently located just down the road from David's apartment complex. At his suggestion, we decided to drop in and say hello, just for kicks of course.

The entertainment was an obese, friendly woman who in many ways resembled a stereotypical, conventional witch pictured in traditional

Hollywood films or children's cartoons. She had a rather large, pointed nose and long black hair pulled back in a ponytail that revealed a prominent, shiny forehead. David and I didn't know what to expect or what was customary with regards to readings, but we were hoping to have ours done together. However, the "witch" wouldn't allow this.

David was the first victim. During his twenty-minute session, he was desperately waiting for the enigmas of our unification to be divulged and unraveled before his very attentive eyes and ears. But instead of revealing insightful, illuminating answers to David, the soothsayer confirmed what he already knew. Amongst other things, she declared that no woman would ever love him the way I loved him.

I was up next.

The clairvoyant fortune teller had me all to herself in what looked like a poorly remodeled kitchen. She immediately apprehended my hand and held it captive. But ironically, the palm reader didn't take one glance at my palm; instead she was steadily and intently fixated on my eyes. The moment our eyes connected, I sensed the pervasive evil that was staring at me from the morbid pits of her portly body.

The medium informed me that she had a vast array of critical information to convey to me, but for some reason she could not elaborate with David sitting outside in the waiting area. She urged me to forgo this particular visit and come back without him; if I desired to hear the privileged and confidential material, I had to come back completely alone. As either a courtesy or bribe, the palm reader did not charge me for my session but she innocuously encouraged me to return on my own. I immediately sensed that she was one of Satan's loyal vessels but I didn't dare hypothesize what her wicked intentions could have been.

David was highly puzzled and intrigued. Why couldn't this prevaricating woman communicate with me while he waited outside? Why was she adamant that I come back unaccompanied? David felt uneasy and sensed something was not right. But how could he possible know what I perceived? How could David understand that this woman and her commanding officer had sinister plans in store for my next visit?

At that time, David was completely oblivious to the eerie supernatural domain and the impact it had on my life, but the times were quickly changing. A vigorous and inexplicable force was emerging and coming to light. A tiny, but mighty, seed had begun to sprout in David's recently awakened and aroused spirit.

Very early on in my relationship with David, I was overtaken by the sudden urge to paint. I had recently added a relatively large, 36 x 24 inch, canvas to my inventory and felt that this was the right time to try it out. I sat in front of the canvas and was overwhelmed by its enormity, as I had typically painted on considerably smaller canvases. Consumed by nervousness, I stared at the oversized white fabric for a good ten minutes. I didn't know where or how to begin.

A glass of smooth Malbec relaxed my nerves as it gently coated my throat. My romantic playlist also assisted me with this daunting assignment. In no time at all, thoughts of David raced through my mind. My fears faded and were instantly replaced by a deluge of love and romance. I felt like I was immersed in a dream, consumed by God's commanding spirit and my love for David. I was entirely engrossed in what felt like an intoxicating trance.

Throughout the entire painting session, my focal point was a single, gold leaf sculpture that inconspicuously occupied a quiet corner of the game room. Inexplicably, I was drawn to the majestic figure that had gone unnoticed for years. In between brush strokes I periodically gazed upon the small golden statue as the Lord's hand forcefully painted through me.

In the end, this particular abstract held a fair likeness to the gold leaf, but on a much larger scale. Instead of gold, He highlighted the veins and lamina of the leaf's body with an exciting array of bold and dramatic colors, including blue, orange, purple, green and red. Since the leaf was lying in a horizontal position, the painting also bore resemblance to an oversized eye. A portal or gateway to another dimension also came to mind.

I was quite happy with the final product but it wasn't worthy of museum status, as I had deemed some of my other pieces to be. There was no doubt that it was one of His special creations but at that time I couldn't have known how exclusive it truly was. I could never have fathomed the magnitude of what lie behind what the dear Lord had just gifted me with.

I would eventually give this painting to David as a token of my love, but the present situation and timing would not allow this exchange. Phillip and the children knew that I wasn't inclined to giving away my paintings; each and every one of them meant a great deal to me. How could I explain spontaneously giving this specific piece away? Perhaps when David and I married I would present the painting to him as a housewarming gift. Until then, the abstract would hang in the upstairs game room where it fit in nicely with the warm, neutral colors and décor.

David was a great fan of my artwork and was delighted to hear the exciting news of a fresh, innovative painting. He was anxious and thrilled to see the latest addition of my burgeoning collection and became even more ecstatic when I informed him that my mind was pleasantly overflowing with uninterrupted thoughts of him throughout the entire sitting. I ruined the surprise and confessed that this painting would one day be my gift to him. David was incredibly grateful for this meaningful, heartfelt promise and understood the existing complications.

Gradually, my artwork became a common theme in our conversations. David began to ask probing questions about my creative gifts and abilities. He was exceedingly curious to know how it was that I came to develop my fervent passion for painting.

Throughout my life, I had been accustomed to guarding the details of my divinely inspired creations. I had various reasons for choosing not to divulge too much information regarding my esoteric painting practices. This was a rare and supernatural experience that was, first and foremost, quite unbelievable. The arcane and spiritual nature of the situation was probably as difficult for me to articulate, as it would have been for anyone else to comprehend. I presumed that most people would label me crazy and I never felt the need to justify my sanity to anyone. Simply put, trying to explain the reality behind my works of art was never worth the effort.

But David was altogether different. With time, I knew he would come to understand. I deliberated briefly but knew what had to be done. I broke precedent and shared everything with David. I divulged every curious and baffling detail, from my complete lack of talent to God's spirit infusing me to paint at His command. I didn't hold anything back; I didn't feel the need to.

Being the skeptic that he was, David was lost and dumbfounded when he heard my outrageous story. He had never heard of such a bizarre and phenomenal account. But he knew that I could not and would not make up such tall tales. Why would I?

Much sooner than I expected, with God's generous assistance, the mystifying conundrum became amazingly crystal clear for David.

As expected, David originally had difficulties processing my transcendent engagements with God, but he wasn't necessarily shocked by my revelation. I sensed that he had a very shrewd spirit that was cognizant of everything going on. It seemed as though David's influential and sovereign spirit made continuous attempts to transmit this valuable communication feed to David's mortal mind and consciousness. Before I even mentioned any of my "special" abilities, David had already recognized that I was a very special person.

Although he couldn't figure out exactly how or why, the purpose that David had intensely searched for his entire life had just been revealed to him. A heavy obstruction had been lifted and David's eyes were suddenly opened. His life radically changed when we were miraculously brought together and he had finally been given the reason why. David's newly appointed mandate was to protect me and to do so at all costs.

David didn't know why I needed protection or from what exactly, but his natural instincts told him to be on guard and keep an eye out for those attempting to infiltrate my circle of trust.

David was intrigued by how easily and effortlessly I seemed to attract people; it was almost magnetic. Individuals often gravitated to me like insects fascinated by and attracted to sources of light. I, of course, was accustomed to these routine encounters since I experienced these forceful attractions most of my life. David, however, had never witnessed the type of human dynamics that I evidently brought to life. It wasn't only men that I lured in, but women, children, elderly, and good and bad souls alike. He observed this spectacle so frequently that he pondered over it quite often.

David considered the lavish notion that I could have been some type of spiritual portal that human beings were drawn to on a nonphysical, subconscious level. My children had also shared similar theories with me, but I didn't dwell on or think too much of their assertions.

After reflecting on David's theory, I thought of Martha and the many other vessels that God had hand-picked and placed in my life to protect me or to convey one of His treasured messages. I knew God was communicating with me through David but I wasn't certain if David was yet aware of the type of information he was actually receiving. Gradually, I began to spoon feed some of my most sacred experiences to David; every now and again, I unveiled long kept secrets relating to God's firsthand involvement in my life.

I learned, very early in our relationship, that David wasn't a strong Christian man; in fact, he couldn't even bring himself to acknowledge that Jesus Christ was the one and only way to salvation. A wandering agnostic, David was lost and had spent the majority of his life in search of the truth. Just like the other millions of aimlessly roving nomads,

David was led astray and naively succumbed to the world of obscurity and deception.

Confusion and uncertainties worked exceptionally well for Satan's selfish initiative. The evil one employed any mechanism within his reach to drive our society as far away from the light of Jesus Christ as he possibly could and David was no exception. I had solemn concern for David's eternal resting place, but our relationship was just in its infancy and neither of us was ready to delve into such a controversial and earnest discussion.

David's entire existence was based on science and logic, not on faith. There was so much I desired to share with him but I knew his adolescent soul wasn't ready to receive the full course meal just yet. He wasn't quite capable of plunging into such an expansive spiritual ocean. A work in progress, David was still developing and maturing. I didn't believe that David's mortal mind could fully comprehend the entire span of my supernatural experiences. There was no doubt in my mind that he would have difficulties grasping God's influences on me.

Despite my natural concerns and reservations, I did feel incredibly safe and comfortable with David. If God had indeed sent him into my life to serve as my devoted guardian, then who was I to doubt? I put my trust in the Lord and convinced myself that David was fit for the job he had been given.

CHAPTER NINE

Difficulties We Faced

As a devoted and inseparable alliance, David and I were the target of many continuous and hostile attacks. But it was our majestic love that sustained our relationship through the most tragic and trying times.

David and I had painstakingly arranged to spend my upcoming, milestone birthday abroad, during an impeccably timed company event slated for the thriving city of London. An enthusiastic David spent many hours meticulously planning and arranging every moment of my festive celebration, from the wee morning hours up to the time our bodies would tire and beg for rest and slumber. He put his entire heart into each and every detail of screening and subsequently selecting the birthday activities that were worthy enough for us to engage in. After all, this was no ordinary day; my happy day of birth was meant to be extraordinary and treasured, despite the scrutinizing audience that would most likely be prowling around the town.

Evading the department staff was the biggest concern David and I deliberated on and fretted over. Fortunately, I had obtained relevant insider information regarding everyone else's scheduled extracurricular activities. We prudently discussed and contemplated the means by which we could flawlessly circumvent all of our coworkers during our clandestine escapade. Our event listing was comprehensive and well thought out; we were confident that our ingenious strategy was nailed down tight and bulletproof. David and I didn't anticipate any other threats or major concerns.

How could we possibly expect that Phillip could somehow intervene from nearly 5000 miles away?

Hindsight dropped by for a friendly visit, slapped me in the face a couple of times and showed me how unbelievably naïve I had been.

I was so absorbed in my relationship with David that I was oblivious to the fact that I displayed any evidence of infidelity in my marriage. But Phillip was well aware of the signals that I frequently and carelessly exhibited. He recognized that I was fully engrossed in my own world of distant aloofness and serene seclusion more often than not. He noticed me responding eagerly to text messages on my cell phone and the growing number of email alerts that I received throughout all hours of the day and night. At times, I even snuck off to make surreptitious calls in the bedroom. I went out with my "girlfriends" regularly.

Even though our marriage was in a state of disarray, the glaring proof haunted Phillip's thoughts. Of course, he had never mentioned or even suggested his strong concerns directly to me, but chose to internalize his persistent fears instead. Phillip was tormented by his suppressed fears and emotions until the night he decided to try to prove himself wrong. Instead, he was shocked to discover that his forbidding suspicions were confirmed.

Overwhelmed by feelings of abandonment, Phillip operated in a hasty act of insecurity and mistrust. He invaded my privacy and stealthily read through my personal email account while I was overseas enjoying my prudently fashioned stretch of intimacy with David. Completely distraught, Phillip called me in absolute disbelief and hysteria. While sobbing uncontrollably, Phillip had repeatedly read through each and every endearing email communication shared between David and me. His desolate heart was crushed and he was severely disgusted by my repulsive, unforgivable sins.

Phillip made several copies of the incriminating evidence that vividly recounted my extramarital affair with David. Overwhelmed with contempt, he threatened to send the condemning email correspondence to our human resource department as well as David's unsuspecting wife. I could lose my job but I couldn't bear it if David was unwillingly removed from his prestigious position. He didn't deserve for his entire life's career to be taken away from him in one thunderous flash of hatred and vengeance.

In sheer indignation and delirium, Phillip even made threats to David's life. My husband considerately offered me one singular exception; he vowed to keep my reprehensible secret to himself and to forget about it entirely if I swore to end my shameful relationship with David. Thoughts of David losing his job, or even worse his life, inundated and drowned me. If my children got wind of my dishonesty and deception, I would be mortified. I had no choice but to concede to Phillip's calculating extortion.

I was in a deep pit of despondency and confusion. Phillip's agony and misery shot rays of guilt and disgrace through every fiber of my body. Witnessing his despair brought tears to my eyes and throbbing pains to my reprehensible, deceiving heart. I never intended to inflict any pain on Phillip; I never wanted this outcome for him or for our marriage. But despite my sorrow and remorse, I had one major problem – my heart belonged to David. No matter how hard I tried, I could not uphold my promise to Phillip.

I immediately called David and explained the situation to him. I described the duress I was under as a result of Phillip's coercions. As expected, David was strikingly upset but not as concerned with any of Phillip's threats coming to fruition. The magnitude of our love was more important than senseless intimidations made in absolute anger.

David and I shared the exact same sentiments; regardless of the severity and complexity of the situation, we could not let this interference stand in our way. The thought of existing without the other was unbearable and impossible to perceive. We were blessed and thankful to have savored the sweet taste of true love. How on earth could we consciously and willingly say goodbye to one of the most precious gifts we had ever received? What kind of hollow and dull life would that be for either of us? We were fully aware that the stakes were dramatically higher than ever before, but our interminable union was well worth the gamble and any other that would come our way.

Without any hesitation, David and I agreed to stay together, but we recognized that we had to take additional and more stringent precautions going forward. We drastically decreased the amount of communication and time spent together, only to find our hearts besieged with aching and longing unlike anything ever before experienced. As in any great love affair, suffering was to be expected.

Decision making became increasingly difficult, as we had to carefully consider the additional risks of Phillip once again uncovering the truth behind our covert relationship. When we had privileged opportunities to be together, David and I generally elected to spend our time alone. When we did choose to wander into the public arena, we took extra security measures. We both appreciated and relished each moment of affection and warmth we were granted. With each second we were given, David and I vowed to hold on to our once in a lifetime love and treasure it forever.

One night, as I sat in a heavenly stream of starry-eyed thoughts and recollections, the painting that silently hung in my game room came to mind. I almost heard it calling to me. Suddenly, a spiritual force came over me and spoke to me with a pristine clarity. For some inexplicable reason, I knew that, regardless of the inquiries Phillip and the children might have, I had to give David his rightful gift. This mysterious painting, that somehow summoned me, was not mine; it belonged to David.

David was overjoyed when Christmas came around and I presented the promised painting to him. He knew this piece of art would one day grace the walls of our home but he expected that day would come at a much later time. Filled with the raw excitement of a child, he cleared a wall just above his main sofa and hung the painting in the center of his living room. The painting was brilliantly illuminated with natural lighting from a sliding door that led to David's balcony. It fit right in and instantly became the central showcase of the apartment.

I was delighted by David's appreciation and adoration of this unique, one of a kind demonstration of my devoted love. He felt that this painting brought us even closer together, as though a part of me or my spirit was residing in his apartment with him at all times. When I physically couldn't be there with him, David somehow felt my presence emanating through the mysterious oil painting.

All was bliss, for a while at least.

Never in a million years would I have predicted that David's soon to be ex-wife, Susan, could prove to be a menace or aggravation. After all, she was the staunch initiator and driver of their forthcoming divorce. I was certain that she would have been thrilled to have her freedom from David and would therefore painlessly let him go without any interference. But Susan had lost sight of her goal the very moment she let jealousy invade and dominate her mind.

Susan was devious and conniving. She pried into my personal life without a shred of shame or reservation. She meddled and snooped and somehow discovered that her husband was involved with a married woman. The crazed woman was beside herself. She had no qualms about informing David of her outrage and position of unqualified disapproval.

I was furious to find that Susan had initiated unauthorized background checks on me as well as Phillip. I used every ounce of restraint humanly possible to control my anger and contain my already envisioned imminent vengeance. As uncharacteristic and exasperating as this was for me, I constrained myself for David's sake alone. The last thing I wanted was to cause any unnecessary grief between him and his daughters. Their parents would soon divorce; this was enough hardship for them to deal with.

Ignoring Susan's cunning actions was considerably difficult for me. Nothing in me could forgive and forget her palpable treachery. I could not bring myself to renounce this woman's criminal acts as easily as David seemed to. As their divorce had not yet finalized, David proceeded with extreme caution so as not to add fuel to an already blazing forest. As expected, Susan's insidious activities spawned an unforeseen and unnecessary amount of tension between David and me.

As we inched along and attempted to move pass this underhanded act of invasion, Susan shocked us with another massive bomb. She discreetly peered through David's computer files and found that I was a member of the department he headed. This time she had solid leverage over David and could cause severe delays to their divorce process. Susan made subtle threats and comments suggesting that she could effortlessly use this newly discovered evidence to her advantage if need be. The enraged and envious woman boldly stated that she was well aware that the consequences of having a relationship with someone in the same reporting line could result in termination.

David intuitively sensed Susan's excessive bitterness and anger with his newfound happiness. For the sake of his children and to avoid any further and unnecessary grievances, he had to act in a conciliatory fashion. David had no choice but to cater to his soon-to-be ex-wife and proceed through the divorce process with grave restraint and attention as best as he possibly could without upsetting our relationship.

Ironically, dealing with the guiles and pressures of our respective spouses may have actually fortified the relationship we desperately strove to defend and shelter. David and I fought these unyielding, arduous scuffles side by side. And with each notable victory, we united and fused together into one cohesive and indestructible unit. We were armed and equipped to take on the world.

But we could never have foreseen the battle we would encounter next.

Maybe we were blinded by our enchanted love or entirely engulfed by one another to notice, but David and I completely failed to see the commotion spreading through our office. Unbeknownst to us, salacious rumors about our "inappropriate" relationship had rapidly made their way throughout the most of the organization. The gossip train carrying mayhem and upheaval had travelled all the way from our department to our human resources division. Much to our surprise, David and I learned that we were the subject of an ongoing internal investigation.

Very early on, David and I had discussed and recognized the full range of perils and risks that we faced as a result of our union. We were fully cognizant of every possible consequence. We knew that if we stayed together we would likely be subject of intense scrutiny and suspicions. Termination was a potential outcome from the very moment I sat next to David on that extraordinarily comfortable and memorable loveseat.

In spite of all of the obstacles we faced, the thought of abolishing our relationship was never up for consideration. David and I acknowledged that we were headed down a challenging, tumultuous path but we willfully chose to walk it. If we had to face judgment and punishment for the love we shared, then we would make that sacrifice.

The entire department was questioned before David and I faced our trial and interrogation. Our relationship was painted to be a debauchery of disgracefulness. As humbling and degrading as this ordeal was, David and I remained secure in our love and we were not discouraged. Despite the tainted stories floating around influencing and shaping the prevailing office opinions, there was nothing detestable about our relationship. David and I experienced the purest form of love imaginable. Sadly, most people could only dream of the type of love we shared.

Finally, near the end of April, after a few drawn out weeks of intense grilling and cross-examinations, David and I were asked to leave the company. The piece of incriminating evidence that sealed the case shut was a text message from David; his communication simply read, "I love you sweetheart xxxxxx."

CHAPTER TEN

The Abstract

Soft facets of sunlight danced frivolously upon the curves of my face while the cool, unperturbed breeze brushed my hair perfectly into place. Dinner was a magnificent feast for two on the private, uninhabited patio that was surrounded by a sheltering panel of plush palm trees. The rich Bordeaux style red blend was succulently smooth and exuded a subtle complexity that demanded further exploration.

David and I toasted in amorous commemoration of our joint termination, delivered to us only hours earlier.

We had just been forced to resign from our positions because of the precious love shamelessly proclaimed in a text message for the entire world to read. There couldn't have been a more romantic or noble reason for anyone to lose a job. David and I weren't celebrating our termination, we were rejoicing in our triumphant love.

What would have been a devastating, earth-shattering experience for most was nothing more than a temporary hiccup for David and me. As one would expect, we were naturally shocked by the circumstances but not at all deterred by them. Throughout our relationship, David and I sensed a pervasive, underlying power protecting and guiding us through every impediment that had been cunningly placed in our way. We somehow knew that, despite the seemingly unfortunate turn of events, everything would work out for us and strategically fall into place.

That enchanting dinner was one of the most tranquil and memorable David and I had shared together. Surprisingly, everything felt frighteningly right; we were completely relaxed and unruffled. As we ate and drank in faithful communion, we were surrounded and enveloped by our sanctified love. It saturated our immediate atmosphere and sheltered us like an unbreakable, invisible force field. Notwithstanding the unfortunate turn of events, the brilliantly lit starry night ended marvelously.

But despite our fairytale like union, David and I did not have any exemptions to the difficulties that all couples endured.

Quite intrinsically, it was only natural for David and me to expect that, when things went stunningly right, our barrage of problems would evade us and stay far at bay. Of course, that was simply our hopeless and romantic naivety taking charge and setting our emotions on cruise control.

But with even the slightest change of the most harmonious wind, a drastic turn of the climate would routinely and abruptly follow suit. David and I had no indication that there was a severely menacing and aggressive front headed in our direction; violent thunderstorms were in the forecast and on the near horizon.

Our ill-fated chain of proceedings modestly began with one tiny, insignificant lover's spat.

Soon enough there were two.

Then, in no time at all, there were several minor quarrels that we miserably failed to conquer and eradicate. Still living and struggling for survival, these apparently inconsequential disputes escalated and mutated into one monstrous and uncontrollable catastrophe.

The interaction between David and I deteriorated with each passing moment. Communication was so prickly and disagreeable that even the thought of being in close proximity was agonizing.

I needed a break from David and I needed it ASAP!

Rather fortunately, a group of old friends had recently asked me to join them in New York City for the upcoming weekend. Although I had originally declined the offer, the invitation had remained open; I could always change my mind.

The solution to my quandary with David was quite simple; I would escape to New York, pull myself together and decompress. I desperately needed time to reflect on the current state of my bleak and distressed life, specifically the surreptitious life I shared with David.

But I was baffled. What had gone so miserably wrong between the two of us?

Perhaps our involuntary resignations had an unanticipated, detrimental impact on us. Maybe the love David and I shared was similar to a life demanding of sunlight for nourishment and sustenance. Could it be that our love flourished and strengthened with time spent together but diminished considerably with absence? Did the distance between us indirectly lead to the onset of our persistent bickering and turmoil?

My mind was not entirely set on ending my relationship with David; however, it was undeniably a highly considered deliberation. I needed my personal time and space to ponder the possibilities and reexamine the jumbled and disorderly track I was aimlessly driving down.

How on earth could David and I continue on this unstable and rickety road? After all, I was still married to Phillip and the shadowy path to our looming divorce wasn't getting any brighter.

Maybe our recent terminations were a sign or message from God; maybe He was actually signaling for David and me to terminate our precious love affair. Perhaps now was the optimal time to dissolve my union with David. It was quite possible that a final farewell was finally in order.

But my great plan didn't turn out as well as I had hoped. When David heard the news of my planned getaway, he was seething and fuming! I had known David to be a very calm and collected gentleman that rarely lost his temper, but this time I had tipped him over the edge. I had never before seen such indignation emanate from an otherwise tranquil and composed individual.

David didn't acknowledge or accept the concept of a "break" or time apart; for David it was all or nothing. I was given one very clear ultimatum; if I opted for the New York trip then he and I were over. There were no ifs, ands or buts about it. There would be no second chances.

I wasn't positive about my future or David's future or even our future together; I was downright lost and confused. The one thing I did know with absolute certainty was that it would be entirely rash and foolish to risk throwing away this one of a kind love without having complete confidence in my decision. Without any hesitation, I said no to New York.

Though we attempted to patch up our misfortunes through a rocky reconciliation, David and I remained fairly distant. Although I stayed in town, I still had to consider the progression or, more likely, regression of our relationship. Distance and time were still very crucial elements that I earnestly believed could help me wade through our deep ocean of struggles.

That weekend, my heart and soul were dedicated exclusively to my precious little angels. I was immersed and hypnotized by my adoring children; any chance thoughts of David were minimal and trivial. Subconsciously, I may have been transitioning and customizing myself to a life without him. I was practically convinced that we were near the end of our journey together.

On Monday, I agreed, albeit lackadaisically, to meet David for breakfast and coffee. The first glimpse of the morning sky was clear and cheerful but the sun was rapidly sheltered by an abundant mass of melancholy clouds. Dense, heavy rainfall poured down immediately after we finished our meal.

David and I happened to be driving my low-sitting car on that drizzly day and the streets were beginning to show signs of flooding. David needed to run some errands but was worried about driving my car through the hazardous high waters. In light of the inclement weather we agreed that his SUV would be the safest bet. We quickly made our way back to his apartment to swap out our vehicles. But before making the switch, we made an unexpected visit up to the apartment. David had something he wanted to share with me.

David sat down in front of his cozy desk and turned on his computer. He tenderly sat me on his lap while he played Sinead O'Conner's "Nothing Compares to You" music video. All weekend long David's shattered heart was heavily burdened with continuous feelings of abandonment and lonesomeness. This song gave him comforting thoughts of me. David told me that I meant everything to him and shamelessly confessed that he couldn't bear to live his life without me. His heavy and downcast eyes welled up with tears.

As David gazed deep into my eyes, I sensed an infinite sea of love and adoration. David and I had grown so accustomed to being with each other every day in the office that the abrupt shift had evidently taken its toll. We realized that this newly imposed time apart had an undesirable impact on us and was destroying our relationship. We talked about various ways we could help keep our bond intact. We vowed to do everything in our power to nurture our rare, one of a kind love.

As we sat restfully in a warm, affectionate embrace, David became curiously distracted and his attention was instantly diverted away from me and our conversation. In a matter of seconds his interest had suddenly shifted; David was entirely immersed in the abstract painting that graced his living room wall. Like an inquisitive child, fully engrossed, he began to tilt his head from one side to the other as though he were trying to adjust his focus or calibrate his gaze.

A dumbfounded David professed to see a man's face in the center of the canvas. He pointed out the anonymous figure to me, as best as he could, without moving an inch from his chair. David was bewildered and zealously asked me if I could see the esoteric image he cautiously spoke of.

It didn't take me more than a few seconds to make out the picture; it was as clear as the day. There was an eye, a nose and a mouth that methodically fashioned a man's profile. The altruistic stranger faced our direction and appeared to be staring right at David and me. He had shoulder length, black hair that looked smooth and well kept.

David was astonished by this newly revealed imagery. At first glance, it reminded him of an exquisitely designed stained glass window that would have resided in a church or ancient cathedral. Handsomely segmented and outlined compartments divided or parted the bigger whole. The abstract had somehow changed colors and the new pigments, still vibrant and concentrated, were entirely different. And then, of course, the cryptic man in the center of it all exuded a great sense of awe-inspiring spirituality and sanctity. It wasn't at all difficult to detect the prevailing religious or pious connotations.

David and I were captivated and intrigued by this mysterious figure and the marked clarity of his features. Who was he and why, after five months, was he suddenly revealed to us?

We spent the next several hours intently examining the painting, although it felt as though only a few trifling minutes had gone by. David and I inspected and studied the painting head on and from all angles. Oddly, the man could only be seen from the side where we were sitting, which happened to be from the left side of where the canvas was positioned on the wall.

David and I stood directly in front of the abstract and then we leisurely made our way to the precise transition point where the face became visible. In one instant, we witnessed the miraculous transformation. The original oil colors used in the abstract changed before our very eyes and the buried, surreptitious figure magically surfaced and greeted us. As the angle of view decreased, the freshly renovated colors became richer and bolder. The definition and details of the face and hair became remarkably sharp and distinctive.

A few of the random shapes in the abstract appeared to make up the outline and form of a dove surrounding or enclosing the man. The first thought that came to my mind was the baptism of Jesus Christ, where God's spirit came down upon Him like a dove.

David and I couldn't comprehend how or why these images were suddenly shown to us but we felt an inconceivable amount of serenity and harmony. We were intrigued; our imploring souls yearned and thirsted for answers.

A fervent charge of exploration took over as David and I scoured the Internet and the Holy Bible in search of the specific events and facts surrounding Jesus's baptism. We discussed many biblical themes but, still, none of them made any sense in light of the circumstances. David scanned through hundreds of stained glass photographs while I researched the meaning of doves. All the while, we found it impossible to take our attention off of the esoteric painting. This was unlike anything either of us had ever experienced; we were completely mesmerized by the sudden transformation and emergence of our newfound companion.

Deep down inside and maybe all along, David and I recognized who the arcane figure was that mysteriously appeared and peered out at us through the painting.

Immaculately framed and featured in the center of David's apartment was a spectacular representation of Jesus Christ. Quietly and peacefully, He dwelled in the very nucleus of the abstract that I had painted and presented to David as a Christmas gift. The memorable day of May 10th marked the beginning of a whole new beautiful world for David and I; Jesus was at its core. But He no longer stood silently in the shadows. He made His pervasive presence known and began to speak to us in a thunderous but gentle voice.

CHAPTER ELEVEN

The Revelation

After its stunning debut, David and I spent most of our waking hours studying the enigmatic abstract for weeks on end. We took hundreds of photographs and analyzed each and every one of them. Consumed by the extraordinary transformation, we were like eager children in search of a great treasure, but, unfortunately, we weren't privy to a legend on a map to help guide us or provide us with any clues. We weren't provided with a rule book or instruction manual, but we didn't let that stop us. Jesus Christ had been miraculously unveiled and revealed to us on a short, unplanned stop by David's apartment; this was the only reference point David and I needed to fuel and motivate our voracious appetites. Beholding the glorious transfiguration was like witnessing Jesus Christ come to life; the surreal metamorphosis was breathtaking and elevating.

From the very moment I stepped foot into David's apartment, my eyes were like magnets, permanently fixed on the exclusive painting. I found it extremely challenging to concentrate on anything other than this soul-stirring work of art. I lost all control and surrendered myself; the piece was alluring and all encompassing. Time even seemed to have altered or shifted gears while I gazed upon His consecrated image; hours felt like minutes and minutes drifted by in mere seconds. An infinite ocean of tranquility covered me while I drowned in His irreproachable presence. My body and mind became peripheral, almost absent. My spirit was revitalized and fortified by the spellbinding power He exuded.

Without any question or discussion regarding the commanding persuasion of the painting, David and I wholeheartedly dedicated ourselves to it. We strove earnestly to understand what was happening. What was going on? What did His sudden appearance mean? None of it made sense; we were beyond baffled.

What was the meaning behind this unbelievably phenomenal sign that disclosed itself to us in the living room of David's small, inconsequential apartment? Why did our painting, created with such great love and passion, majestically transform before our very eyes immediately after one of the most turbulent times David and I had ever gone through?

This mysterious canvas had slept inconspicuously on the wall for many months without signaling or summoning us. Why did the one and only Jesus Christ present himself to us so unexpectedly and magnanimously on that overcast and rainy day?

We yearned for the answers to these questions and so many more. Fortunately, David and I were both unemployed and had sufficient time to seek understanding and enlightenment. We solemnly sought and we generously found, or, to be exact, God benevolently provided.

After intense scrutiny and experimentation, David and I discovered that the remarkable conversion to Christ only occurred in natural lighting and only when the skies were cloudy or overcast. If the brilliance of the sun shone in full force, Jesus remained concealed; the original abstract was all that could be seen, regardless of the angle. We experimented with artificial lighting at all intensities and levels, but there was never any change in the imagery. It seemed as though the enchanted, surreptitious treasures buried inside the abstract came to life and could only be awakened with precise settings.

It was only a few days after the astounding premiere of Jesus that God began to communicate with me in a distinctly different manner than He had previously done. He spoke to my spirit in a blindingly profound fashion that I had never before experienced or could even comprehend; His words were solid and resounding. He steered me to precise Bible verses and stories that ultimately provided me with the insight and wisdom that He lovingly desired for me to have. And even more innovatively and imaginatively, God began to reveal and explain the secret encryptions and messages scattered throughout the supernatural painting He created through me.

The staggering work of art was not only created by God's ethereal hand, but it was also fully infused with His holy breath and essence. This phenomenal painting was His revolutionary and inventive "Revelation" sent to our world as a beacon to a faithless, debased society in dire need of evidence and confirmation. There was much to behold inside the walls of His precious gift and He was there to guide us through each of the many manifestations and their respective meanings.

He began his instructive enlightenment with Jesus Christ.

One half of Jesus' shield-like chest was blue and the other was red; these were well-established, preeminent Holy colors that held great biblical connotation. The blue represented Jesus' divinity and the red represented his humanity, as well as His ultimate sacrifice for the salvation of the human race. These divine and highly significant colors only appeared within the transformation view; in the native abstract, these areas were purple and orange. Jesus' black hair was originally a bluish hue in the abstract. His shoulder length, perfectly intact hair instantly took me to my vision of Jesus in the celestial garden.

I was wholly absorbed by Jesus' galvanizing stature that I initially failed to see beyond His prodigious image. But God embraced me in His arms, like a loving father, and gently guided me. Kindly, He opened my eyes to a glorious kingdom beyond my wildest dreams. The Almighty led me to extraordinary images that my mortal mind could never have concocted or conceived. And He did it all in His infallible time.

The first illustration that God highlighted for me, shortly after Jesus' dramatic opening exhibition, was that of a young, angelic female figure. The delicate looking, celestial being appeared in the bottom right quadrant of the arcane "Revelation" and was positioned just to the right and slightly in front of where Jesus stood. David thought that Jesus could have been carrying the girl but it was difficult for us to determine with certainty. Either way, the girl was nestled safely beside Him, out of harm's way.

The angelic girl was noticeably smaller than Jesus; this was also reminiscent of my heavenly garden vision. She was bright white and radiated a soothing glow of an almost saintly purity. The ivory girl had long flowing hair that seamlessly rolled down one side of her face in a very graceful and elegant manner. When I first saw her I was somewhat fearful; I didn't know what to make of this new ghostly presence. Thankfully, God quickly relieved my fears and explained that that this nebulous individual was, in fact, a depiction of me.

What on earth was going on? How could I, a mere mortal, be standing right next to Jesus Christ in this phenomenal painting crafted by God's very own hand? Was this another one of His prophetic paintings? I was dumbfounded by the shocking account but my inquisitive mind raced with possibilities.

I considered the vast realm of options that could be in store for me. Like an excited child eagerly awaiting the next chapter of a captivating bedtime story, I was zealously enthusiastic for His word. I wasn't aware of it at the time, but God was steadily and judiciously preparing me for the privileged knowledge that He would soon convey to me. I had to wait patiently for His divine communications; I had to sit still until the Lord was ready to connect with me.

As I waited on God, I was struck with a heartfelt and humbling epiphany. I realized that I had it all wrong. Throughout every phase of my life, it was actually God that had been waiting on me! This morsel of divine wisdom changed my outlook, improved my relationship with the Lord and helped me on the odyssey that was soon to come.

One afternoon while we were casually perusing through our immense collection of photos, David looked up towards the "Revelation" and noticed something new in the painting. He thought there was a slight chance that I could be frightened by this new image so he treaded the waters very carefully.

David pointed out a rather large face that was looking in the general vicinity of the delicately illuminated girl. One dark, pronounced eye and a parted hairline that gave way to flowing layers of short, wavy locks were clearly evident. David outlined massive wings that spanned across the entire top half of the canvas. Right before our very eyes was a stunning and grandiose angel ingeniously positioned just above Jesus and the small girl; this overarching angel seemed to be shielding and protecting them. The spectacularly arresting depiction was a beautiful representation of love and asylum.

David and I browsed through our vast collection of photos so that we could thoroughly examine the angel's specific features. As I prodded through the assortment, I was distracted and held captive by the authentic "Revelation" hanging before me. I felt an immeasurable amount of energy and love emanating from the unimaginable depths of the canvas. Suddenly, the Holy Spirit spoke to me and I began to receive an incredibly powerful communication.

A few months before she passed away, someone in the family photographed the most beautiful expression of love that I had ever seen on my grandmother's face; she happened to be looking at me when this priceless and poignant moment was captured. Her eyes sparkled with palpable emotion. Her genuine smile and unassuming visage were glazed with a youthful warmth and soft glow. I was enamored with this emotive depiction of my grandmother and carried it with me always.

I reached into my purse, grabbed my wallet and retrieved the notable black and white photograph. I was amazed by the similarities between my grandmother and the imperial angel in the "Revelation." In a most uncanny fashion, the angel's facial structure and hair greatly resembled my grandmothers; even the partition down the middle of the angel's head was exactly identical to the photo! The angel was facing the girl, who, as I had just been informed, was an illustration of me. Likewise, in the photograph of my grandmother, I was sitting to her left as she beheld me with such candid affection and fondness. I couldn't believe my eyes!

David scanned my grandmother's photo into his laptop and superimposed her image directly on top of the angel in one of the photographs of the "Revelation." David was stunned by the startling similarities. The guardian angel's identity had just been declared. David and I were left speechless and without any doubts.

Though I had sensed her spirit with me continually, that moment was exceptionally different. I felt my grandmother in a much more profound and tangible manner. I experienced an incredible closeness to her. I recognized her presence there in the room with me as I was overtaken by raw spiritual sensations and sentiments. Unrestrained tears rolled down my cheeks as I fully took in and grasped the inconceivable announcement that my beloved grandmother was the angel in God's painting. As I stood there standing next to Jesus, she hovered overhead, guarding us with her expansive wings.

I cringed at the thought of having to part ways and say goodbye to the depiction of my angelic grandmother displayed on David's living room wall. Although she wasn't a tangible being, though I couldn't touch her skin or hear her voice, I knew that my grandmother's presence in the "Revelation" was a message of love from my heavenly Father. He had confirmed what I believed all along; he showed me that my beloved grandmother was with me always.

My aching heart longed to see her countenance every day; I desired to have her with me in my own home where she could be easily accessible. I couldn't contain my feelings of concentrated grief and melancholy. The thought of having to part with my grandmother one more time was heart wrenching and unbearable.

I went against my principles of gift giving and selfishly asked David if he would consider relinquishing his gift. Because he graciously used his heart to answer my question, David didn't think twice about my request. He gave me one sympathetic look of compassion and without any reservations or objections, he altruistically replied with a simple, selfless yes.

We kept the "Revelation" at David's apartment for a few more days until we could arrange for a secure handover. David and I recognized that our intimate trio would soon be divided, so we seized every opportunity to study the painting together for as long as we could. Once the "Revelation" was transferred to my home, we were well aware that David could not tread near without great risk of exposure.

God revealed an astonishing set of new images to us while the "Revelation" still adorned David's living room. On the bottom left quadrant of the painting, there was a large hand behind two small devilish looking spirits. The trifling demons were in full flight, swiftly headed in the direction of the girl. Auspiciously, the hand, about four times the size of the demons, visibly blocked their path and thwarted their efforts.

It didn't take long for us to realize that the hand and arm were the exact same shading as the angel towering above Jesus. The angel's shielding hand swept around Jesus and the girl like a protective cocoon, keeping them safe from the reach of Satan's minions.

This was the first indication of an ominous presence residing within the walls of the "Revelation." Although I was somewhat comforted by the message of protection, I couldn't help but wonder why this level of security was even necessary. Why were there even demons dwelling inside of this hallowed canvas?

Why was the devil targeting me? I had spent a lifetime of being on guard and evading him. I felt his foreboding presence within my reach on many occasions. After all that I had sensed and experienced, I now had a perfectly clear illustration of my enemy's pursuit in God's supernatural painting.

Something didn't feel right. Trepidation crept in. I began a journey of intense reflection as I pondered over the obscurities of God's perplexing painting. At this point, we had very little insight into the enigmatic "Revelation" and I was naturally fearful.

I poured my anxiety and misgivings out on David and he lovingly comforted and reassured me. He encouraged me and reminded me that it was I who was stood next to Christ in the "Revelation." Regardless of how dark the situation appeared to be, I would always remain safeguarded.

Despite the fact that I was painted as the devil's bulls-eye, I still felt an overriding need to have the mysterious work of art in my home. I believed that there was a superior significance behind the divine imagery and that, in time, His purpose would be revealed.

David didn't think twice about returning the "Revelation" to me because his pronounced love for me was unconditional and self-sacrificing. The incomparable painting held a special place in David's heart because it was essentially an extension of my spirit residing with him at all times. He didn't fully comprehend how or why, but David felt my spiritual presence stem from the painting the very moment it moved in and made itself comfortably at home. This inexplicable feeling comforted David during our difficult times apart.

Above all, David knew, beyond a shadow of a doubt, that this fascinating painting was a treasured and rare gift from God Himself. This outspoken conviction couldn't even alter David's noble decision. He believed that our salient love would win through in the end. David had firm faith that, one day, the "Revelation" would grace our home. At that time, neither of us would ever have to suffer from the categorical pangs of separation anxiety.

David didn't regret his chivalry, but he certainly didn't expect what subsequently followed. Inexplicably, the "Revelation" had brought a unique and ubiquitous spiritual dimension to David's apartment; David made this discovery as soon as he returned the painting to me. Emptiness and bleakness invaded and subjugated immediately after the "Revelation" vanished. The wall where the "Revelation" once lived had become as barren as David's lamenting soul.

Although highly enthralled by the mysteries of the "Revelation," the Lord amplified our interest and insight into His incomprehensible work. As David paddled through his tremendous loss, I found an inconceivable amount of fortitude and solace in the presence of the hallowed "Revelation." I did my best to support and console David through this chapter of withdrawal and lonesomeness.

Fortunately, neither of us was alone. God was there with us every step of the way, even when we least detected His presence. When we needed it most, He generously provided us with a speck of His mighty strength and endurance. David experienced His interventions firsthand during a visit to England.

Out of the bluest of skies, the Holy Spirit joined David for a relaxing stroll along the decorative, rolling English countryside. It was on this memorable walk that David received a once in a lifetime communication from God's throne. He heard the echoing, resounding words that he would desperately cling to for the rest of his life.

CHAPTER TWELVE

Divine Messages

The God of wonders and His wondrous "Revelation" cleverly intervened in the most delicate and precarious situation that David and I had ever encountered as a couple. Just before the stunning transformation of the abstract, our fragile relationship was cruising on incredibly thin ice. We came to an abrupt and unexpected 4-way junction and, like unassuming deer in the headlights, we froze in our tracks. Miserably lost, David and I were filled with hopelessness; we didn't know what to do or where to turn.

Our combined consciences were overflowing with sinner's guilt, so it didn't feel right to run to God for help; seeking His guidance didn't give off that warm and fuzzy feeling. However, staring in the face of our mounting trials, we recognized that our one of a kind love was worth fighting for. David and I needed to preserve this precious and exceptional gift at all costs. We could have never suspected that God was actually on our side and also fighting for the same cause.

The salvaging power of the commanding "Revelation" dove straight into our trying times and lifted us up to an entirely new elevation. David and I soared to new and exciting peaks as we opened our hearts and souls to God's domain and, more importantly, His dominion. God had fundamentally repaired and resurrected our broken relationship and offered us the keys to ascension.

David was accustomed to living a so-called "normal" life that was void of the inexplicable events, miraculous manifestations and God-given gifts and visions that I had gradually grown accustomed to over the course of my existence. The cutting-edge "Revelation" had opened David's eyes to a new and exciting realm where God manifested Himself freely and communicated openly. As David took his first wobbly steps into the spiritual and supernatural dimension of our world, God came alongside him and gave him a gentle, encouraging nudge.

While prospecting for a position in a large international corporation, David paid a visit to his brother Arthur, who lived in a small, quaint English village. Early one morning, the two brothers chose to bond and unwind with a long peaceful stroll through the scenic, rustic countryside. About halfway through the hike, David, unaccustomed to such long treks, grew with exhaustion and began trailing behind Arthur. While taking in and appreciating nature's glory and the attractive grounds, David found himself in a deep meditation with reflective thoughts of our love. He missed me desperately and ached to return home to me.

At the exact same time, on an entirely different continent, Phillip and I were in one of our customary heated disputes. I sat nonchalantly on the edge of the bed while Phillip shamed and chastised me for my immoral affair and indifference towards our marital vows. I didn't utter a single word; my silence provoked an already furious husband. Again, I sat silently as Phillip unleashed his indignation. In time, he withdrew, surrendered his out lashing and stared at me with utmost grief and disgust.

Phillip urged me to talk to God. He encouraged me to go out and find a beautiful garden or countryside far away so that I could spend quality time with God and earnestly pray to our Father for direction.

My thoughts immediately sailed overseas to David; in that exact moment he was in a lovely countryside far away and I longed to be there with him. I envisioned myself strolling beside him, hand in lover's hand. I imagined the gorgeous topography laced with charming flowers and reeds swaying in the mildly perfumed zephyr. I closed my eyes and felt the warmth of the sun penetrating my pores. My heart ached for my dear David.

I waited for Phillip to leave the bedroom and then jumped towards the telephone. Maybe the sound of David's sweet, uplifting voice could help extinguish a morsel of my pining; any ounce of relief would help.

There was no answer. Perhaps he was in an inaccessible area and unable to receive any communication. I waited about five minutes and attempted another call. This time my call was a success.

For the first time in our relationship, it was I who was on the receiving end of a supernatural account; David had just been preoccupied with a divine spiritual visit!

As he wandered despondently through the serene Bluebell Wood in England, David suddenly felt a gentle hand softly embrace his waist. He felt the strong sensation of being elevated up and into the glorious peaks of the "Revelation." His mind immediately recalled the radiant girl that appeared to be lifted in Jesus' arms. David wondered if he could have been experiencing a similar or parallel manifestation. But the girl in the painting was being carried on the opposite side of the canvas as David felt he was being raised. Completely oblivious to what was happening or why, a blanket of wholesome peace encased David's body as tears engulfed his eyes.

David heard a pacifying voice tell him not to worry about anything; he was about to receive an enlightening and eye-opening message from God. The spirit that swaddled David mentioned my name and explained that evil forces were attracted to me because of that which resided inside of me. It also indicated that I was abundantly filled with God's spirit when I was with my children and when I painted.

There was more.

We found out that, in comparison to most people, David's good spirit was much more prevalent in the world and his God-given task was to bring out more of my good spirit in the physical world. The heavenly host cautiously warned David that when he was not in my presence that evil prevailed over me somehow. The divine messenger also confirmed David's notions regarding his puzzling and rather unanticipated divorce. David and I were impressively brought together by God's masterful design; our preordained union was the ultimate motivation behind David's failed marriage.

Finally, the heavenly manifestation mentioned the much acclaimed "Revelation" and expanded on its elaborate and sophisticated significance. The informative spirit conveyed that the exceptional painting contained a wealth of rich symbolism and meaning but that it was important to note that all interpretations were correct. It delighted David to hear that God intended for His astounding "Revelation" to serve as a unifying element between the two of us; He expected our alliance to grow more robust as we jointly experienced the phenomena and miracles associated with His extraordinary painting.

As the spirit communicated, David's doubts vanished and his faith surged. He was certain that he was somehow being held inside of the confounding "Revelation."

As David described his metaphysical encounter, his voice resonated with euphoria, conviction and unparalleled hope. At that moment, nothing could bring him down or crush his elevated spirit. David had just been touched by the hand of God.

The spiritual presence that lifted David's body and spirit was an invisible entity. Initially, David supposed that the angelic messenger could have possibly been my spirit but then he thought that it could have been my grandmother's. Not at all familiar with how God operated in this astonishing yet unfamiliar territory, David even considered the notion that the Holy Spirit had paid him a friendly visit. In the grand scheme of things, the spirit's identity was secondary; what mattered above all else was that the critical communication came directly from the Almighty God.

David and I were tremendously impacted by this eminent supernatural visitation. We were both equally awestruck, not only by the miraculous life-changing event, but also by the impeccable timing of it all. Phillip had just insisted that I find a place somewhere in the quiet countryside to seek God's voice and counsel. How could we have supposed that on the other side of the world, across multiple time zones, at the exact same time, God would reveal Himself to David on the quiet pastoral woods of England? David and I knew that this profound incident was not coincidental; it was exquisitely and immaculately contrived.

Prior to this momentous day, I had unlocked the doors to and invited David into my own covert supernatural world; the top-secret dimension of my life that I had once vehemently fought to keep concealed from all family and friends. Although I knew he never doubted me, David couldn't possibly conceive what each unique occurrence actually felt like.

How could he have possibly felt what it was like to be God's very own paintbrush? How could he have experienced the incredibly humbling effect of Jesus's towering power as He walked in the garden with me? How could he ever fathom the incapacitating sounds of a demon's terrorizing and agonizing growls?

David listened attentively as I vividly recounted each of my paranormal incidents, and though he solemnly attempted to grasp the complexity of my experiences, he could never truly taste the raw substance of the words I zealously spoke of. He needed to have his own induction into the nonphysical realm to fully appreciate the depths of the pervasive spiritual dimension that co-existed with us at all times. During David's memorable walk in the woods, God had given him just that, a first-hand introduction to the spiritual domain. This well-timed, transcendent event was vital to David's future resolve and perseverance.

Simultaneously, as God thoroughly worked on David, the Almighty was also effectively operating on me. His Holiness explained that the "Revelation" that He altruistically sent down to our world had two primary messages; one was for the whole of humanity while the other was explicitly for David and me. At the time, He didn't disclose too many details or specific information; the particulars would come at a later time, in His perfect time.

I learned, very early on, that God delivered His supreme knowledge to me in a piecemeal approach in order to allow my mortal mind the necessary processing or digesting time. My capacity to handle His grand and superior wisdom was extremely limited. The Lord also gave me the requisite grace period I needed to prepare myself for the marvels He would divulge next.

Time and time again, God encouraged me to abandon my trepidations and forebodings; He assured me that He would always serve as my protective force field. Amorously, He declared that I had nothing to fear. As heartening and comforting as His promising words were, fulfilling His request was not a simple endeavor. It proved to be one of the most difficult challenges of my life.

How could I just let go of and abandon what I had contained inside of me for so long? Or rather, what had contained me? More than anyone, God knew the history and intricacies of each and every one of my apprehensions. He was well aware of the torments that had plagued and crippled various areas of my life. I dreaded the fact that I was the object of the devil's affection. Still, I didn't have a clue as to why he shadowed and pursued me since my early childhood. I had been left in obscurity for all of my life. Only God knew the motives behind Satan's devious prowls.

Shortly after the "Revelation" was revealed to us, David and I began pursuing God's interventions in our lives on a daily basis. We embraced His preeminent leadership and infinite wisdom. Fervently, we clung to each one of His priceless words. Unbeknownst to either of us, God had us securely detained and shielded in His hallowed bosom. We were His malleable clay; He was skillfully morphing and molding us into His liking.

Regardless of the situation or circumstance, the miraculous "Revelation" continually made its way to the forefront of each of our conversations. Morning, noon and night, God's sanctified painting consumed our minds and thoughts. Our souls were profoundly stirred by its complexities and spellbinding spirituality. David and I ardently strove to understand, if humanly possible, the magnitude of this heaven-sent creation.

During one of our afternoon lunches, David and I examined our vast collection of "Revelation" photographs. We prudently studied each one in hopes of discovering more clues to this mystifying puzzle that God had just laid out before us. Nothing stood out.

Then, in the blink of an eye, the Holy Spirit came over me and struck me with enlightenment. He informed me that there was a message inside the face of Jesus; a written communication intended for all of mankind. My already heightened sense of anticipation and enthusiasm intensified to even greater depths.

I fervently broadcasted the remarkable news to David only to be disheartened by his apparent lack of faith. He listened considerately, but he couldn't fully accept or comprehend the concept of what had been conveyed to me.

What on earth was I talking about? Filled with doubt, he supposed that I could have somehow misunderstood or misinterpreted the Spirit's message. David believed that the Spirit may have meant that the alleged message in Jesus' face might have been a symbolic one rather than a literal, inscribed one. This incredibly outrageous notion was just too fanciful and extreme for David's constrained mind to consider as a viable option.

I didn't bother with vain attempts to persuade or push David. After all, that wasn't my job; I was certain that God was working on him.

David's young spirit and emergent faith were in the preliminary stages of growth and development. He simply needed more time to blossom.

David's strong reservations failed to influence or sway my unquestionable conviction. Without any ounce of disbelief, I wholeheartedly fell captive to the Spirit's communication. I knew there was a message masked in Jesus' lacerated face and one day it would come to light. One day His communication would be seen by all, including my skeptical David.

The Holy Spirit's firsthand tip-off fueled my desire and my excitement levels surpassed the heavens. God had recently indicated that the "Revelation" had two key messages; the Spirit's critical announcement could prove to be an integral piece of evidence necessary in unraveling this mind-boggling conundrum. I was bursting with intrigue and curiosity, but I was forced to exercise my patience.

I was informed that there was a message, hidden inside the boundaries of Jesus' face, for the entire world to see and that was it. No other information was disclosed to me. I didn't know what to do or how to proceed with this limited knowledge.

Should I search for clues? Was the message scrambled? Was there something I needed to decode? I was obliviously confounded by my many scattered inquiries.

I carefully surveyed His image time and time again but to no avail. Weeks went by but nothing else concerning Jesus' face was relayed to me. I decided to contain my interest and zeal, and for the most part, didn't mention the subject to David. But one day, the Holy Spirit stimulated my attention and motivated me once again; this time I lost all form of composure and self-control. I found that my patience was no longer sustainable.

David and I were casually watching a movie at his apartment when the Holy Spirit spoke to me. The film's central theme focused on encrypted messages meant to help the human race at the predestined time of destruction or Armageddon. The Spirit kindly reminded me of the message concealed within the confines of Jesus' face. I was told that this exclusive, still undiscovered message also served to help mankind during times of great peril and distress.

I was fiercely motivated and determined to solve the enigmatic case of God's hidden message. As soon as the movie ended, I expressed my keen enthusiasm and conviction to David. He still wasn't convinced but he elected to humor me.

I had gazed upon and admired Jesus' striking face in the "Revelation" thousands of times, but nothing stood out. I couldn't distinguish anything other than His already obvious facial features, nothing but blood and lacerations. I thought that the message could have possibly been written using a distinctive alphabet or maybe even ancient symbols that I was unfamiliar with. David and I decided to run with this preliminary idea, as we had nothing else to go on.

David assisted me as I combed through the internet for hours on end. We researched a swarm of ancient alphabets including Greek, Hebrew, Latin, Sanskrit, Sumerian and many others. We studied early pictographs and hieroglyphs. If we came across anything related to communications or languages of biblical times we didn't hesitate to investigate; we simply dove right in and explored.

I couldn't leave any stone unturned; I had to quench this all-consuming, overwhelming thirst! David was patient and accommodating, despite the fact that his beliefs were not in line with my own. He loved me and did his best to indulge me. David tried to prevent any disappointment I might have had by repeatedly pointing out that the message the Spirit referred to could have been a symbolic one. Maybe the message had to do with Jesus' demeanor or expression. Maybe it was as simple as that.

Notwithstanding David's failed attempts to influence me, my faith remained rock solid and could not be cracked or broken. As soon as I got home I continued my quest for the truth. Hour after hour, I diligently concentrated my efforts on investigating the ancient scripts. In hindsight, I really didn't have a choice; I felt as though my actions were completely out of my hands. I operated in an almost robotic state, as though programmed to calculate or formulate an answer to an unsolvable theorem. My brain was on hyper drive and I couldn't take my heavy foot off the pedal. At times, my mind spun and raced so fast that I even began to question my own sanity.

Even so, my faith remained undeterred and intact.

I forced myself to cease my unproductive research efforts; my exhausted brain deserved a respite. The children were watching one of their favorite TV shows so I squeezed in and joined them. Immediately, I felt the warmth and peace that they unfailingly unleashed and decorated me with. At last, my mind, body and soul were completely at ease. I didn't care to watch the show; instead I focused my energy and thoughts on my beautiful children; I was fully absorbed by their presence.

Maybe this was the precise moment the Lord was waiting for. Maybe He was waiting for my heart to finally take charge over my opposing mind, because it was at the exact moment of true submission when God spoke to me in His governing voice.

Earlier that week, David had sent me a new snapshot of the "Revelation." As I sat there completely focused on my children, God spoke, instructing me to open this particular photograph on my cell phone. As soon as the photo appeared, I witnessed a miracle! God meticulously outlined and highlighted the message in Jesus' face so that I could see it clearly and without question. The featured message was written vertically through Jesus' face and spanned from the pinnacle of His forehead all the way down to His chin; it clearly read "PS 512." A distinctive font was used to write the two letters while the numbers were bundled together in a different type of bubble font.

In an instant, I froze with wonder and adoration. God's very own writing was permanently engraved in one of my modest paintings! I needed time to absorb and digest this riveting inscription and its significance. I came out of my initial shock and sighed with utmost release and deliverance. The message I had frantically sought after was right before my eyes all along, but it took God's power to reveal it to me. Although my physical eyes were open wide and keenly searching, my spiritual eyes, for some reason or another, had been sealed shut.

As I pondered over the possible meaning behind the cryptic characters, God spoke to me. He indicated that His divine inscription represented the bible verse "Wash away all my iniquity and cleanse me from my sin" (Psalm 51:2, NIV). At long last, His primary message for humanity had been revealed! This phenomenal painting and its miraculous contents were a call for all of God's children to come to Jesus Christ!

I sat in humbled reverence as the Almighty God infused me with His knowledge and illumination. In the very center of the "Revelation," the explicit visage that represented Jesus' crucifixion was dark red with striations dispersed all throughout. His blood stained faced was a graphic portrayal of His magnanimous sacrifice and crucifixion. Only Jesus' blood could wash away all our iniquities and cleanse us of our sins. I couldn't imagine a verse more compelling or a more innovative way to communicate His redeeming message to the world!

Titillating tingles raced down my spine. This unbelievable and jaw-dropping sign from God was beyond astronomical; it surpassed anything and everything that I had ever known or heard of!

I was instantly taken back to the Old Testament of the Bible and reminded of how God carved the Ten Commandments to help save His people from the clutches of sin and depravity. This time was different; this time He was aiming to save His children from the ravaging clutches of hell and eternal damnation.

God's glorious love poured down from His throne and engulfed me like an unruly tsunami; I was drowning in a world of euphoria. I exalted Him and His immeasurable magnificence and splendor. I thanked Him for His unsurpassed love, a love marked by the sacrifice of Jesus Christ. I thanked the Father for revealing His critical message to me; I vowed to do all that I could to help distribute His imperative dispatch to the masses.

As soon as I collected myself and came back from my epic dialogue with God, I gave David a summary of the intriguing exchange and outlined the "PS 512" for him. David was fascinated and engrossed by God's jaw-dropping exposé. Just as the Spirit had conveyed to me, the message foretold of was, in fact, a literal and written one meant for all of humanity to see. David was fixated by the mind-searing imprint and never doubted again.

David rushed to research Psalm 51:2 and fatefully encountered the story of David and Bathsheba. The similarities between their historic account and our relationship were startling and remarkably inspiring.

Bathsheba was a married woman who committed adultery with David. Although David and Bathsheba had sinned before the Lord, they shared a pronounced love. God forgave their flagrant immorality and blessed their highly favored son.

The incredible sin and love David and I shared was an obvious and unmistakable parallel. Similar to David and Bathsheba, David and I also shared a profound, intrinsic desire to bear a child together. We never quite understood why we felt so strongly or where this inherent compulsion originated from. The one truth we knew with absolute certainty was that our aspirations to conceive grew with each passing day.

"PS 512" not only served as a testimony to the Crucifixion and soul-saving blood of Jesus Christ, but it also shone as an illuminating ray of hope for David and I. God's edifying message brought light to and reinforced our inexplicable yearning for a child. David and I would one day be blessed with an extraordinary son and He would be exceedingly favored in the eyes of the Almighty.

CHAPTER THIRTEEN

I AM

The sudden onset and downpour of God's overriding presence, coupled with His consuming "Revelation," inundated me in an overwhelmingly dominant manner. The puzzling and concentrated powers of the inscrutable "Revelation" mysteriously unlocked a dormant part of my spirit that had been trapped unsuspectingly since my early childhood. His cryptic oil painting served as the master key that cracked open the conduit of communication with the one and only Almighty God of the universe. The truth was that my Creator had been calling out to me all of my life, but, unbeknownst to me, something or someone was deliberately obstructing the channel.

Soon after God unveiled His treasured "Revelation" to me, I embarked on a journey of gradual release from my insulated, soundproof prison and began to hear God's roaring voice and gentle Spirit as clear as the crisp, morning songbird. At last, the portal was open; God and I were finally on the same frequency.

All of my life, I had recognized God's unmistakable love for humanity. After all, I was no stranger to His written word. Since my obedient early years of daily Bible reading sessions at my grandparents' humble home, I had always believed in God's great love for the world, as so prominently demonstrated by the sacrificial Crucifixion of Jesus

Christ. How could there be a greater display of unadulterated love than this altruistic and unparalleled act?

But after the sudden arrival of the "Revelation," I began to sense and savor God's magnanimous love in a way that I never knew could be possible. My soul experienced a dramatic metamorphosis and His love became exceptionally personal and tangible. As God began to speak to me and guide my every move, I recognized a massive transformation emerging from deep inside of my core. I felt His everlasting love infiltrate each of the millions upon millions of fibers and cells that molded my body. The Father's unconditional love permeated and bounded me in a most beautiful way and I couldn't help but surrender myself to its authority. I became its willing and beholden prisoner.

Completely overtaken and overjoyed by God's infinite pool of mercy and affections, I, oftentimes, found myself sitting alone, quietly, basking in the glorious sensations that inundated me, only to be awakened by gushing tears streaming uncontrollably down my face. The love-filled tears flowed effortlessly with unblemished and incomparable happiness, peace and comfort.

I suddenly began reflecting on John the prophet and his poignant teachings. On several occasions John referred to himself as the disciple whom Jesus loved. Although some had mistakenly misinterpreted John's writings, he never actually declared himself to be the only disciple loved by Christ. John must have felt God's never-ending, all-consuming love in a very pronounced manner in order to make the unflinching proclamations of the love he felt from his influential Teacher.

I quickly realized that, upon truly perceiving and subsequently embracing the magnitude of God's love, it was quite difficult not to proclaim it as John often did and as I began to do. I felt His inexhaustible love so immensely that it was almost impossible to imagine that one God could love each and every one of His billions of children with the same level of passion and purity as He bestowed upon me. But in all of His vastness, He did.

For the first time in my life, I knew of the intimacy John openly pronounced in his writings; I felt God's love so intensely that I could boldly shout out to the world that I was the one loved by God; I was favored in His eyes.

Those were the most beautifully searing thoughts to have ever entered my unpretentious mind. I clung to them in the direst of times.

God navigated and steered me through a thrilling course of discovery and enlightenment. After all, this was His imperial flight and I was merely His compliant passenger. I was destitute and directionless without His calculated guidance. As I concentrated on His glory, the flight became easier and the destination came into clear focus. He was the final stop. The more I saw of Him, the less I saw of myself.

In no time at all, I grew with the wisdom of the ancients. I realized that my trivial life on earth was undeniably empty and meaningless unless God was my sole centerpiece. He was my only light and life, my nourishment and sustenance. He was everything and without Him I was nothing, absolutely nothing.

Though I had always loved God and His profuse spectrum of dimensions, for the first time in my life, I found myself falling passionately in love with Him. I was in love with all that He stood for, all of His merciful goodness and all of His immeasurable love.

For a couple of days, my spirit became entirely fixated on His majestic "Revelation." My interest was specifically engrossed in a chalky white region that was situated just to the left of and adjacent to Jesus' blood-stained face. My spirit sensed that there was something obscured in this area calling out to me and longing to be exposed. The Holy Spirit directed me to a precise photograph of the "Revelation." He asked me to turn the picture upside down and He then showed me a riveting image that I never could have dreamt of witnessing; it was the sacred and venerable face of the Living God!

His Holiness beamed with raw wholesomeness. His esteemed, white visage was embedded in and surrounded by a bed of plush, delicate clouds. It looked as though God and the clouds were an extension of each other, as though they were one entity that morphed and transfigured.

God's large eyes resembled hollow, black holes but the delineation of His left eye's features was remarkably clear. His snowy white hair and beard extended and merged into the cottony pillows bordering Him. God's pious expression looked eerily similar to traditional illustrations of some of the more classical depictions of God.

Shockwaves and tremors incapacitated my body! How could the God of the universe, the Creator of all things, reveal His blinding and consecrated face to me? I was exceedingly humbled and gratefully honored. For a while, I was in a dreamlike state, preoccupied by His inconceivable greatness. I was mesmerized by His stunning countenance and couldn't help but wonder why or how I could be so privileged and blessed.

Who was I to the God above all gods? Why would He reveal Himself to me in this astonishing manner?

As my love and regard for the Lord grew, He continued to fascinate me with incessant insight into the unrivaled "Revelation" and into His vast, magnificent kingdom.

Early one morning, as we sat and spoke, He asked me to read about Moses and the burning bush. I had likely read the celebrated story dozens of times before, but this instance was unlike any of the previous readings. For the first time in my life, I took in and absorbed each of the verses with a different set of eyes and a recently resuscitated spirit.

I envisioned a meek and modest Moses speaking to the one sovereign God; I felt Moses' absolute veneration and humility for His supremacy. I understood why Moses was equally paralyzed by both fright and adoration. I even identified with his extreme fury and repulsion with the sinful nature of an immoral civilization.

As I sat in reflection of God's inspiring manifestation to Moses, the Holy Spirit directed me to one of my recent abstracts; this particular piece happened to be just a few feet away from where I sat. There was a small, red tree or bush in the center of the canvas. A glowing orange illumination was suspended inside and throughout the center of the tree but it was not a part of it. The radiant internal entity spread out within the branches of the tree with a wing like shadow, similar to that of a large bat. God explained that this illustrious painting was actually a depiction of the consecrated burning bush written of in the book of Exodus.

I was stunned! Tingling sensations and vibrations danced up and down my skin as His enchanting essence flowed throughout my entire body once again. Using my unskilled hand, God had painted His very own rendering of the distinguished burning bush that He piercingly spoke from thousands of years prior!

Before the majestic gift of the "Revelation," I modestly prized and appreciated each distinctive painting that He created through me. Despite my deep regard for each of them, I never stopped to analyze or give meaning to any of his delightful designs. It had never before crossed my mind that our paintings could hold such massive significance. I had seen the "Burning Bush" nearly every day, but never recognized what it represented. When God unveiled its staggering meaning, its opulence suddenly shone like the dazzling North Star.

As I admired His glorious work of art, He instructed me to resume my reading. I once again picked up the Holy Bible and continued from where I had left off. The Almighty stopped me as soon as I reached the words "I AM who I AM." I meditated on His galvanizing words for several minutes while I marveled in His vastness and omnipotence. His enormity was incomprehensible and beyond all human understanding.

"I AM who I AM" echoed through my mind over and over again.

I was fully taken in and intoxicated by the mere thought of Him when He directed me to a particular photo of the "Revelation." On the top left area of Jesus' head were the three letters "I AM". The renowned letters were capitalized and carbon black. They were upside down just like God's face in the clouds. The words were positioned in an inverted, reversed style. The letters needed to be flipped over in order to see them correctly.

God had strategically placed His divine footprint on His transcendent masterpiece filled with an immense array of wonders and mysteries. How could the same treasured painting bear my lowly, insignificant name as well as the name above all names? How could I be so blessed and privileged?

But above all else, how could any of this be real?

At that moment, I felt as though I had been thrust into a fairytale or fantasy world, but I was very conscious of the fact that this new world, no matter how surreal, was now my stark reality. God's marvelous miracles inundated my new life; His profuse love and brilliance consumed me so heavily that His heavenly light could have secreted from my pores and I would not have been at all surprised.

I couldn't contain my range of passionate emotions nor could I translate my feelings into paltry, inadequate words. Streams of tears surged from my eyes as an ocean of love poured out from my captivated heart. This was the only way that my concentrated, unsurpassed emotions could be released. This was the only means by which I could process the overwhelming impact of God's transcendent presence and supernatural manifestations.

Yet, as saturating and consuming as His company was, there could never have been enough or too much of Him. There was still so much more of His grandeur to come; little did I know that this was just the beginning of the prodigious and infinite I AM.

CHAPTER FOURTEEN

Signs of the End Times

Though God's miraculous painting accented and adorned my modest home, its true dwelling place was well within the confines of my beating heart. In no time at all, I progressively and passionately submerged myself into the cosmos of the bewildering "Revelation." Our unprecedented relationship morphed into a living, breathing one.

I was fully aware that one day, thousands upon thousands would travel to the ends of the world to behold His glorious, modern day miracle. One day, civilization after civilization would appreciate His supernatural creation and many would come to believe in His glory and might. One day, once lost souls would come to believe in the one true savior, Jesus Christ. Until then, I vowed to safeguard His masterpiece and harness every ounce of spirituality and goodness that it exuded.

As I stood in reverence of God and His spiritually infused "Revelation," the Holy Spirit informed me that, although "PS 512" was a major milestone, it was merely a small component of something much greater; God had an even superior, monumental message for His beloved children. I was baffled! What could be greater than a symbolic, God-inscribed Bible verse embedded on the blood-stained face of Jesus Christ in a painting crafted by the very hand of the Almighty?

My eager, rapidly pumping heart soared with anticipation, but I knew I had to wait tolerantly for His perfect timing. By then, my aptitude for forbearance had graduated to new heights. I had learned that He communicated with me as He so desired, at His own pace. Any form of communication from my Father was like an exceptionally exquisite symphony composed and played exclusively for me. Like a jubilant child, I took great delight in waiting for the next harmonious rendezvous with my Creator.

I found myself relishing in God's presence quite frequently. One of our favorite meeting places was at my homely, wooden kitchen table, under the soft light of the dawn's graceful and elegant brilliance.

One early morning, while worshipping and praying, the Holy Spirit directed me to read the story of the two beasts in the book of Revelation. When I finished reading, He informed me that the "Face of God" painting, which had been hanging innocuously on my living room wall, was a graphic illustration of that biblical foretelling.

God urged me to study the painting as He cautiously navigated me through its many unturned leaves. Similar to His approach in accenting the "PS 512" in Jesus's face, God clearly exposed the beasts of Revelation to me. He began the suspenseful unveiling with the "leopard" like creature with a wounded forehead. In the "Face of God" painting, the ghastly beast eerily resembled a brown and black leopard and the two slash marks that represented its' wounds were clearly impressed on his forehead. His black, sinister eyes seemed to prowl and peer out at me through the canvas. This uninviting, grossly unnerving beast appeared to leap out of the bottom left corner of the painting in a rather obnoxious fashion.

The next image God pointed out was the most disturbing and petrifying of them all. Right next to what I had already "known" to be the face of the Almighty was His defiant arch enemy, Satan himself. Meticulously hidden inside what appeared to be red and black noise, Satan's hideous face was revealed directly along the right side of God's face. God and Satan faced each other with irrefutable contempt and rage. It was evident that Satan's bloodcurdling red horned face was considerably smaller than God's.

Discreetly and cleverly embedded within the lower portion of Satan's appalling face was the second beast referenced in the chilling book of Revelation; this was the beast with horns like that of a lamb. However, his faint features were not easily discernable nor was he nearly as arrogant as the first beast.

Each of the revolting images was incredibly alarming and distressing. How could I never have noticed the dreadful creatures that had inconspicuously resided on my wall for so many years? Unlike the "Revelation," where the buried imagery was only exposed with precise lighting and positioning, the images in the "Face of God" were evident head on.

The painting that had plagued me with many months of agony and sleepless nights clearly showed God, Satan and the two beasts from the end times. Without any indication whatsoever, the Spirit of God had imbued me to paint the final face-off of Armageddon!

I was reminded of the staggering "Revelation" with all of its mind-boggling wonders and mysteries. It took God's gentle hand to open my eyes to the painting's special contents. Similarly, although I had examined the "Face of God" hundreds of times before, God did not allow me to see it for what it was. I thought back to the day we painted the "Face of God;" my discerning spirit immediately knew that there was a distinctive, nonphysical energy emanating from this piece. My reverent fear and restless nights were now put in perspective. Albeit frightening, the haunting past was beginning to resurface and make sense.

The images were crystal clear and I couldn't help but wonder why I had never seen them before. Maybe, up until this point in my life, I was not yet ready to appreciate the truth of what lie lurking within the "Face of God;" perhaps I first had to renounce my impeding fears. I was a work in progress but I stood firmly on the fact that I was God's work; He was my grand architect. As my mighty strength and comfort, He strategically helped me cast aside each of my prevailing fears and He did so using various approaches and techniques. I had to fully understand and appreciate the evil and darkness that pervaded our world in all of its calamitous capacity in order to conquer and expel it from my life. One of God's illuminating tools was the "Face of God," but on various occasions He also used dreams and visions to help edify and push me along.

One night, God gave me a disturbing yet realistically convincing nightmare wherein He showed me two distinctively different parallel worlds. One was the world I was accustomed to living in and the other was a vile, lifeless dimension of it.

One minute, there were vibrant and colorful gardens swaying to the sweet lullabies sung by the small and genteel birds that inhabited the region. Green bushes and bright sunlight were prevalent. Then, in the next moment, all signs of life and hope were gone, as though everything good and living had been instantaneously sucked out of the planet. The setting or foundation was exactly the same but the gardens were replaced by extremely dry, cracked earth, dirt and rocks. Withered, decaying branches were all that remained of the bushes and trees previously full and flourishing. The chillingly crisp air was surrounded by a dense gray, haunting sky. The missing sun no longer gave off its rays of light.

God showed me many other snapshots of our present day world; He showed me residential areas, schools, forests, lakes, skyscrapers and business parks. Each of these everyday glimpses was then immediately trailed by its wretched, dead version, void of any goodness or light.

Finally, at the end of the nightmare, He showed me the magnificently adorned mountain ranges.

There were a plethora of luscious and thriving mountainous peaks and valleys spanning many miles. Then in one swift, sudden overhaul, God showed me the other end of the spectrum, the evil version of the grand landscape that I had just taken in and appreciated. Again, all that remained was a dreary and decrepit barren wasteland. There were no signs of life atop of the mountains; their exteriors were dark, stony and desolate.

I was then taken into one of the canyons and was shaken by the disturbing discovery. A few of the mountain sides had hundreds, if not thousands, of demonic beings trapped halfway inside the interior mountain walls. The upper halves of their bodies were protruding out of the mountains and their lower halves were cemented in place, not at all visible. The demons were dark and grotesque; dirt and grime covered their flailing and writhing emaciated arms and torsos. Their long, stringy black hair flung about as they repeatedly floundered and squirmed with false hopes of freedom. Their mouths moved as though they were screaming and shrieking but their muted cries were inaudible and wasted.

The dream then ended abruptly.

When I awoke, the nightmare consumed me as I deliberated on its many possible meanings. I came up with several likely interpretations. My first and predominant notion was that God wanted me to observe the evil dimension of the present day world, the world that I was a part of. Was He showing me that, despite all of the beauty and outer facades we observed with our physical eyes, that evil and wickedness crawled creepily underneath it all?

After all, Satan had been granted dominion over the world; he was the true ruler of the earth we inhabited. Could the perilous images God exposed to me in my nightmare reveal the very sinister foundations upon which all of society lived and existed, but casually ignored?

The other option that came to mind was that God was not showing me another dimension of our present world but rather a future, demolished state of it. Perhaps He was revealing an ominous view of another time, a prophetic preview of the ubiquitous darkness and evil that would eventually prevail.

I also considered the possibility that these previews could have been a trailer of the dire state of existence during the dreaded time of the antichrist's appointed reign otherwise known as the Tribulation. Or, even still, the bleak and breathless world in my horrendous nightmare could have been the abandoned world after Christ's triumphant return and harvest of His faithful followers.

Any of the possible scenarios was frightening and upsetting; the thought of residing in this morbid, evil dimension, where death and demons dwelled, was terrifying and sent chills down my spine.

About a week after this gripping and eye-opening account, God sent me another midnight message. This announcement was drastically different; it was very pronounced and required little to no interpretation.

As I tossed and turned in bed one restless night, I was awakened by a peculiar light source originating from the bottom right corner of my bedroom window. My heavy eyes opened sluggishly to find the phrase "THE END OF THE WORLD" suspended in midair just a couple of inches above the window's ledge.

The dramatic distress signal was a glowing bright blue that radiated like a neon sign meant to attract the masses. The alarming dispatch was motionless as it floated serenely, like a lost ship in the midst of a still, tranquil sea. The communication was visible for no more than one minute and then, in the blink of an eye, it vanished into the cold night air.

I was astounded, but not at all perturbed, by the blistering, prophetic words that God impressively displayed before me that night. I didn't ask God to clarify this message as the blazing caption spoke for itself.

I prayed solemnly for a couple of hours, but had difficulties sleeping after God shared that the end times, detailed by John in the book of Revelation, were imminent. He didn't specify a date or time period but He did stress the impeccable timing of and relevance of His "Revelation." Again, He instructed me to spread His critical messages in the

"Revelation" so that all of the earth could witness His glory and partake in deliverance through Jesus Christ.

It became rather evident that David and I were involved in an intricately woven and complex blueprint much larger than we could have possibly understood; greater than any human being could ever have fathomed. We couldn't begin to measure or rationalize His intentions or plans.

God's transcendent "Revelation" unleashed the floodgates of the spiritual dimension onto our physical world. Rather abruptly, and without any prior indication, we were summoned into a spiritual battle between good and evil. David and I were chosen to fight in the war above all wars; the concluding finale between God's angels and Satan's demons.

David and I were God's very own anointed, earthly foot soldiers; we were given the crucial and heavy task of disseminating God's message of salvation through Jesus Christ, before it was too late. At last, the final quest for the ultimate dominion of souls was upon our fallen and oblivious world.

CHAPTER FIFTEEN

Sanctuary

Our divine mandate was unbelievably monumental and the consequences of failure were nothing short of catastrophic. As I came to grips with the world that I was suddenly thrust into, my laden heart began to pump with sincere concern and compassion for every person I knew and the billions of strangers that I would never cross paths with. The very souls of the entire global population were at stake. In the end, there were only two possible outcomes, eternal life or eternal damnation; both were definitive.

There was absolutely no room for defeat; I could not disappoint the Lord, my God. After all, He had chosen me for this prodigious campaign. I had no idea why but He did. And when the times became insufferable and my purpose seemed unattainable, the God of the universe had confidence in me. Even when, in my unworthiness, I felt entirely inept, He assured me that I was fully capable.

When I first came to grips with the severity of the situation, I wrestled with internal demons and debilitating reservations. I lacked self-confidence and felt small and incompetent. I suffered through many overwhelming moments wherein which I felt completely daunted by the crucial, decisive commission that had been assigned to me. Lifelong fears continued their attempts to taunt and torment me; their primary goal was to hinder my determination and weaken my faith. And, to top things off, I was a guilt-ridden adulteress. I couldn't understand why God had chosen me, an undeserving and contemptible sinner.

As God shared His magnificent insight and vision with me, He simultaneously worked to chip away and erode each of my apprehensions and worries. I had to be completely fearless and courageous to progress and accomplish His will and my mission for Him on this earth. The Almighty God repeatedly emphasized that He was with me always; He would never leave my side. With full force and authority, He blatantly told me that I was not strong enough to accomplish a single one of the tasks set before me, but that His boundless strength within me could and would accomplish all things for His grand purpose. Together we would conquer and triumph; that was the only way to achieve victory.

God worked diligently to encourage and build me up. He offered me His commanding strength and fortitude and I accepted it with a grateful heart. With Him by my side, I was able to renounce and bid farewell to each of the suffocating fears that had imprisoned me for so many years. God removed my strangleholds, lifted me up and cradled me in His loving arms. My devoted Father assured me that He would never let me go.

The Lord comforted me by accentuating the fact that He chose David and I; neither of us had a choice in the decision making process or our inconceivable destiny. More importantly, I didn't need to understand His mysteriously complex ways or motives; I simply needed to accept His decisions as fixed and absolute.

As His promising wisdom began to take root and flourish inside of me, the Holy Spirit took me to my memorable vision of Jesus serenely watching over and directing me in the heavenly garden. I was reminded that, in His all-seeing eyes, I was wholesome and untarnished. As sweet as the floral bouquets that surrounded me on my unassuming, celestial walk with Christ, in that very moment, I could almost smell the fragrant taste of release and freedom. My lifelong associates, the enemy's rusty old chains of bondage, were being crushed by the hands of the Almighty.

But the process of full restoration took a considerable amount of time; time to wash away a lifetime of viscous, tenacious debris and time to renounce all of my worldly afflictions. I desperately needed time to heal the wounds and encumbrances that had monopolized my mind and entrenched themselves in nearly every facet of my life. And that's exactly what God gave me; He gave me His precious time and concentrated, attentive care.

And just like that, it happened.

The moment I knew that I was completely free from the clutches of fear and sin was during one of my early morning engagements with my Father. I spent the morning browsing through several recently uploaded photos of the "Face of God." I was astonished by the remarkable end-time illustrations that had just been revealed to me and eager to examine the details and imagery behind each of the new images. My keen spirit sensed that there was much more to this painting. Zealously, I hoped that He would confirm my notions.

I briefly glanced at Satan and his two despicable minions but found that my true concentration and fixation fell upon the scorching rage swimming in God's bewildering eyes. I was mesmerized by the penetrating eyes that brimmed with unassailable authority and fury. I zoomed in on one of the magnetic beacons and was submerged into it. Eye into eye, I felt like I was a miniscule grain of sand caught up and lost in the all-expanding universe or cosmos. I humbled myself before the Lord as I sat in wonder and appreciation of His inconceivable vastness.

As I ventured for morsels of clues or some speck of clarity I thought about enhancing the green color of His eyes. And then, in one inexplicable flash of heavenly intervention, God supernaturally took charge of the situation. The Lord seized control of my computer the very moment I clicked on the edit button.

The computer monitor went black for a few seconds and then a random photo of me appeared on the screen. Then there was another. Two seconds later, another snapshot of me appeared. I was alone in each of the photographs, no family or friends accompanied me. God must have presented me with at least a dozen of my stored photographs before He reached His critical main message. After my personal and very intimate slideshow, He reached the peak of His divine interception with a poignant video specially designed just for me.

During the first few moments of the broadcast, I trembled, inside and out, with concentrated, agonizing fear. I didn't recognize the contents of the transmission and I suspected that the sly devil could be up to his cunning trickeries yet again.

I was completely alone; no one was in the house. I struggled to regain any semblance of composure. Although I was overcome by gut-wrenching angst and torment, something in me was still compelled to understand the situation. I forced my focus on the supernatural prompter directly in front me.

I couldn't believe my eyes and ears when I finally realized what was going on. My Father, who had been steadily building me up and urging me to fully trust in Him and His protection, played the sweet tune of God Will Take Care of You, as I watched the computer monitor in disbelief and astonishment!

The grand finale of His miraculous exhibition was a single photo of an oil painting of my precious grandmother. The Holy Spirit and I had painted this meaningful piece shortly after she went to be with the Lord. I immediately thought of the guardian angel in the "Revelation;" this angelic beauty represented my grandmother's protective spirit.

I was frozen and speechless. Paranormal, inexplicable events like this happened on the big screen, but not in real life. As outrageous as the chain of events seemed, the truth was that this was not fiction, this was my reality. The supernatural dimension had been opened up and revealed to me and there was no escaping its inexhaustible reach.

I embraced the God of wonders and all of His gifts, especially His love for mankind. I couldn't begin to conceive the magnitude of His profuse love, its immeasurable depths or unreachable heights. But I certainly felt its lasting mark on me. His love was eternally sealed on me and could never be washed away. I laid down my life, fell in complete devotion and surrendered my entire existence to God. I felt all of my fastidious fears meticulously swept away by a massive monsoon of His inexorable love.

God nailed and drove His riveting message into me in such a remarkably unique and dynamic way! In that instant, I was made new and whole; I was never again the same.

Simultaneously and rather harmoniously, God had also been fortifying David's sense of security and faith. He cleverly bridged David's renovating spiritual encounter in the quaint English countryside to the astonishing "Revelation." During his renewing walk in the woods, David felt that he was carried and lifted up inside the "Revelation," but he never expected to find that his supernatural experience was, in fact, a phenomenal foreshadowing of what was soon to come!

In one startling exposé, God showed us an uncanny, crystal clear image of David lying down inside of His astonishing "Revelation." David faced upward, positioned just to the right of Jesus. With eyes sealed shut, he looked to be in a tranquil, restful slumber. The Lord appeared to be carrying David as He watched over him.

This graphic illustration was a beautiful bit of insight into the transcendent painting that the Lord had bestowed upon us. Not only was I on Jesus' left side but He had also established that David was to His right! Speechless and dumbfounded, we couldn't begin to fathom what all of this could possibly mean.

On David's unforgettable walk along the serene countryside, the Spirit had communicated that the stunning "Revelation" would serve as a cementing, unifying element for David and me. How would we ever expect to find that we were actually the supporting characters in His extraordinary painting? In this world and in the mysterious realm of His divine illustration, David and I were bounded together by Christ Himself!

David and I were overwhelmed by this beautifully stirring sight! We were filled with awe and amazement! We were enthralled by God's profuse goodness.

Just when we were coming down from our colossal high God immediately shot us right back up. He pointed out that Jesus' right shoulder was moderately elevated just behind David's body. It became rather evident that our earlier notions were correct; Jesus was actually carrying David in the "Revelation" in the exact same manner that David felt to have been raised and held during his divine visitation in England!

By this stage in our valiant odyssey, David and I were anxiously prepared for God to dispense a drop of His infinite knowledge on us at any given time. Each of His magnificent manifestations was breathtaking and unbelievable but we knew that there were no parameters or constraints to God's glory. The "Revelation" was His masterfully generated work of art and there were no limits to its highly prized contents. Though He had already revealed some fascinating facets of His exquisite work, David and I were ready for more of Him; we thirsted for more of the "Revelation." Filled with enthusiasm, we waited for God to shower us with unequalled artistic grandeur.

And then He did.

Soon after David's arresting appearance in the "Revelation," God candidly introduced us to another member of the "Revelation" cast, the Holy Spirit. The Holy Spirit's splendid image resided just a few inches below David. His venerable face was a perfect snap-shot of the modern day, traditional depiction of Jesus Christ. His slender, elongated face flowed meekly in a sinuous, spiritual fashion. His gentle, soft features gave off a powerfully serene and soothing, albeit intangible, quality.

The Holy Spirit's portrait was quite unique compared to the rest of the imagery we had been accustomed to in the "Revelation." He could only be seen at a very precise, narrow angle. When the slant was too large, the Holy Spirit's face was fragmented and disjointed. But, as the angle decreased, the individual facial components magically fused together to create His graceful presence.

According to the Holy Bible, the Holy Spirit represented the outpouring of God's spirit onto the earth after Jesus ascended to His Heavenly throne. This phenomenal representation in His divine canvas was another pivotal piece of God's grand message for the world.

Just above the Holy Spirit's head and lying snugly on top of David's chest were my lovely children. They were comfortably packed together, sleeping peacefully as David's protective arm held them tight.

Though quite intrigued, I was still slightly concerned. I couldn't help but wonder why my children would be captured in God's painting. Why were any of us in His divine creation? His Spirit spoke to me and graciously granted me His reassuring comfort. I was instantly reminded of His imperative campaign; God made it very clear that His "Revelation" carried two principal messages and one of them was expressly for me.

The Holy Spirit directed me to a thick, white canal or passageway that spanned from the middle left side of the "Revelation" to the middle right side. This channel cut through the bottom of Jesus' chest as it made its way across the painting. God informed me that this strip was actually a spiritual energy flow that followed a defined trajectory. Upon careful inspection, it was evident that the energy flow travelled in my direction and originated from the Holy Spirit, David and my children. God's inspiring illustration and message captivated me.

The Lord explained that the spiritual stream was white because it represented God's goodness and His untainted spirit. In essence, the Holy Spirit, David and my children were all inflating me with God's spirit and protection.

Again, this sublime rendering was concurrent with David's consultation in the Bluebell Wood. It was on this utopian path that the

Spirit informed David of the moments in which I was predominantly filled with God's spirit - when I was with my children and when I painted. It was also on this trail that David was assigned the tall order of filling me with more of the good spirit.

By this time in our relationship, David was faithfully aware that the Holy Spirit overcame and saturated me each time I painted, so he naturally connected the dots.

The Spirit spoke to David of three critical mechanisms by which I was filled with God's spirit and each one was ingeniously delineated in His impressive canvas. Well-defined representations of my children, David and the Holy Spirit were unmistakably nurturing me in the Almighty's consecrated construction.

I felt incredibly blessed and honored to have God innovatively emphasize His holiness gushing towards me and fueling me with His spirit. Similar to the torrent of goodness racing towards me in the "Revelation," I felt God's love flowing down on me from His heavenly footstool.

Though God had recently liberated me from each of my fears and provided me with some sense of what was going on, I still couldn't help but wonder why I was caught up in this miraculous, enchanted whirlwind of a tale. Why did God care for me so profusely that He would choose to use this distinctive medium as a means to communicate and reveal the sacred secrets of His kingdom with me? Why did He stress the significance of His omnipotent Spirit invigorating me? Why did He introduce me to my guardian angel while simultaneously revealing that she shielded me from ghastly evil spirits soaring in my direction? Why did the Almighty assure me that Jesus and His angels would always provide me with an impenetrable barrier against all evil and harm?

The Lord's motives were well beyond my mortal comprehension. The only thing I understood, with great clarity, was that whatever it was that I was involved in was extremely noteworthy and paramount to His overarching plan. He made it perfectly clear that I stood by Jesus' side with full armor and protection. God's desire was to fill me with His good spirit; He even took it upon Himself to illustrate lavishly the mechanisms by which His spiritual flow was most prevalent in my life.

I quickly became inundated and overwhelmed by the "Revelation's" explicit imagery and the Lord's accompanying communications and explanations. Then, with a pronounced and commanding conviction, I suddenly felt my divine purpose greatly increasing in scope.

CHAPTER SIXTEEN

A New Dimension

The parallel messages deeply entrenched in the supernatural planes of the "Revelation" were becoming progressively influential and meaningful as God eloquently shared tidbits of His divine insight with me. His brilliant and glorious painting was well beyond anything this world had ever encountered and up until then, it was the most astounding artifact that I had ever seen or even heard of. It was impossible to fathom that there could have been even more to this magnificent treasure, but I quickly found that my limited knowledge was in its infancy. The truth was that there was substantially more in store for David and I. Similar to our intricate and multifaceted Creator, the cosmic "Revelation" also carried the same exclusive multidimensional DNA as its maker.

Just when I thought I had seen it all, God blew me away with absolute astonishment and wonder. He showed me that His grand masterpiece completely and metaphysically transformed and morphed into exclusive new dimensions! These exciting, uncharted terrains paved the way to entirely new formations and associations.

Anxiously, in pursuit of exploration and further discovery, David and I decided to take extra photos and videos of the "Revelation" to add to our mounting collection. We were hoping to discover breathtaking new imageries and meticulously concealed messages just waiting to be unearthed. As we eagerly sorted through the new photographs, we were shocked to find an impeccably clear and dynamic depiction of a monstrous looking creature consuming what appeared to be a defenseless human being!

The beast resembled a ferocious tiger. Its oversized mouth brutally devoured an innocent-looking head as the beast's supportive black paw pressed the smashed face securely within the grasp of an unyielding clutch. The helpless target was in unmistakable pain and agony. The impact of the beast' blow on the prey's left cheek was strikingly evident; the victim's head was firmly detained in place while the savage beast viciously demolished a portion of his face.

David and I noticed that the illustration of the unruly beast was located in the precise area of the painting where David, my children and the Holy Spirit once resided. But in this new realm they were gone and not at all detectible. In this new and somewhat frightening domain, we could only see the predator and its captive casualty. David and I had just been introduced to an entirely new breadth of God's unbelievable painting!

Immediately after examining the new imagery, David and I viewed one of the new videos we had just taken of the "Revelation," where we observed from a changing azimuth rather than from the right to left view that had unveiled the original transformation and face of Jesus Christ. We were blown away by the incredible transformation and sudden emergence of the insidious beast. We saw the original transformation where Jesus and the other inaugural images initially appeared at their precise angle. David, my children and the Holy Spirit were perfectly intact in this view. Then, as the camera slowly moved up to a slightly different azimuth, David and I miraculously witnessed these images vanish before our very eyes as the beast and its victim materialized in plain sight!

God highlighted that there were two profound meanings behind this advanced and extraordinary facet of the "Revelation." He explained that this explicit imagery represented the perturbing, nightmarish period, also known as the Tribulation, divined by John the prophet in the confounding book of Revelation. The Tribulation was the prophetic age in which Satan and his loyal beasts would be granted complete dominion over the world; goodness would be subjugated as darkness and evil would prevail and triumph. Not surprisingly, this new unearthing turned out to be another fragment of God's elaborate admonition for humanity.

God also underscored a very personal and relevant aspect of my life and relationship with David. He clarified that the dreadfully disturbing sight of the beast-like creature was a portrayal of the provisional moments when evil conquered over me and fundamentally drained me of God's spirit and goodness. It was remarkably apparent that, as the illustration converted to the newly introduced "tribulation" view, the white spiritual conduit that advanced towards me from God's three chosen sources, transformed to form the victim's white, innocent head.

God had just presented us with an unequivocal spiritual depiction of Satan depleting me of God's righteousness!

In this upsetting "tribulation" view, Jesus still stood in the center of the canvas but His face was no longer pacifying and uplifting; wrath and indignation were written all over His seething countenance. His furiously daunting rage had mounted as Satan's forces triumphed in the end times as well as when they temporarily seized control over me. God emphasized that His desire was for me to be consumed with His spirit at all times; this was absolutely essential for fulfilling His will.

Sadly, on a number of occasions, I found it extremely difficult and lacked the required diligence needed to stand up to and painstakingly combat the savage evil influences that were constantly attempting to derail me from my divine purpose and destiny.

Without question, I understood God's personal decree for my life, and although I desperately wished to please Him, I didn't exactly know how to go about accomplishing His instruction. I was bewildered and found discouragement crawling in at a feverish pace. However, the startling new dimension of the Lord's consuming canvas provided me with some fresh insight and enlightenment.

More than ever before, I had increasingly begun to sense the precise moments when evil crept in and overcame my mind. The enemy's surreptitious attacks began to occur on a more frequent basis, and although I was immediately made aware of the infiltration, it was still extremely difficult to prevent and defeat the devil's concerted energies and labors. I felt the demonic forces shadowing and honing in on me on an almost daily basis, but for the first time in my life, I was beginning to understand why. Satan was giving his best and all; his primary goal was to prevent me from achieving God's superior mandate.

Soon after this powerfully impactful exposé, God blessed me with a graphic dream that supported His recent disclosure.

In the dream, I fell asleep and was awakened by a gorgeous, picture-perfect morning. The luminous sun lit up the freshly renewed sky with a soft, pacifying glow. The jubilant, carefree birds sang delightful, inspiring melodies to further brighten the already flawless day. I stepped out on to my front porch to breathe in and enjoy the refreshing morning that God had graciously bestowed upon us.

Much to my surprise, I found many of my neighbors, hundreds of them, already outside standing in their front lawns or nervously casing the sidewalks. Their heads were raised and intently looking up into the clear, blue sky. Following suit, I too looked up towards the heavens; I was eager to see what all the commotion was about.

Far, far away in the very distant sky, I detected a tiny black speck swaying from side to side as it slowly but steadily advanced downward. I couldn't make it out but it gradually grew in size as it made its way towards us.

What on earth could it be? Everyone's eyes were fixed on it; we all needed to understand what this bizarre object was and why it was presumably headed in our direction. As the curious entity came closer to our atmosphere, its identity became evident; it was an enormous black shark casually swimming with ease in midair, as though the arid heavens were its boundless ocean.

The massive shark eventually made its way down to just about 30 feet above my home. As it threateningly swayed over my house, its motions and patterns eerily resembled a vulture circling around, waiting for its next meal. The neighbors stayed put for a few hours until they came to the realization that the shark meant them no harm. Slowly, one by one, they trailed off and went about their day.

Unlike everyone else, I was horrified. This vicious visitor from outer space came to our world and decided to hover around my house; it was apparently interested in me and no one else. Panic-stricken, I rushed inside to find some shelter within the confines of my home. Throughout the day I periodically looked out of the windows; each time I sneakily peered out, I was shocked to find the shark still "swimming" directly overhead.

The next morning was another lively one. I cautiously walked outside expecting to greet a normal day, eagerly hoping to find that the shark had retreated. Instead, I found about half the number of neighbors examining the skies yet again. I immediately looked up and saw the microscopic shark commencing its trek towards the earth. The neighbors eventually withdrew their concerns as they once again saw that the black giant's sole interest was in me. I, on the other hand, was consumed by fright and sped inside of my protective abode. Again, the atrocious shark lurked above my house until I went to bed in the evening.

For the next few days, the shark began its routine morning voyage just as soon as I stepped outside of my front door. With each passing day, the number of neighbors slowly dwindled down until, one morning, not a single person came out to observe the unusual heavenly activities. Everyone in the neighborhood had lost any and all fear of the menacing creature because they had each discovered that I was his single target; the rest of the world was invisible to it. Unfortunately, I, the shark's helpless prey, could not escape its sight.

After a few weeks of intense prayer, I was able to relinquish some of the heavy chains that had kept me a prisoner in my home. Emboldened, I decided to pursue my freedom and stop living like a slave. I was determined to go out and function in a manner I was previously accustomed to, as best as I possibly could with an enormous prowling predator soliciting my every move.

As expected, the shark, casually swaying back and forth in its customary location, greeted me as soon as I left the house. I quickly walked to my car and slammed the door shut, but found my relentless hunter oscillating its way towards me. I fought the many fears urging me to retreat as I had done for so long. I prayed for strength, started the engine and took off.

I thought it would be nice to surprise my mother with a lovely bouquet of fresh-cut flowers; my first stop would be the local florist. I had hoped that this kind gesture would lift both my spirit as well as my mothers.

The tenacious shark actively pursued me during my travels; it was a constant marker in my rear view mirror. I ran errand after errand and the unflinching shark remained intently on my tail. When I decided to call it a day, I noticed that my staunch stalker followed suit. The uninviting ogre leisurely made its way to its new permanent resting place above my residence.

The next few weeks and months were difficult and trying. Each morning I woke to find the shark waiting to torment me with his traditional salutation. If I remained indoors, it lingered above me, steadily watching guard above my home. If I left my house, the black giant shadowed me and didn't let me out of its view.

With time, I eventually adapted to my new life; a reality where a terrifying, colossal shark observed my every move. But, despite the behemoths taunts, with time and earnest prayers, each of my fears disintegrated and decayed.

I reached a turning point and no longer desired to live the life of a forsaken captive. Prayer was essential. I turned to the Lord for faith and encouragement; I needed to know, with absolute certainty, that He was there shielding me from my enemy. He immediately opened a new door and changed the playing field. The dreary circumstances I had grown accustomed to for so many months had precipitously taken a sudden, sharp turn.

Instead of waking up in my own home, on the very last morning, I woke up in an entirely new, but familiar, environment. Instead of stepping out onto my front porch, I instead walked out from my grandparents' front door.

I was once again welcomed by my inauspicious shark, but this time he didn't make his routine trek from the heavens. My ill-boding foe sat listlessly on the street just a few inches outside of my grandparent's wrought iron fence. This was the closest he and I had ever been. His titanic and terribly intimidating face silently stared at me through the small holes in the fence. His inaudible yet vehement beckon caused me to stop dead in my tracks. I briefly hesitated but I pressed on, towards my uninvited guest. I had no apprehensions and bravely marched directly in front of the leviathan. The fence was the only structure between this horrific creature and me; he was in such close proximity that I could have reached out my tiny hand and touched its filthy, leathery black hide.

I peered into the shark's large, incriminating eyes and it into mine. The mammoth had something to say to me; it desperately longed to connect with me but it didn't know to communicate in a way that I could comprehend. Or maybe it just was not allowed to do so. I didn't know what its message was but I somehow knew that this creature's principal charge was to capture and harm me. Rather fortunately, I also knew, without a shadow of a doubt, that I was under God's continuous watch and protection and the shark was forbidden from imposing its wrath on me. In that moment, the shark understood that any and all fears I once had had been completely overturned.

The gargantuan ocean animal and I stood there in complete silence, face to face, as the rest of the world carried on naively.

I finally woke up and it was all over.

God used this graphic and illuminating dream to embolden and fortify my position. He advised me that, because of my critical assignment, the devil would never deflect his concentrated attentions from me. He would diligently surround and pursue me with close proximity. Satan's mission was to infiltrate and destroy me, but my Father urged me to remain steadily on His path, despite the enemy's vast array of weapons and tactics that would be used against me. I needed to fully grasp and appreciate that God's impenetrable, shielding forces and powers served as a permanent barricade against all evil.

I was incredibly encouraged by God's inspiring and fortifying promise. As I bravely settled in the safe haven of His love and protection, I keenly perceived and harnessed my spiritual gifts on an even deeper level. I was ever cognizant and confident in God's graciousness and special endowments. My acute senses were amplified and I began to deploy each of my skills with greater tenacity and poise.

I began to notice an even greater number of lost, menacing souls congregating towards me. The enemy's armed forces started to pop up out of thin air and plainly manifest their sinister intentions to me. The immoral reprobates had no regard for those surrounding me; they came after me when I was alone or in the presence of friends and family. I even detected the enemy's reprehensible attempts to infiltrate my domain when I was with my darling, innocent children.

After an exhausting morning of running errands, the children and I stopped to grab a quick lunch at a nearby fast food establishment. Our intent was just to sit and eat but we were immediately interrupted by a seemingly friendly, elderly female employee. The woman was welcoming and kind but my spirit was on guard; I knew there was intense darkness dwelling inside of her. As she commenced with innocent small talk, she became increasingly fixated on me and never even turned to look at my children. My focus, however, was on the kids. I politely tried to dismiss this woman's invasion of my quality, family time, but the woman exhibited a great deal of resilience and persistence. She was cemented in place and would not budge, not one inch.

The Holy Spirit covered me like a cool mist on a blazing, hot day. I lifted my head firmly and peered straight into the intruder's unscrupulous eyes. Chills raced down my spine as I observed the disgusting filth that flourished deep inside of her conquered soul. This woman was one of Satan's loyal, practicing followers.

I was resolute. Fearlessly, I gazed well beyond the imposter's physical eyes and spoke silently and intently to her forlorn spirit. Using only my mind, I simply said, "I know you are evil and you need to leave now. Get away from me and my children." The woman obviously heard my command, gave me a disturbing grin and walked away without uttering a single word.

This smooth circumvention proved to be one of my easier accomplishments. However, some of the other nefarious situations I faced were not so easily evaded.

I found myself caught up in one of the most precarious positions I had ever encountered during a routine drive down one of the city's busiest freeways. I enjoyed the magnificent morning as uplifting, energizing music pumped through my veins. In spite of the heavy traffic that surrounded me from all directions, I still took great delight in my own little festive, yet tranquil, world. While driving along, listening to my revitalizing playlist, the Holy Spirit surged me with an electric-like jolt. Danger was nearby.

I immediately turned to my right and panicked with sheer horror and fright. With his mouth wide open, panting and drooling like a ravenous animal, a deranged man, obviously possessed by a demonic force, was staring at me with a ferocious intensity. His head was hanging halfway outside of the window of his beaten down, maroon pick-up truck. The stalker's steady hands were fastened to the steering wheel but his death-defying eyes were glued on me.

At all costs and ignoring all other dangers, and including the risk of a catastrophic highway collision, I knew I had to lose the hideous monster. Without any thought or hesitation, I slammed my foot on the accelerator and immediately swerved into the next lane. I looked to my right and the salivating fiend was there again, his bulbous eyes still latched onto me. I raced and battled through the narrow lanes and heavy traffic for several more minutes but no matter what I did, the dark red truck magically appeared right next to me each and every time. It didn't make any logical sense. Despite each of my dare devil tactics, Satan's coldblooded marionette effectively maneuvered his way through the traffic and amazingly found his way to me.

I couldn't recall exactly how I succeeded, but eventually, without causing any accidents, I evaded my devious and calculating pursuer. My heart pumped so heavily that I had to exit the freeway to calm myself down and regain my composure.

I sat in complete hysteria and shock for quite some time. This crazed man was controlled by a higher order of demon in Satan's hierarchy; it was quite possible that, not just one, but a legion of demons could have resided in his vanquished soul. The savage animal never once stopped to inspect the highway or the cars surrounding us; he didn't break his concentration on me for even one hair of a second!

I pondered over this perplexing event throughout the day and eventually came to the realization that what I witnessed that morning was not humanly possibly; it was completely impossible for someone to propel down the freeway without looking forward at least once! There was no doubt in my mind that this daring and dangerous exploit was one of Satan's heavy-duty attempts to eliminate me!

I recounted these two sobering, paranormal occurrences to a compassionate and sympathetic ear. David hung onto my every word and attentively listened with grave concern and an increased urgency to guard and defend me. We both knew that David was commissioned to protect me while I fulfilled God's mission. After all, David was directly cemented to me and to God; it wasn't my purpose, it was our purpose.

By this time, David was no stranger to bizarre or inexplicable events that frequently marched their way into my reality. He was certain that I was personally chosen by God for some greater purpose, but he could not yet fathom how favored I truly was. How could he, when even I remained oblivious?

But God kept preparing us and kneading our spirits to His liking; He continued to communicate and captivate us with marvelous signs and wonders.

One of the Lord's more random and unexpected signs came alongside a street corner as David and I headed out for a romantic evening on the town. We caught the red light at a heavily congested, major intersection. There were dozens of pedestrians coming and going from every direction, but David and I were simultaneously channeled to a middle aged man that stood alone at the crossing. The gentleman paid no attention to David but concentrated his firm gaze upon me. He looked right at me but there was more to it; this complete stranger was somehow looking beyond the exterior and staring deep inside of me. Like a laser, his eyes seemed to penetrate through my physical body and into the very foundations of my soul.

Like a dramatic movie scene, the disorienting act and setting seemed to move in slow motion. With our eyes stuck on this starry-eyed wanderer and his gape fixed exclusively on me, he leisurely elevated his hand into midair and motioned the sign of the cross.

David and I were both taken back by this deferential symbolism pointed directly at me. Did this transient see Jesus Christ as he gazed upon me? David, stunned and perplexed, gave me a look filled with love and admiration.

I didn't know what to make of this reverent, expressive gesture, so I just took it all in stride. I had turned to the All-Knowing for meaning and interpretation for each of the cryptic and inexplicable circumstances thrown my way, but maybe this incident didn't require any further explanation. The unequivocal sign of His holy cross spoke for itself and was more than enough for me to take in.

CHAPTER SEVENTEEN

Introductions and Awakenings

David and I knew that we needed to broadcast the vigorous and inspiring news of the "Revelation" to the ends of the earth, but we were also fully aware that God's comprehensive message for humanity was still incomplete. We both waited patiently for His divine word and precise direction. Our hearts yearned for the missing components of His grand plan, but we expected that they would come in His perfect time, as He had shown us time and time again. I knew, with absolute certainty, that my heavenly Father would notify me when His all-inclusive message was ready to be publicized to the world.

As we waited for God's full-blown announcement to come to fruition, David and I decided to produce a video and use it as a means of introducing our families and close friends to this sacred treasure that we had kept securely veiled and sheltered for so many months. We thoroughly examined and discussed every aspect of the "Revelation" that had already been exposed to us, but decided that it would be best to keep the video succinct. We understood that Godly manifestations of this proportion were not an everyday occurrence and could possibly invoke great fear and terror, even amongst close relatives. David and I chose to focus our efforts on the original transformation and simply outline the "PS 512" inscribed in the blood-stained face of Jesus Christ.

David spent a substantial amount of time and energy accumulating and merging the individual stills and visuals that would eventually come to construct the video. In the end, his industrious labors culminated into a stunningly elegant and deferential exhibit of God's miraculous work of art.

All across the board, the responses to the video were comparable; everyone who bore witness to the magnificent transformation was stunned and astonished by God's work! The breathtaking message in Jesus' face rendered most speechless! The consensus was that the vast majority of our captive audience was emotionally and spiritually moved; they irrefutably accepted that this canvas was brushed by God's very hand.

But this consecrated work of art had the most influential and lasting impact on three very special people, my precious gifts from God. My amazing and adored children were never quite the same after witnessing the Lord's phenomenal glory shine through the painting.

My kids were struck with riveting jolts of exhilaration and euphoria the very moment they saw the video of God's "Revelation." I had never before seen them filled with so much zeal and enthusiasm. But how could they not be?

Their young, physical bodies housed very mature and wise souls; their discerning spirits immediately recognized God's infusion and proclaimed His painting to be a momentous sign for the entire world to behold. They danced with delight and sang joyful songs of worship and praise. Each of the children repeatedly thanked God for His spectacular gift, especially for painting it through their beloved mother. They highly esteemed and prized the sensational miracle that graced their humble home.

Naturally , the children exhibited many curiosities and were faced with many unanswered questions. They regularly probed into the mystical world of this fairytale-like painting. They pondered over its grand significance and postulated over why it was sent to the earth. The inquisitive youngsters wondered why God had chosen their mother to paint through and began questioning God's rolling wave of communication with me.

I relished their enthusiasm and openly poured out some of His privileged insight into their fervent and receiving hearts.

My compact, yet heavyweight, spiritual powerhouses were completely absorbed and overwhelmed by the "Revelation" and, of course, by God Himself! They lit up like brilliant, pulsating stars as they jubilantly exalted their Maker. My cherished children passionately exclaimed that we were the luckiest family in the entire world; we were an integral part of God's blessed, royal family!

My faithful and devout children were convinced that God had a special assignment for me. But somehow, their intuitive spirits were aware of this well before the "Revelation" even came to light; they weren't nearly as surprised by God's luminescent manifestation as I would have imagined that they might be. They took everything in with elegant grace and composure, almost as though they had been expecting something extraordinary to happen all along.

During one of my dynamic discussions with the children, the Holy Spirit gracefully interjected and asked me to open up the suite of "Revelation" photos that I had recently saved onto one of my flash drives. I was steered to one specific frame and was greeted by a much cherished friend. The face of Jesus Christ, in His physical, human form, was staring right at me! His consecrated visage was so realistic and lifelike that it looked as though it was superimposed onto the painting using advanced technology. His startling, sacred image took my breath away!

Jesus Christ, our Lord and Savior, was suspended in the white, clouded area of the "Revelation," right next to God the Father. In fact, a quarter of Jesus' face was concealed behind the face of the Almighty and both images appeared to extend from one another. Father and Son, side by side, decorated the rising white clouds of the heavens in a painting that I had painted! The celestial scene was beyond human comprehension and tremendously inspiring! My ardent spirit raced with enthusiasm and unrivaled rapture!

But I didn't just see His magnificent face and make bold assumptions. How could I audaciously assume that I was beholding the Son of God? The Holy Spirit relayed this privileged, insider information to me firsthand. This new disclosure was a lucid picture of the Son of Mary; the human form of God who had walked on our earth over two thousand years ago. The revered face that, millions upon millions had only imagined and dreamt of beholding, was divinely sketched before my very eyes, in a phenomenal painting that I was fortunate enough to have in my possession.

I was elated; what I experienced was beyond this world, beyond surreal! My entire body tickled with His saturating presence as I felt His quintessence pumping through my veins, saturating the very core of my being.

In that moment, I was compelled to share the revolutionary and lustrous likeness of Jesus with my children. Without any slight intimation or suggestion, I innocuously showed them the nameless face and casually asked them who they thought the man in the clouds was. Their deeply intuitive spirits did not hesitate. They didn't require a moment to decipher or interpret; each of my children knew instantaneously that the man they gazed upon was none other than their savior, Jesus Christ.

The kids couldn't believe their eyes! They were fanatically overcome with enthusiasm and hope. Alexandria and Allison immediately announced that this new image was a sign from God; a beacon that Jesus would soon return to our world to save His faithful flock. Their passionate conversations about His return quickly turned to the

Rapture; they each longed for the day that we would escape the charges of death and claim resurrection with our Lord.

To fuel their excitement, I decided to dazzle them with the Father's face in the clouds. Alexander instantly exclaimed "Wow, that's God's face!" In God's defense, a stupefied Alexandria stated that Alexander didn't know what God looked like, no one did. But my son stood firm and unyielding. In response to Alexandria's comment, he boldly proclaimed that he knew what God looked like in his heart and he had no doubt that the face in question was the Father's!

No mother could have been more honored and proud.

As I sat, delightfully observing and listening to my children authoritatively preach of Jesus and the end times, I began to hear His commanding voice yet again. The Spirit led me to the scriptures, "After he said this, he was taken up before their very eyes, and a cloud hid him from their sight. They were looking intently up into the sky as he was going, when suddenly two men dressed in white stood beside them. "Men of Galilee," they said, "why do you stand here looking into the sky? This same Jesus, who has been taken from you into heaven, will come back in the same way you have seen him go into heaven" (Acts 1:9-11, NIV).

The Holy Spirit indicated that this groundbreaking component of the global message not only represented the Ascension of Christ, whereby He went up into the clouds after His resurrection, but the astounding imagery symbolized His final return as well!

The individual constituents of His stupendous design were finally piecing together and beginning to make sense. It was clear that His astonishing "Revelation" showcased various events or stories of the New Testament of the Holy Bible. So far, David and I had been enlightened with graphic depictions of the Crucifixion, pouring out of the Holy Spirit, Tribulation, Ascension and glorious return of Christ. But as unimaginable and stupefying as these images and their respective connotations were, the Spirit informed me that there was still more of God's mind-blowing message advancing my way.

I went back to look through the hundreds of other photos, specifically upon the area where the Father and Son resided together in the clouds. In most of the snapshots, Jesus' face could not be seen. In only a couple, His face was faint and barely visible. The one superb shot that the Spirit led me directly to was the only photograph in the entire collection where Jesus' facial features were meticulously crisp and discernible!

Our God was beyond amazing; He had led me straight to where I needed to go! But I shouldn't have been at all surprised since I was already very acquainted with His superior methods of communication. Without question or hesitation, I laid myself down to His direction each time He engaged me. I simply did as I was told.

David, on the other hand, was not so familiar with the Lord's inscrutable strategies or interceptions. But, on occasion, God took it upon Himself to direct David's steps as well.

Soon after David and I revealed God's breathtaking masterpiece with my family, Thunder, my devoted Miniature Schnauzer, became terminally ill and it was advised that he be put to sleep as soon as possible. When I moved away from my parents' home to start my own family, I thought it best to leave Thunder behind. It saddened me to have to say goodbye to my dedicated, little companion, but I was well aware that my younger and even more attached brothers would have been devastated without Thunder's loyal and playful company.

The family briefly discussed the matter but it was an easy decision to make; to shelter Thunder from unnecessary pain and anguish, we decided that the veterinarian's advice was the best route to take.

Just a few days after Thunder was laid to rest, God directed David to another photograph of His "Revelation," in which the image of a large black and grey Schnauzer was haphazardly captured. Intrigued, David immediately sent the photo my way for examination. At first glance, I had to sit down to contain myself. I found myself saying hello to my dear Thunder, who was scrupulously illustrated in the upper left quadrant of the canvas, right next to my beautiful grandmother.

I didn't quite comprehend the reasoning behind this unforeseen unmasking. How could my precious Thunder dwell within the boundaries of God's miraculous painting and, more importantly, why?

I was astonished but enormously reassured and comforted. Because of my grandmother's presence, I had come to believe that the upper division of the "Revelation" represented another realm other than the corporeal. I felt that the area above Jesus symbolized heaven or a representation of those that had moved on from our physical world into the spiritual. Thunder had just died and his carbon copy considerably reinforced this staunch conviction!

I didn't hesitate to send the emotive picture of Thunder to my mother and each of my brothers. With the photo I included a caption of "Guess who?" There was no question in anyone's mind that they were looking at our honorable Thunder; he had a uniquely wise and judicious look that was superbly mirrored in the "Revelation."

My family had already acknowledged and grasped the "Revelation" as God's divine creation, but suddenly they were given another enticing facet to consider. They now witnessed, first-hand, that God had incorporated a very personal aspect of my life in His painting. The timing of it all was undeniably impeccable.

But just what was it that God was attempting to convey by revealing a depiction of Thunder just a couple of days after his death? Thunder's timely introduction invoked a new avenue of emotion into my family's collective consciousness. Fear crept in as they each began to ponder over the esoteric depths and intricacies of the now frightening "Revelation."

After Thunder's debut in the painting, my family rapidly followed suit and came on board with my supposition that the upper half of the canvas was a representation of a heavenly or spiritual dimension. But as spectacular as this theory was, the family was also terrified that this supernatural, unworldly painting could be prophetic and ominously predict the deaths of my loved ones!

My family's trepidations didn't ignite any repressed anxieties or concerns regarding my sentiments for the "Revelation." God's manifestation was magnificent in all of its dimensions; every individual feature and component of the painting came directly from the Lord. Whatever He had to say, in whatever form or fashion, was especially welcomed and embraced. If His splendid masterpiece also happened to foretell of death and the afterlife, then there was a valid reason for it. For me, this was just another exceptional element of its profuse complexity and grandeur.

More than anything in the world, my parched soul yearned and ached for God's extensive array of signs and wonders, for His sovereign illumination and merciful assurances. Any gesture from my Creator was never short of splendor and inspiration.

But, in spite of all of God's glory and beauty, the enemy remained a constant thorn in my side. I recognized Satan's pervasive presence and determination coming through in a most powerful way. For extra comfort and security, I longed for the Lord's warnings and premonitions. At times, His unrivaled and inconceivable communications and manifestations inflicted brief stints of fright, but after everything I had seen, it was fairly easy to fall right back into His safe, sheltering arms. Despite the alarming content and nature of some of God's forewarnings, I actively sought His guidance and prudently took heed.

However, like a child in learning, on a rare occasion I did require more than one serving of His prudent counsel.

Perhaps the most alarming and personally significant admonition came to me in the middle of an unusually cold, still night. In the middle of a deep sleep, I was awakened and greeted by an appallingly familiar face. There were no sudden noises or any type of commotion in the bedroom, but something surreptitiously disrupted my slumber; I was convinced that it had to be his permeating, sinister presence that woke me from my rest.

Positioned on my left side, I opened my listless eyes to the horror of one of the appalling end-time beasts. The leopard-like beast from the book of Revelation, the exact same atrocity that eerily protruded from the "Face of God" canvas, was intently staring at me from just a couple of feet away from my face!

The gruesome character looked as though it had implanted and positioned itself on the back side of Phillip's head; it was insidiously discreet and stationary. His shadowy, black eyes watched me with contempt and loathing. I was frozen solid and could do nothing but stare back. I wondered whether this beast would come to life or try to attack me. Filled with terror, I prayed earnestly.

My heavy breathing and racing heart eventually normalized as I ultimately came to the conclusion that this hideous omen could not harm me. Albeit horrifying, I understood that this was another sign from God. But in that formidable moment, its relevance remained a mystery. In time, I made my way back to sleep and eventually forgot about the abhorrent interruption.

But what I earnestly strove to forget, He forcefully impressed upon me again. Of course, I should have known better. When God sent a sign, any sign, there was usually a very good reason for it. He wasn't going to let me off the hook that easily. So, to refresh my selective memory and awaken my perception, God sent me a friendly reminder.

Just a few weeks after the beasts' initial appearance, the Lord showed me another monstrous creature on the back of Phillip's head. But this uninvited visitor was a newcomer; this was a new evil spirit that God had recently shown me in the "Revelation." In the painting, this revolting black beast was also swiftly travelling in my direction and like his fellow companions, was stricken away by the angel's protective hand.

I wasn't at all frightened or troubled the second time around. I knew what was going on; God was bestowing His wisdom upon me. The Lord was cautiously alerting me that there were some demonic spirits residing in my husband's soul. He had been conveying this communication to my spirit for many months but I had casually brushed it off and ignored His guidance. I didn't want to believe that Phillip could have drifted and turned away from the light; I just did not want to accept the disturbing reality.

The truth was that my troubled mind was clouded by massive loads of guilt. Maybe by not acknowledging Phillip's corruption or iniquities, I could easily overlook or swallow the terrible pain that I had inflicted upon him. Maybe, without conscious knowledge, I felt partly responsible for my abandoned husband's straying from the Lord's path.

Did a small fragment of my subconscious believe that I could have pushed him into Satan's receiving and deceiving arms?

Whatever reasons I once had for refuting reality were no longer valid. God was no longer allowing me to disregard or hide from the truth, His truth. He had advised me of Phillip's drastic shifts, but I stubbornly refused to take heed. So what did God do? He used a very resounding and blunt tactic to showcase Phillip's meticulously concealed corruption; He exposed the sign of the beast on his head!

God had repeatedly, via various methods, cautioned me regarding Satan' prowling forces; there was no doubt that I was his prime target. After God had informed me of Phillip's new allegiances, I realized that the stakes had been drastically raised. I made some obvious connections and concluded that I had to make some immediate changes.

The cunning devil had slyly infiltrated my private lair and was stalking my every move, even from the vicinity of my own home!

CHAPTER EIGHTEEN

The Testimony of Christ

The stress and anxiety of making a drastic, life-altering change was beginning to take a heavy toll on my mind and weigh me down physically. But my concern wasn't at all to do with my life or Phillip's; I was confident that we would each wade through the trying times of the divorce and ultimately prevail. My titanic heartache and distress was for my children; the thought of causing them any ounce of grief or sadness was soul crushing and unbearable. The sole reason I had remained incarcerated in my marriage for as long as I did was for their sake alone; I had chosen to spare them the agony of a divorce, even if that meant a bleak and unfulfilled life for their mother.

But the tables had drastically turned as my former life had become virtually obsolete and nonexistent. I was in love with David and Jesus Christ served as the unifying and concentrated center of our blessed union. We had a God-given assignment that involved spreading the good news of Christ via His anointed "Revelation," the phenomenal painting that would one day claim the title of the most prized and sought after religious artifact of our time. Pronounced and immediate changes were in order and God was ingeniously paving the way to a new and promising future.

God gave me the first push to independence by displaying the two beasts on Phillip's head. I knew I had to leave my marriage and had every assurance that God would help me deal with the aftermath of my decision. He would ensure that the impact on the children would be negligible; their transition into their new lives would be seamless and comfortable.

As my faith ripened and matured, I stopped questioning, or even wondering about, God's motives for bringing David and I together. God had repeatedly advised me to trust completely in His supreme authority, even though I lacked sufficient understanding. So, with time and a growing childlike faith, that's precisely what I did.

I could have never imagined the monumental destiny that God had preordained for David and me. No human being alive could have ever fathomed our massive purpose.

With the priceless gift of His glorious painting, David and I clearly recognized that we were a part of something that measured epic, biblical proportions. Still, we were left puzzled for quite some time. I pondered over our recent chain of supernatural events often but inevitably found myself drowning in His written word. Each time my thoughts turned to the compelling writings of the Bible and its outstanding stories and characters, I would inevitably lose myself. I spent countless hours envisioning or recreating the magnificence and vigor of its remarkable contents. I always felt considerably close to His word, but I could have never gaged just how close I truly was.

The day we received confirmation and enlightenment, that unforgettable day David and I found out that our lives were actually foretold of in the sanctified pages of the Bible, we were left speechless and thunderstruck!

David and I were very aware that we had a firm obligation to spread the word of God and His revolutionary testimony, depicted in and through the rich colors of the inexplicable "Revelation." We also knew that, because of our unique experiences with His unfathomable work, that we were the only two people in the world that could possibly accomplish this sacred mission. The assignment would be daunting, but God would be right there beside us through every debilitating obstacle and challenge. Our enduring expedition would be a grueling one, but David and I really didn't know the half of it. The full extent of our lifelong quest was well beyond our wildest dreams and human comprehension.

Our imperative task was a global one. I was rather composed and unruffled when God first unveiled our true identities. He had already informed us that through His glorious "Revelation," David and I would impact millions of souls and win many over to Christ.

So, when the Holy Spirit informed me that we, David and I, were the two witnesses that God referenced in the book of Revelation, I wasn't nearly as surprised as one would have expected. David also took the remarkable news with a great calmness. We both felt that God had been preparing and fortifying us for this resplendent awakening for quite some time.

The Holy Spirit directed me to the eleventh chapter of the book of Revelation as He boldly proclaimed David and me to be His two witnesses. God established that He sent His awe-inspiring and wondrous painting for us to use as a powerful and prophetic tool; this transcendent medium would attest to His glory and the eternal salvation through the blood of Jesus Christ.

As I read through the chapter, the Holy Spirit stopped me at one specific verse, "If anyone tries to harm them, fire comes from their mouths and devours their enemies. This is how anyone who wants to harm them must die" (Revelation 11:5, NIV).

The Almighty God steered my attention to the preeminent "Revelation" and astounded me with a new remarkable image. Just below the white spiritual channel flowing towards me was another source of my protection. God exposed one of His good spirits shielding me from the small demons that were charging in my direction; what looked like a surge of black and white flames escaped from my new defender's wide open mouth. It was already obvious that the angel's protective hand secured me from the evil forces, but now I could clearly see that the large hand was actually thrashing the wicked minions into the mouth of this new protective entity.

God explained that Revelation 11:5 was a spiritual reference and not a literal one. The fresh image of the fire-shooting spirit was a depiction of this verse. He warned me that the devil's foot soldiers would ceaselessly attack us but David and I would always have the Lord's impenetrable ammunition; layers of defense that we could never envision or comprehend. God urged me never to fear or lose sight of Him. Just like He astonishingly portrayed in the "Revelation," Jesus would carry David and I through each of the many trials and hardships that would surface throughout the course of our arduous, yet honorable, calling.

Just a few days after this momentous, life-changing announcement, God gave me an accompanying dream to help seal in and solidify our assignment. In my dream, He showed me a rendering of the "Revelation" where a fully armed and austere Jesus stood at its center. Jesus looked as though He was prepared for battle as He fiercely held two weapons, one in each of His hands. In His left hand, He gripped a long, white sword while a small, white dagger graced His right side. Though both weapons were white they were noticeably different. The larger sword was a polished and intense white while the dagger exhibited more of a dull, lackluster appeal.

God explained that David and I were the dagger and the sword, respectively; we were His two mighty weapons on earth. In the intriguing "Revelation" of my dream, a fierce Jesus held the two swords tightly in His hands just like He held David and me securely in His arms in the authentic "Revelation!"

As His devout witnesses, the Lord would use David and I, His obedient, humble servants, to disseminate His authoritative word, the testimony of Jesus Christ. After all, the word of God was one of the most powerful weapons forged against the enemy.

I felt incredibly blessed and invigorated as I exalted Jesus and His great name. His power and authority were overwhelming and incomprehensible, so much greater than us. Yet, He chose us. Why He did was well beyond me.

According to the book of Revelation, at the end of our earthly lives, David and I would gallantly die for the One who died on the cross for us. I couldn't imagine a sweeter departure from this crestfallen world. I couldn't envision a more noble entrance into everlasting paradise with our Lord!

The powerful metaphor of the two swords was a part of God's private and personal instruction for David and me, it was clearly symbolic of how He would use David and me to spread His message to the masses. However, the prominent illustration of Jesus Christ carrying His people in the "Revelation" also held considerable significance for the rest of the population.

The majestic portrait of Christ carrying a man and a woman also served as a beautiful representation of the Rapture. This divine, supernatural occurrence served as a symbol of hope for the elect and faithful disciples of Christ. For those who believed in this biblical prophecy, this paramount and cosmic event would fashion an inconceivable and inexplicable escape from physical death. This specific component of His luminous painting was another chief element of God's crucial announcement for humanity.

The Lord had just granted us one more magnificent piece of His message.

The significance and splendor of this passionate scene was captivating and heartening. The promise of deliverance from the horrific tribulation period was painted by the Lord for the entire world to see and cling to for inspiration and encouragement. Those filled with conviction and obedience to His everlasting word would claim the keys to victory in the most dreadful and atrocious era in all of history. The devoted and loyal followers of Christ would graciously be given a fee admittance pass into His celestial kingdom.

My thankful heart was overjoyed and elated. How could we fathom God's abounding and immeasurable love? He had already sacrificed His only Son to save us; it was His blood, and His alone, that washed away all of our iniquities and cleansed us of our sins. It was His celebrated death that opened the doors to eternal life.

Was this timeless gift not enough to prove that His love for humanity was beyond measure? Were there no limits to His grace and mercy? He was the Almighty God and didn't have to do a single thing for our redemption, but in all of His resplendent righteousness He did. And moreover, He then offered the priceless gift of the Rapture for those who would believe in Christ and willingly receive His endowment.

But, with this sublime thought, my heart began to singe with a penetrating pain. I was overtaken by anguish and sorrows for the millions who would never come to know and appreciate His brilliance. They would never receive emancipation from the unimaginable terrors that would emanate during Satan's atrocious reign over the earth. They would beg for mercy and death but their cries would not be answered. They would suffer excruciating torment and plagues, all because their hearts had been hardened and their eyes blinded to the One Truth.

For a couple of downhearted weeks, I wallowed in despair and compassion for the deluded and lost souls that would remain after the Rapture; they would be forced to exist in the ubiquitous and inexorable squalor of the devil's dominion. God offered me His welcomed comfort by assuring me that the dreadful age of the tribulation would last for a fixed period but that the suffering would eventually cease at His predetermined time. All things would come to their end at His great command.

And then, my merciful Father presented me with the final fragment of His extensive admonition for mankind.

He took me to the haunting tribulation view of the "Revelation." I noticed the fury in Jesus' countenance as He looked with rage upon the devouring beast. The Holy Spirit directed me to an area just above Jesus' fuming face and directly beneath the guardian angel. He pointed out a thin, sharp, arched object that had a handle on one end and was crimson red on the other.

The Holy Spirit took me to the sacred pages of the bible. I gasped as I read the resounding words of John, "Then another angel came out of the temple and called in a loud voice to him who was sitting on the cloud, "Take your sickle and reap, because the time to reap has come, for the harvest of the earth is ripe." So he who was seated on the cloud swung his sickle over the earth, and the earth was harvested" (Revelation 14:15-16, NIV).

The instrument God highlighted for me in His glorious painting was the sickle from the Harvest; this renowned tool belonged to the angel hovering just above it. The deep red coloring on the end of the blade represented the bloodshed of all of the civilizations of the earth. It was chilling to see that the blood only appeared on the sickle in the tribulation view; in the original "Revelation," the sickle could be seen clearly but without the dripping blood.

The Harvest represented the final judgment of mankind; it was the absolute end of the world. The Bible proclaimed that the angel of the Harvest would come and reap the earth at the end of the tribulation; Christians would be granted eternal life and non-believers would be sent to dwell in eternal damnation and unrest. After the Harvest, there would be no more chances for redemption or repentance.

I sat frozen, in a state of complete reverence and humility. I had never been more amazed and mesmerized by anything in this life. Nothing in the world could compare to God's miraculous masterpiece. His intoxicating tapestry was flawlessly woven and beautifully articulated by His very hand. In His extraordinary "Revelation," the God of yesterday, today and tomorrow had effectively and meticulously illustrated the New Testament of the Holy Bible! What David and I had spent countless hours, days and months examining and marveling in was the abundant and everlasting testimony of Jesus Christ!

Direct from heaven's throne, God had provided us with distinctive images of the Crucifixion, Ascension, outpouring of the Holy Spirit, Rapture, Tribulation and Harvest; key events that spanned from the gospel of Matthew all the way through to the hair-raising pages of the book of Revelation! The personal testimonials written by His prophets were graphically recounted in this supernatural painting. The comprehensive message meant for all of humanity was essentially a chronicle of the New Testament! But instead of using written text, this time the God of the universe produced a magical multidimensional oil painting to showcase His glorious word!

It was finished; His all-inclusive announcement had been revealed. The great and mighty I AM had finally disclosed His sweeping proclamation. The "Revelation" was a final call for all of humanity to come to Christ! David and I had to distribute this unbelievable story to every tribe and every nation. Every person alive had to be granted the opportunity to witness His inconceivable and spiritually infused manifestation.

But the task was a daunting one. How would we begin to spread His glorious message?

We chose to create a new, extensive video and distribute it to the masses via the World Wide Web. David worked on the video content and presentation while I asked God to kindly bestow His fluency and wisdom upon me. I prayed for His Spirit to speak through me while I attempted to communicate His imperative dispatch. But the delivery proved to be much more difficult than I had anticipated. As I struggled with the messaging I continued my supplications.

The stealthy devil crept in and attempted to impede me using weapons of discouragement and self-doubt. He filled my mind with insecurities and reservations. The furtive enemy tried to convince me that, regardless of my efforts, I would fall short and disappoint God. He emphasized that I was not worthy enough to speak for the one true God. The master of lies piercingly pronounced that people would not believe in the painting's genesis; my energies would be wasted on an already defeated people. The devil's cunning trickeries were so forceful and masterful that I came incredibly close to walking away from God's critical instruction.

I struggled with my malicious opponent while David persevered in his undertaking. He worked diligently and painstakingly to create a reverent and influential production that impeccably captured the essence of God's "Revelation." David impressively showcased each event of the New Testament with great modesty and untainted character.

I believed that God conscientiously worked through David and smiled upon his final product.

I shared my internal conflicts and misgivings with David. He encouraged me and we both fought the devil with the strength of our combined prayers and faith. God lifted me up and opened my eyes to the devil's deceptions and self-seeking intentions. Satan did not want God's message to reach a single soul; the enemy was frantically attempting to thwart any and all communication regarding the heaven-sent "Revelation."

God released me from the dreadful influences that were deterring me from completing His assignment. He countered all of Satan's attacks and restored my confidence. He assured me that, despite what people publicly acknowledged or proclaimed about the painting, in the deep confines of their hearts, most would see God's glory.

The Creator of all things empowered me with His valor. When the time came for me to complete my commentary, God provided me with the exact Bible references to use and He spoke boldly through me! I was simply a conduit; His eloquent prose flowed naturally and directly from His Spirit and out of my mouth. He intoxicated me with His presence in the same fashion as when He painted through me supernaturally.

The end result was a beautifully illustrated demonstration of God's indispensable declaration. His innovative rendering of the New Testament was available and accessible online for each of His children to behold and appreciate. Enthusiastically, David and I began distributing the staggering video to friends and family; we prayed earnestly that His crusade would spread like rapid wildfire.

Together, over the span of many months, David and I felt and experienced every supercharged ounce of power and essence that the "Revelation" had to offer, but we never grew accustomed to it or tired of its magnificence. We could never stop rejoicing in its incessant splendor. With each passing day, our uncontainable passion for it and its Creator grew astronomically. We vowed to deliver His message and proclaim the Name above all names to the very end of our days. That was our purpose in this life and we were stubbornly determined to succeed.

But we were so captivated and blindsided by this supernatural and glorious wonder that David and I did not consider anything beyond this grand, elaborate design. But we should have known better; His Majesty's intricate and complex strategies and campaigns could never be fathomed by any human being. God had just declared that we were His two chosen witnesses of the end times; this enormous responsibility consumed us and was more than enough for our mortal minds to process. Our simple brains didn't have the mental capacity to contemplate a more superior or distinguished commission than this! How could there even be anything greater than this?

But God had something else in store for us; a charge so imperative and monumental that He would send down His fleet of angels to serve as our personal guardians and protectors.

Very early on in our relationship, God had planted a deeply ingrained, microscopic seed in each of our hearts. Though we had both heard His resounding voice and penetrating, yet startling, message, the truth was that David and I were too terrified to speak of the matter, even to each other!

CHAPTER NINETEEN

John, the Great Prophet

I never claimed to be a Bible expert. In fact, I considered myself very far from the scholarly ranks. Though some of the Holy books were relatively straightforward and easy to decipher, others were incredibly complex and not as intuitive. Particularly, I found the obscure texts of the book of Revelation to be the most cryptic of them all. The confounding and impenetrable forewarnings of John, the prophet of end times, were unmistakably meant to leave any and all readers with a great sense of wonder and mystery.

The All-Knowing made it very clear that specific apocalyptic events and prophecies that He openly disclosed to John were to be intentionally undisclosed to the rest of humanity and therefore omitted from John's powerfully telling writings as he boldly declared, "And when the seven thunders spoke, I was about to write; but I heard a voice from heaven say, "Seal up what the seven thunders have said and do not write it down" (Revelation 10:4, NIV). Further in the same chapter, the Bible declares "But in the days when the seventh angel is about to sound his trumpet, the mystery of God will be accomplished, just as he announced to his servants the prophets" (Revelation 10:7, NIV).

No one, other than John, could have possibly conceived or even begun to imagine the grand and monumental design that God had in store for our fallen world! Could we ever have expected that at some other appointed time, some of God's heavily guarded blueprints would actually be revealed to anyone else? The concept was simply foreign and unimaginable!

In the few short weeks after God had informed me of my meek appearance in His elaborate "Revelation," I carefully studied my image in the painting and began to notice some unusual anomalies in my facial features. The slight aberrations seemed to come and go with incredibly minute variations in the canvas' angle. Though I knew that there were no limits to the depths of His cosmic masterpiece I was, nonetheless, left startled and bewildered.

During the early phases of discovery and examination of His painting, I was a nearly aimless toddler stumbling and fumbling around, just learning to use my muscles and beginning to crawl. I knew that God had graciously opened the gates of heaven and sent down His precious testimony to grace our lost and decaying world. I also recognized that, in bestowing and entrusting me with His priceless treasure, I had to be directly linked to its divine secrets and ultimate earthly purpose. With time, I did learn to walk, but each bit of new information required digestion and an ample amount of processing time.

Though David and I were His two chosen witnesses with great assignments on this earth, I couldn't fathom that my physical, mortal existence could hold unimaginable and transcendent ties to His eternal, celestial kingdom.

Throughout the course of many conversations shared between me and David, I had passionately expressed my extreme regard and likeness to John. I understood and genuinely felt the overwhelming love John proclaimed to have received from Jesus; a love so concentrated and pronounced that it was almost impossible to conceive that there could have been enough of it to go around for anyone else!

I was certain that a timeless and unspoken bond, albeit an intangible one, existed between me and the distinguished diviner.

One afternoon, as I carefully inspected the bottom left corner of the "Revelation," I was struck with an abrupt illumination. I knew what I had seen but, for some reason, I was highly disconcerted; too disturbed to even bring this new image to David's attention. I was greatly perturbed by the likeness of a judicious, elderly man that called to me from another world, his very distant world. Part of this fresh image overlapped with the image of me.

God's gradual and impeccable interventions calmed my concerns and trepidations. The man's shrewd and saintly features began to grow on me as I increasingly examined his facial structure. His stern expression and full, flowing beard conveyed a great sense of knowledge and piety. The sagacious image extended from inside of the left side of my face, as though we were somehow interwoven or connected to one another, but he only appeared at a precise, narrow angle.

Who was this man and what was our connection? My abounding curiosity grew and was only satisfied when the Holy Spirit informed me that the composed gentleman beside me was none other than John, the ancient prophet of the Lord!

The Holy Spirit kindly explained that the reason John's image was intricately embedded with my own in the "Revelation" was because our union was a spiritual representation of John's spirit residing inside of me. My mind immediately turned to the scriptures. Just before the two witnesses are mentioned in the book of Revelation, the Lord declares that John was to prophecy again. The great I AM had just enlightened me and let me in on one of His luminous secrets; He informed me that John would prophecy again through me and my paintings!

The same John, who stood side by side with Jesus Christ as he humbly walked on the earth, sat inconspicuously beside me in God's multifaceted and boundless piece of consecrated art. The same John, who witnessed the heart wrenching crucifixion and miraculous resurrection of Christ, was alive in our very day and age, dwelling inside of me, preparing me for my honorable mission! The same John, who lived long enough to see the horrendous proceedings that culminated to the ultimate demise of our world, would once again prophesy. Only this time he would use one of the Lord's very own witnesses as his personal vessel!

I was completely beside myself! In light of the recent disclosure, I finally began to understand the deep, heartfelt affinity and fondness I held for John.

I had just been endowed with one of the great mysteries of the Bible! So many of the enigmatic puzzle pieces were beginning to fuse together perfectly!

Though, day by day, it was becoming more evident that the end of our world was soon approaching, my heart rejoiced and I took solace in the wonders of the Almighty God.

My discerning spirit recognized that even more astounding surprises were making their way down from His throne and I couldn't help but to look up with a receiving and grateful heart. I couldn't take my steady eyes off of the Lord. I found it extremely difficult to focus on anything other than Him and the epic destiny that He had just introduced me to. I was consumed by all of the recent revelations and I couldn't keep my anxious mind off of the mysterious marvels that would come next!

CHAPTER TWENTY

My Special Life

The children were astonished by the spellbinding and poignant new video David and I had just broadcast for the entire world to see. Although the detailed and explicit content and associated messaging could quite easily have frightened them, God assured me that sharing the full production with them was the right thing to do; their spirits were highly evolved and adept to handle His news, both good and bad. And, as one would expect, He was right.

They cherished all aspects of His urgent proclamation, the promising and frightening equally. Filled with fervor, my children believed that this unbelievable, multidimensional painting was an indisputable sign of Jesus' highly anticipated return. They marveled incessantly at the overwhelming "Revelation" and were oftentimes transfixed by God's wondrous work of art. They gazed upon God's regal creation with wholehearted admiration and veneration. There was no room for doubt in their devout hearts.

My faithful children were blindingly transformed by the impressive "Revelation" and its numerous connotations. Their already advanced spirits were given a turbo boost after experiencing God's manifestation; after basting in the brilliance of the "Revelation" they were inundated with God's spirit in a remarkably noticeable manner. Each of my dear children began to reference God with an effervescent purity. They couldn't help but speak of God's extraordinary celestial painting and how it would radically impact the world and change many lives. They believed that the word of the Living God, via the vibrant colors of the "Revelation," would reach millions of lost souls and that His glorious painting would acquaint them all with Jesus Christ.

But my children were only familiar with the specific components of the "Revelation" that David and I shared in the public domain, the summary of the New Testament, from the Crucifixion of Christ to the Harvest of the earth. I didn't divulge God's personal notices for David and me. How could I have? Though they recognized that their parents suffered from a struggling marriage, my innocent and trusting children didn't have any indication that there could even be another man in my life. That's why I was completely caught off guard and surprised to find that Allison was privy to some of the discreet information that David and I had closely and heavily guarded!

Allison and Alexander were playing a game of make believe while I was in the kitchen tidying things up a bit. They sat in front of me as they took on the roles of two highly energetic and enthusiastic newscasters. Their cover story, feature of the day report was on the phenomenal "Revelation." Allison informed her captive audience of one that God had sent a miraculous sign to the world, a notable and outstanding painting that He had created through her mother.

My natural expectation was that my enlightened daughter would next comment on the recently released video or the specific events of the New Testament that God had inventively infused in the painting, but she did not. Instead, Allison proceeded to state that this incredible painting, sent from Heaven, contained all of her mother's spirits. My daughter's incandescent eyes beamed as she proudly declared that the painting was, in fact, a story about my special life.

She left it at that. Nothing else was said.

I smiled in awe as my curiosity ran wild. My little angel was not consciously aware of all the spiritual beings that God had surreptitiously embedded in His expansive canvas. Allison had no previous indication that I was the blessed woman who stood at Jesus' side! My daughter had no clue that God's spirit flowed through to me from her and her siblings, David and the Holy Spirit. She had no knowledge whatsoever that I was one of the two witnesses foretold of thousands of years prior! Allison had no earthly idea that, since the "Revelation's" exquisite debut, God had been using it as a fail-safe mechanism to convey inconceivable and profound personal messages about my life!

There wasn't a need to for me to communicate any of this classified information to my daughter because her heightened spirit had already been illuminated by the Holy Spirit. The All-Powerful had just shared the fascinating news with her. God had been using Allison to relay His sagacious messages to me for years, but I couldn't fully appreciate exactly how or even how often. After the "Revelation's" arrival, I witnessed His glory glisten through her like never before.

Alongside Allison's intuitive commentary and sudden spiritual infusion, I soon detected striking metamorphoses in Alexandria and Alexander as well.

Alexander became considerably attached and devoted to me. My son constantly reiterated that I was a very special person. With an unshakeable conviction, he frequently claimed that I was the best mom in the world, even better than Jesus' mother, Mary. I recalled these outrageously bold claims from the past, but they didn't carry as much substance back then. This time around, Alexander's resounding assertions carried immense passion and motivation. Without fail, Alexandria and Allison loyally agreed with their brother's staunch position regarding my motherhood.

Strangely, each of the children spoke fondly of Mary and Jesus, as though they were present during the Savior's life on earth. It humored me to hear each of my children compare my maternal aptitude to

Mary's, with such great lucidity and certainty. But on another note, their incredibly courageous, outrageous declarations were an accolade to their intense love and respect for me. Their resolute testament stirred my spirit and was permanently branded in my heart.

The clairvoyant method of communication shared between Alexandria and I had drastically kicked up a notch and the frequency had also increased. After the rise of the "Revelation," my daughter and I communicated telepathically on a regular basis.

And Allison continued to receive and transmit thought provoking messages from our Father's heavenly kingdom.

One day, out of the blue, Allison decided to write me a very endearing letter that any mother would cherish forever. The substance of the note had to do with her unwavering love for me. It was a lovely, heartfelt message, but what stood out the most was her reference to God. In her letter Allison declared that I had a special gift from Jesus and God; there was something that God had placed in my heart that I wasn't yet aware of. Allison insisted that I had a very special spirit but she wasn't going to tell me exactly how special it was because I had to figure it out for myself.

In that very instant, I was incited by the Holy Spirit; I was awakened to the fact that God was speaking to me through my daughter, Allison. Confusion crept in; I was already well aware that He considered me special since He had hand-picked me to be one of His witnesses. I was destined to spend the rest of my life spreading the awe-inspiring testimony of Jesus Christ cloaked throughout the "Revelation." And, I would suffer the same fate as the faithful disciples who were slain for His name. What was I missing?

I was beyond baffled and couldn't understand what else there could be for me to decipher. God had clearly and strategically outlined the blueprints of my life. What else did the Almighty have in store for me? How could there be anything greater than serving as His devout and committed witness?

That very same night, God gave me a very unique and unforgettable dream, an animated, cartoon dream. The vitalizing dream was out of this world and completely bizarre. I didn't even know it was possible for a human to have a dream in a cartoon fashion but the Lord showed me otherwise. I believed that He constructed the dream in this peculiar style to add color and emphasis to its supreme significance. Perhaps it was customized to be incredibly distinctive and outrageous so that it would be memorialized in my mind forever. Needless to say, it was.

Cartoon or not, the dream was sufficiently extraordinary and momentous in its own right that I could not escape its penetrating influence.

The fairytale-like dream started with a grand commemoration of my son's birth; it was a festive and joyous occasion. My newborn son grew up to be a delightful child filled with unrestrained love and a prolific appreciation for life. The dynamic animation moved on to showcase and capture his life's major milestones, such as his birthdays, graduation ceremonies, entrance to college, etc. With each distinct event, time had passed and my son had aged appropriately; I witnessed him grow up and accompanied him through every one of his life's achievements. I loved my son dearly and was proud of his virtuous life and succession of accomplishments.

The enchanted dream ended with the biggest life event of them all. All of a sudden, my son was a grown man; he must have been in his early to mid-thirties. He had long, wavy brown hair and a matching full beard. A pristine and unadorned white robe lined with a simple gold sash delicately enveloped his body. At this allotted time, my modest son revealed to the world that He was Jesus! I wasn't shocked by my son's audacious news; as his mother I somehow knew that his announcement was imminent. I was overjoyed and thrilled that His time had finally come.

I sensed a fierce global excitement and vehement rejoicing. Though I could not actually see any of the festivities, I knew that epic celebrations were occurring all across the globe.

When I awoke from the collection of grandiose chronicles, I felt a sweeping sense of joy and peace. Throughout the day and in each of my routine activities and actions, I walked in His magnificent grandeur, as though He were there, in the flesh, walking beside me. A massive transformation stirred inside of me, but I couldn't pinpoint exactly what had happened to me. God had just given me the most colorful and sensational dream wherein I was the mother of Jesus! It was as heavenly and stimulating as my vision of Jesus walking gallantly with me in the rich, ornate heavenly gardens.

Even though the messaging seemed quite obvious, I didn't dare presume to know its connotation as I was a God-fearing woman. I didn't have the audacity to make such impudent assumptions!

I reflected on the euphoric dream and my thoughts were rapidly redirected to Allison's eye-opening letter. Were the two related? My racing heart began to thirst for answers and I desperately sought His wisdom. I asked God for forgiveness for some of the intrepid thoughts His dream had impressed upon me. I humbled myself before the Lord and respectfully confessed that I was in dire need of His divine counsel and clarity. We both knew that I couldn't figure out anything on my own; I needed His direction and leadership. God heard my solemn, unassuming supplications and He generously sprinkled His illumination upon my parched and thirsting soul.

Avidly, I surrendered myself to His cardinal word and instruction. But there was no way I could have braced myself for the astonishing array of communication that was soon to follow.

First and foremost, He urged me to read the twelfth chapter of the book of Revelation, the enigmatic story of the woman and the dragon. This woman was to have a male child who "will rule all the nations with an iron scepter" (Revelation 12:5, NIV). The Lord impressed this phrase upon me and then led me directly to another verse, "Coming out of his mouth is a sharp sword with which to strike down the nations. "He will rule them with an iron scepter." He treads the winepress of the fury of the wrath of God Almighty. On his robe and on his thigh he has this name written: KING OF KINGS AND LORD OF LORDS" (Revelation 19:15-16, NIV).

The Almighty God clarified that both of these biblical references were alluding to the same person, Jesus Christ. The Holy Spirit stated that, similar to Jesus' first arrival, for His prophesied second coming, He would be born again on earth. Jesus would live and dwell among us as a normal human being until the preordained, but undisclosed, time of the miraculous unveiling of His true identity. Then, at that glorious and supernatural moment, all of the world would gasp, in awe, in the presence of Jesus Christ!

We then took an intimate stroll to the treasured "Revelation;" the richly populated painting had become some sort of road map or guide for most of our conversations. Again, the Lord prompted me to one specific photograph, one out of hundreds. God opened my eyes to a beautiful baby with what resembled a crown, or multiple crowns, resting on the top of his head. The peaceful child was comfortably swaddled in a blanket and to his right was the warm face of a harmless, newborn lion. The baby and lion were positioned in the area just above my head and were the same bright white coloring as I was.

When I gazed at the serene and stunning imagery, my heart began to melt. David had previously noticed this baby in a few of the snapshots but I was never able to discern its incredibly delicate features. I simply put the obscure imagery aside and disregarded its significance. I realized then that I must have needed God to highlight the child for me at His designated time. David, alone, was unable to open my eyes to its paramount relevance.

Although my shaken spirit had already been cognizant of them, God then relayed the unforgettable words that I dared not speak.

He strategically channeled my thoughts to the unyielding disciples of Christ. As His unassailable followers, they zealously devoted their life's efforts to preaching the truth of salvation through Jesus Christ. God emphasized that the disciples willingly gave up their lives and died because they personally *knew* the Son of God. After His resurrection, they were so convicted and loyal to Jesus that they could not consciously live their lives without disseminating His message of truth. The Lord explained that David and I, His two witnesses, would also have a close and intimate relationship with Jesus, and we would personally *know* Jesus Christ. Just like the disciples, we would be so steadfast and dedicated to Him that we would incessantly and resolutely testify to the Name above all others.

David and I would love Jesus to the death because of the unique, intimate relationship we would have with Him. I would pledge my entire existence to Him because I was the woman foretold of in the twelfth book of Revelation; I was destined to give birth to Him! In the last days of the world and of our fleeting lives, David and I, as His faithful witnesses and parents, would be executed for our son and savior, the returned King, Jesus Christ!

The Holy Spirit overcame me in such a sensational manner that my body tingled, almost to the point of trembling. My mind, body and spirit were completely fascinated and transfixed by what the Lord had just divulged to me. I was rooted in God and His word and could not think with lucidity. My brain capacity was sluggish and may not have been fully functioning. I was stunned into a type of physiological paralysis. Though physically present in this world, I sensed that my spirit had departed from my body and entered another dimension. I was entirely enraptured by the Spirit of the Living God.

It took me several hours to fully absorb and process His intriguing and staggering correspondence. I didn't know how to respond to this prodigious and astronomical responsibility. I laid myself down before the Lord and could do no more than exalt Him and give Him thanks.

I meditated on the Holy Scriptures. Was the galactic truth behind Jesus' return one that John was forbidden to write of? I was directed to His enigmatic words and began to receive clarity from His throne. I pondered over one specific verse, 'The seventh angel sounded his trumpet, and there were loud voices in heaven, which said: "The kingdom of the world has become the kingdom of our Lord and of his Messiah, and he will reign for ever and ever" (Revelation 11:15, NIV). Some of His most clandestine mysteries were beginning to make sense as He steadily lifted layer after layer of protective cloaking from my blind, naive understanding.

I thought of Mary and, for the first time in my life, considered how she must have felt when she first heard the mind-blowing news that she would give birth to the Son of the Almighty God. I wondered if He gave her as many glaring signs and indications as He had given me. My brain activity slowly regained its capacity and replayed each of God's supernatural interventions and communications.

None of the paranormal events and manifestations seemed real but, mysteriously, the Lord's interventions were more tangible than the blood that pumped through my veins. His word was more palpable than the air that I took in.

But there was still more. One more vital piece of information was disclosed to me immediately after I came out of my initial state of shock.

God took me back to the pages of His Holy Bible and urged me to read more on the woman and the red dragon, "Then another sign appeared in heaven: an enormous red dragon with seven heads and ten horns and seven crowns on its heads. Its tail swept a third of the stars out of the sky and flung them to the earth. The dragon stood in front of the woman who was about to give birth, so that it might devour her child the moment he was born" (Revelation 12:3-4, NIV). He then informed me that the red dragon referenced in these verses was the Satan portrayed in the "Face of God" painting!

This Satan, this heinous red dragon, had been pursuing me my entire life and I finally understood the reason why. His malevolent motives were finally brought to the forefront. My chief adversary was a relentless monster that would always be there lurking in the dark shadows, anxiously waiting for me to give birth to his ultimate conqueror!

In that very moment, I knew that the terrifying, bone-chilling growls that I had heard many years before, as I stood alone in my living room, had come from this very red dragon!

How did I not make out this atrocious image before? God had already shown me Satan's beastly face right beside His in the "Face of God," but I just hadn't put two and two together. Satan's ghastly red face with one visible horn was obviously not that of a mortal man's; I had recognized that this was a spiritual or otherworldly depiction of the hideous monster. However, I didn't postulate that this could have been the depiction of the red dragon vividly described in the book of Revelation.

The telling tale behind the "Face of God" was suddenly becoming quite lucid. The red dragon and his two beasts were chief characters in the final and definitive battle against the undefeatable and triumphant Jesus, my future son!

I was completely beside myself and astounded by all of the groundbreaking information and evidence that God had generously fed me. Suddenly, the name of Jesus held a brand new meaning for me. I had always loved and revered Him but my love was beginning to morph into a maternal one as well. There were no words to describe the intense range of emotions that stirred up inside of me; I could hardly contain myself. I was saturated with love from Him and for Him.

How could I be so blessed? How could John, the divine, have prophesied of my destiny so long ago? How could I be the mother of the returned Jesus? And how on earth could I articulate everything I had just learned to David?

I decided to wait until David and I were together next before unleashing the torrent of astonishing news on his unknowing ears. When the time was right and in the exact sequence as God had revealed to me, I shared every detail with David. Much to my surprise, David remained incredibly grounded. He took in every word with great composure and an unexpected calmness. Without any ounce of doubt or reservation and at all costs, David vowed to do all that he could to protect me and our precious child.

Since the beginning of our union, David and I both carried an insatiable and inexplicable desire to have a child together and we somehow knew our child would be exceptionally special. But after the unveiling of the "Revelation," David felt that our child would surpass extraordinary. Though he had a budding suspicion, he was too frightened to acknowledge that he had also believed our child could be Jesus born again on earth! So, when I exposed our commendable and monumental fate, an ecstatic David welcomed this validation with elation and exhibited no signs of shock.

Several significant memories instantly entered David's train of thoughts. The first noteworthy event that came to his mind was the very day that God first showcased His celestial tapestry to us in David's humble abode. David and I were first introduced to Jesus and His testimony in the miraculous "Revelation" on May 10th. This memorable day was essentially the day of the painting's birth. In light of the astonishing news of our coming Son, it was interesting to note that several countries permanently celebrated Mother's Day on May 10th!

Very early on, when we decided to unmask the true nature of God's canvas to close friends and family, David shared a slideshow of the "Revelation" to a very dear friend of his. James, a well-respected, longstanding man of the church, immediately recognized the stunning transformation and the preeminent image of Jesus Christ. He acknowledged and appreciated that what we held in our possession was a marvelous manifestation from the Almighty. But, instead of concentrating on Jesus and the message recorded in His face, James was overcome by an inordinate sense of birth. His attention was drawn to the white passageway that God had later revealed to be His spiritual energy flowing towards me. But at that time, neither David nor I were aware of the stream's unimaginable significance. James repeatedly stressed that this incandescent channel was reminiscent of birth, but just whose birth remained a great mystery to us all. His spirit was discerning, even when David and I were still swimming in a vast ocean of oblivion.

David also recounted his entrancing venture in the English countryside. The Spirit that communicated with David had informed him that I was constantly pursued by evil because of what resided inside of me. Allison's letter stated that God and Jesus gave me a special gift and there was something that I had inside of me that I was not yet aware of. As outrageous and blasphemous as the words sounded, I carried the sacred seed of Jesus Christ inside of my very body!

This confounding awareness helped me rationalize why Satan and his obstinate army had been after me since my early childhood. At last, the truth about my life had been unveiled to me in its entirety. God helped my coming to grips with and processing of the spectacular news by shedding some illuminating light on the matter.

Early one evening as I sat quietly at the kitchen table, God drew my attention to the "Face of God." The daunting canvas happened to be visible from where I sat, so I simply lifted my up my head and looked in its direction. I was startled and nearly jumped straight out of my chair when I saw what God had just revealed to me; it was a carefully crafted realistic portrait of a man!

The flesh colored visage bordered the top of the canvas and nearly spanned the width of the entire painting; the true to life image was positioned just above God's sweltering green eyes. The man's eyes were closed and he was facing down; the newcomer appeared to have been sleeping or in a relaxed meditation. His facial structure was solid and very well defined; he exuded an aura of inherent authority and confidence. This eerie figure's features and profile were remarkably captured and demarcated. The only obscure area surrounded the man's mouth. I couldn't easily make out the shape of his lips because a hazy protrusion appeared to be bulging out of them.

I sensed an uncanny and intense familiarity, a strong feeling that I knew this complete stranger even though I had never seen him before. I felt an unusual intimacy with him and speculated whether this could be a prophetic view of my future son, but I knew it was not Jesus. Alexander didn't come to mind either. I sincerely considered the possibility that this could be another son.

I was astonished that I had never before noticed this haughty and overwhelming lifelike presence. His face seemed to project from the canvas in an almost three dimensional fashion; it was unsettling but not at all frightening. I stared at this fresh image for hours on end. I was astounded by the precision of his picturesque and mysterious appearance.

I examined the painting from every possible perspective but it seemed that the phantom only came to life from the left side view of the canvas, similar to the extraordinary imagery of the divine "Revelation." Remarkably, there was no hint or suggestion of a man's existence from any other slant or angle.

I opened up some of my "Face of God" photographs and carefully scrutinized them. Again, I perceived an exceptionally powerful acquaintance but I couldn't trace its origin. I studied the foreigner's mouth and noticed an abnormal and sinuous substance flowing from his lips; two black, bulbous eyes protruded from the secreting material. I detected a deep significance and pondered on this esoteric imagery overnight.

The next morning God enlightened me. Again, He took me to one particular bible verse, "Then I saw three unclean spirits like frogs coming from the dragon's mouth, from the beast's mouth, and from the mouth of the false prophet" (Revelation 16:13, NIV). I immediately went back to the photographs. It was evident that the murky discharge from the man's mouth did indeed resemble a frog or amphibian! The ghostly guest residing in this cryptic painting was none other than the coming antichrist!

How did I not connect all of the pieces together before? The other key players had already been introduced and made their ominous presence known in the spiritual canvas. The antichrist was the missing pawn of the battle of Armageddon. On that glorious, sunlit day, Satan's right-hand man had suddenly made his haunting debut.

How could the red dragon, two end time beasts and antichrist be suspended on my living room wall for years without ever having been seen? Amazingly, despite all of the dark and menacing characters, I was not troubled or distressed because my prevailing and triumphant Savior was also there, larger than life and at the center of it all!

The Holy Spirit cautioned me; He made it clear that He provided me with a precise depiction of the antichrist for my protection. God warned me that the devious antichrist would attempt to sway and deceive me but, regardless of the circumstances, I must never let down my guard. He stressed that the highly intelligent false prophet would be remarkably manipulative but I must not be influenced by his shrewd tactics. The Lord Almighty had just given me the upper hand; the antichrist's shrewd face was permanently seared in my mind. I would never forget it.

As additional facets of my unimaginable purpose were disclosed to me, it became apparent that both of His heavenly treasures, the staggering "Face of God" and the intoxicating "Revelation," were intricately tied to one another and went hand in hand. Our inventive and ingenious God utilized both of these spiritually infused paintings to emphasize the looming end times and the pivotal role I had to fulfill during this horrific period. The critical charge laid at my feet was beyond my imagination and wildest dreams.

David and I were destined to tread down a hazardous road crammed with roadblocks and obstructions, but God gave us a comprehensive roadmap to help guide us through the perilous voyage. He securely wrapped us with an indelibly sanctioned bond to help us endure and triumph. He blessed us with an inebriating and overflowing love so that we could liberally impart it upon our Son.

But above all, just as He superbly expressed in His celestial canvas, Jesus was there with us, carrying us confidently on our apocalyptic journey. Our Lord and Savior had actually been there all along. How could we ask for anything more?

CHAPTER TWENTY-ONE

Affirmation

David and I routinely discussed our arcane and imperial destiny but for obvious reasons we kept our dialogues and deliberations closely guarded. We knew what our future held but we didn't have the slightest idea how we would go about getting there. Needless to say, the two of us had a considerable number of unanswered questions.

Where would we live? How would we guard the sacred testimony of Jesus Christ, meticulously embedded throughout the "Revelation," while simultaneously sharing its blessings with the world? How would we successfully spread His message to every man, woman and child? But the most important and pressing question was related to the care and security of our Son; how on earth would David and I protect the returned King?

It didn't take us long to realize that we didn't have any answers. Despite the long list of uncertainties that confronted us, David and I thought it best to sit back, relax and let God take full control of the driver's seat. In His perfect time, He would get us to where we needed to be. His loving hand would be our unfailing guide.

We made every attempt to live our lives to the fullest and enjoy our scarce time together; we aspired to savor and appreciate each day and every moment we could afford in each other's company. David and I knew that at some obscure future date, with the birth of our Son, our lives would drastically transform and never again be the same.

David and I had to remain sound and stable which, at times, proved to be extremely difficult and exasperating. After all, the divine knowledge we were granted wasn't just handed down to our world every day. In fact, the last time the Lord had made such a firm and revolutionary declaration was more than 2000 years ago!

For our mental stability and so much more, David and I leaned on God's supernatural strength and resilience. Without Him and without each other, we both would have spiraled into and been trapped inside the unrelenting whirls of insanity!

During one of our arcane discussions, God gave David the hallowed name of our beloved son; He would be called Jeshua. I instantly thought of the name's history and relevance, of which David was ignorant to. Jeshua was the English name of the Hebrew name Yeshua or Jesus. The name Jeshua represented a savior or deliverer. David was delighted to hear of the name's rich and fitting origins. His declared name was impeccably suited for His second coming.

I could not have chosen a more appropriate name. But selecting His name was neither my choice nor prerogative. I had quickly come to the realization that all of the thousands of choices in my life were not actually mine to make. None of my decisions were in my hands; I was so naïve and foolish to think that they ever were. My wisdom and awareness had deepened considerably post "Revelation." I began acknowledging God's authority and influence over each and every move I made, regardless of how small. The silly adolescent notion of me being in control of my own life was a huge façade; recognizing it as such was a sweet release. Accepting and understanding God's total dominion and governance over my life made it incredibly easy for me to succumb to His every directive and command. I relinquished every aspect of my existence to Him and I absolutely loved it!

I found that after I willingly surrendered myself to Him, His holy presence became much more paramount and palpable.

God had revealed so much of the spiritual and prophetic domains to me, archived and cryptic information that could have easily terrified or plagued anyone for a lifetime. But the Lord's supreme love drove out any room for fear. Progressively, He built me up and prepared me for his highly classified assignment. Instead of conceding to worries or trepidations, my heart found peace and refuge in His warm, welcoming embrace. I bathed in His copious grace, mercy and love. The Lord was my sanctuary of protection. And though my mind was peacefully at rest, His generous Spirit continued to comfort and anoint me with even more reinforcing signs and assurances.

One night I woke to find a softly illuminated, ethereal hand hovering directly above me. I was positioned on my back, facing up, so the levitating object appeared in sight as soon as I opened my eyes. The elegant hand was no more than ten inches away from my face. It rotated back and forth systematically with an enchanting grace; it was soothing and relaxing. Besides its revolving motion, the lustrous hand remained steady, suspended in the exact same position above my head. The gentle, rhythmic movement was so lulling that I was reminded of a baby's pacifying crib mobile. The chivalrous curiosity radiated with a concentrated, hypnotic tranquility that sent me right back to my slumber.

I noticed that the conspicuous anomaly extended from a thin, glowing white arm that appeared to originate from inside of my body. At first sight, I searched for both of my hands and lifted them into the air to assure myself that the majestic hand was not my own. When I saw three hands in the air instead of two, it became rather obvious that the glowing hand did not belong to me. I wondered if the beautiful and refined hand was that of an angel's or if it belonged to Jesus Himself. Despite the rightful owner's anonymity, this phenomenon was an ameliorating and inspiring sign from His kingdom. The Lord's luminous love and refuge was with me at all times, guarding me even while I slept.

I was incredibly grateful to have so much of God's commanding presence in my life. He showed me priceless glimpses of Himself and showcased His profuse love in a multitude of imaginative and novel ways. He repeatedly emphasized how special and sheltered I was; the Lord reiterated this so much that my once dominant fears became extinct and forgotten. In light of His extraordinary and vital will for my life, it made perfect sense that the Lord and I shared such a divine and royal intimacy. After all, in caring for and safeguarding my holy child from the enemy's reach, I would need all the spiritual and physical defenses that He could provide. He assured me that our Son would be heavily guarded at all times.

The Almighty also reinforced Jeshua's well-being and safety in a vivid and realistic dream.

The scene opened inside of a small, secluded mountain cave. The world outside was dark and despondent. The skies seemed to be gray all throughout, as though the entire atmosphere could have been saturated with ash. Pandemonium and lawlessness were prevalent but I did not know the details or origins of the chaos. Savage and clamorous battles were fought on the horizon but I could not see the war.

A mighty angel of the Lord, with large expansive wings, sheltered my innocent baby in his muscular arms. The well-built angel spoke to me and said that he was sent from heaven to protect Jeshua; safeguarding my child was the angel's sole purpose on earth. He told me that I didn't need to worry about Jeshua because he would be with Him and shield Him every moment of His life; no harm would ever come to Him. The assuring angel urged me to continue fulfilling God's will, despite the portentous circumstances that surrounded me. With a resolute and brave confidence, I left Jeshua in the arms of His devout champion and exited the cavern. I had to carry on with my commission and conquer the impediments that came with my God-given purpose.

The next morning, I reflected on the perplexing dream. I recognized that this was a prophetic glimpse of my world to come; a clamorous time where everyone, including Jeshua, would be surrounded by a dark world of despair. Could this have been a preview of the tribulation period? Or was the gray and troubled world simply a metaphor for the obstacles that I would soon have to overcome and defeat?

Spreading the testimony of Jesus Christ through the "Revelation" and mothering Jeshua was going to be extremely challenging and arduous, but, despite it all, His will would be done. God was fueling and enabling me for the heavy journey that I would face as His witness. He gave me every assurance that He and His angelic armies would be right beside me and help me through it all.

Although the world recently revealed to me was grim and filled with adversity, the dream was quite uplifting and encouraging. It was heartening to see my beautiful Jeshua securely nestled in His guardian angel's capable and brawny arms. My love for my unborn child was evolving and substantially multiplying, as was my love for my heavenly Father. Without fail, I continuously felt His uninterrupted affections cascade down and submerge me.

The God of wonders continued to show me stunning hallmarks and a plethora of new symbols intricately embedded throughout the miraculous "Revelation." But unlike before, where every illustration pertained to the testimony of Christ, the new signs and manifestations began to point directly to me and my ordained mission.

Much to my surprise, He uncovered a clear and crisp image of a small scroll securely nestled on the top of my head. I was stunned by this insignia and its supreme biblical significance. The two witnesses, scrolls and alarming prophecies of the book of Revelation were all connected, in some way or another, to this fascinating new symbolism in the "Revelation."

I pointed the miniature scroll out to David and he, too, was captivated by its precise placement and the pious implication it held.

David eagerly skimmed through some other photographs in our collection and discovered something equally intriguing. He found that, in some select photographs of the breathtaking painting, the scroll had transformed and been replaced by a simple, unembellished chalice! The mesmerizing goblet was positioned on its side; upon close inspection, David and I noticed a dark substance gracefully pouring out and drizzling down the side of my head!

I brimmed with absolute amazement and disbelief! Was this a rendering of the cup of life, the consecrated and sought after chalice that Jesus drank from before His crucifixion? This was an intoxicating and potent illustration of His life-giving blood covering and protecting me!

Just minutes after the enormous shock of the chalice, the Holy Spirit unveiled another emblem directly linked to the end times. He highlighted the white horse of Revelation; the valiant horse that Jesus would victoriously ride on in the battle of Armageddon. The head of the white horse appeared just underneath my face; his body was nowhere to be seen.

I was astounded by the remarkable new images that irrefutably pointed to the return of Christ; the scroll and chalice on the top of my head and the white horse just underneath it! Amazingly, these compelling and significant depictions were there all along and could be seen in nearly all of the "Revelation" photographs. But, like many times before, God had closed my eyes to them. I was not allowed or privileged to see the staggering images until He was ready to present them to me.

The Lord God Almighty had just dispatched the biggest broadcast of my life; Jesus Christ was returning to earth as a human being and I was to be His mother! Maybe I was finally prepared to grasp and appreciate the prophetic metaphors that supported my calling as His mother and witness.

I adored the manner in which God communicated with me; I cherished His marvelous insight into my life and His unraveling of the mysteries of His sanctified "Revelation." I was certain that my ever mounting love and appreciation for Him physically reached the heights of His throne in the heavens. I was in love with Jeshua and the slightest thought of Him, at times, brought me to tears.

I especially treasured the unforgettable moment that God revealed Jeshua's childhood face to me.

Long bangs draped His forehead and nearly concealed one of His big, bold eyes. His chubby cheeks maintained their structure and definition. My handsome son smiled with His big, full lips as though He didn't have a single care in the world. Jeshua couldn't have been more than seven years old in the captivating picture God had painted of Him in the "Revelation." This childhood depiction of my Son appeared just underneath my image in the cosmic painting.

Like an overpowering and uncontrollable waterfall, a copious love gushed out of my heart and penetrated the entire room as I smiled back at my charming Son. I felt His stream of love for me emanate from the very core of the painting; the priceless scene was surreal and entirely magical.

I replayed the animated dream where Jeshua grew up and developed right before my eyes. In my dream, He was an amiable child, very similar to how He was sketched in God's celestial canvas.

I sighed with joy as I thanked God for this moving and unforgettable moment of togetherness with my Son. I cried tears of happiness as I held His dear image near my heart. I felt His imperial presence so forcefully and concretely. He was there with me; He had been since the beginning.

And then, the Omnipotent spoke to me again; there was something else I needed to see.

Just to Jeshua's right was another new arrival, another lion! The first lion shown to me in the "Revelation" was a newborn and it was situated just to the right of Jeshua's baby image, both just above my head. God had now introduced a young lion that was not fully grown, as evidenced by his lack of a mane. I wondered if this lion could have been the same age as Jeshua.

The Holy Spirit explained and clarified that Jesus was not only His sacrificial lamb but, for His victorious return, He was also the Lion of God. My future Son, Jeshua, was the mighty Lion of God! Though I had already embraced this truth, the reality of the situation was beginning to sink in and take root!

Similar to my dream, the two parallel images of Jeshua and the lion highlighted His growth and development. I sat in complete awe and marveled at His phenomenal masterpiece. There were no words to describe His magnificence, genius and supreme wisdom; every aspect of Him was infinite and entirely inconceivable!

How could so many individuals not believe in Him when there was so much evidence in support of Him? How could so many perish because of their lack of faith?

The God of wonders had shared so much of His Excellency with me and had transformed my life. I had lost all control of my tears; my deep and indescribable love for Him had taken over this once manageable physiological function. I was speechless and could do no more than humbly and affectionately worship and thank Him. With grave sincerity, I prayed that I would never fail Him or my Son.

Very soon after Jeshua greeted me from the metaphysical spectrums of the "Revelation," the Holy Spirit blindsided me with another stunning hallmark presentation.

I had just recently received a new, highly advanced digital camera for my birthday and was influenced to take additional photographs of the bewildering "Face of God." I felt that my existing collection was sufficient but, as I was compelled by the Holy Spirit, I obeyed without question.

I took about ten random snapshots and promptly uploaded the files to my laptop. As soon as I opened up the first photo, God directed me to the antichrist's forehead where I was shown lucid and legible writing! The thin, red font was crisp and the letters appeared to be etched or scratched onto the canvas with a nail or some type of sharp object, rather than painted on with a paintbrush. The inscription was discernable but only came into pristine focus at an increased magnification.

Initially, I had some difficulties identifying the exact letters but it soon struck me that the writing was actually upside down. I rotated the photograph and the letters "DAC" suddenly appeared. These three simple letters, inscribed by the very hand of God, were the antichrist's very own initials!

The fact that David's initials, DPC, were very similar to the new inscription caused me a brief stint of grief and concern. A slight jolt of paranoia infiltrated my thoughts. Was it possible that David could have had another name that I was not aware of? For one microsecond, I pondered the farfetched notion of David as the false prophet. But this fleeting theory was a fanciful and ludicrous one. The antichrist's portrait didn't bear any resemblance to David. I immediately cast out the senseless idea and called David to share the intriguing discovery with him.

We were equally amazed by this sensational finding! Not only did God provide us with the antichrist's mug shot, but He also offered up his initials as well! There was no room for error or judgment; God sealed it in airtight. Satan's very own agent would be incredibly adept with his trickery and deceit; masterfully, this sly fox would charm and coax millions of people into believing that he was God on earth. If David or I ever held any doubts regarding the antichrist's true identity, his initials would serve as the conclusive and irrefutable determining factor!

When my Father assured me that He would defend and shield me against all of Satan's forces, He very well meant it. I never doubted His words or promises. I especially understood the need for my impervious fortress of protection after my prodigious destiny had been revealed to me. But I never imagined that the Lord would equip me with such valuable and priceless tools and knowledge. I recognized that there were some people on earth that would kill to get their hands on information this sensitive and classified! The unveiling of the antichrist's initials was a supreme and unparalleled heavenly leverage handed down to me by the Almighty God.

The severity of the situation had just intensified. David and I were fully aware that we had to secure and safeguard both the "Revelation" and "Face of God" paintings; both of these telling masterpieces were constructed by the very breath of the Living God! Each of these miraculous jewels had unlocked previously forbidden secrets and fundamental keys to His coming kingdom and the end of the world we knew! We needed to preserve His prized works at all costs, but there were obvious challenges in our way. And then of course, there was the stark reality that I was still a married woman!

Stresses began to surface and pressures began to mount. David and I had to deal with a barrage of complications and impediments that seemed to attack our relationship from every direction; we were surprised to find that the biggest obstruction happened to be Satan himself!

Early on, when God acquainted David and me with the tribulation dimension of the "Revelation," He had also interpreted its parallel and very personal meaning for my life. I could never forget that the scene of the horrific beast devouring the human head was also representative of the devil conquering over me while consuming my good spirit.

David and I experienced the intense demonic clout and influence firsthand. We faced many episodes of distress, but always overcame these short periods of disorder. The enemy successfully inflicted havoc and turmoil on our already strained union but rather fortunately for us, these dilapidating uproars had been fleeting.

But then, something terribly odd happened; our customary minor upheavals began to morph into catastrophic turbulences. The true mutiny began only after David and I were blessed with the unprecedented news of Jeshua's coming birth.

CHAPTER TWENTY-TWO

Possession

Though I had been blessed beyond belief and the good Lord had bestowed me with many of His unfathomable celestial gifts, I couldn't help but operate and function as a modest human being with a simple, sometimes weak, mortal mind. Though my kindled spirit was strong and I often heard the voice of the eternal God, I still experienced crippling moments where I did not have the ammunition or wherewithal to ward off or combat the devil with my own defense mechanisms. There were times when I was completely subverted and incapacitated by dexterous forces far beyond my control.

On numerous occasions, in a continuous effort to support me in my colossal crusade, God had offered me many of His soothing assurances. He reinforced the existence of my impenetrable protective citadel, meticulously constructed and cemented with the Holy Spirit, Jesus, angels, my children and David. It was highly likely that there were other cohesive and defensive agents that I was not even aware of. Though there were many bolstering forces in my fortress, my extensive army of defense couldn't completely cloak and render me impervious to my enemy. The one thing that these advocates could not do was cautiously and consciously safeguard my susceptible mind; no one, except me, could accomplish this great feat. Sometimes I triumphed, but regrettably, there were many more times wherein which I conceded to the unqualified invasion of evil spirits.

At times, I found myself guilty of not placing enough diligence on my efforts to combat them. Unfortunately, my negligence led to periods of decline and disastrous breakdown. After all, they were always near and only needed a tiny crack or opening to worm their way in and raid my thoughts. And once the sneaky, little devils were in, they made themselves at home and extended their stay, as most unwelcome guests often did. Nothing short of an act of God could evict them.

Love was the key.

However, the biggest challenge was actually finding the right key; there was not one enchanted, universal key that we could grab onto and deploy. Oftentimes, in the midst of pronounced distress, David and I had to try out hundreds of unique keys and pray that one would work to our advantage!

I had always believed that spiritual possession, in both its good and evil forms, was a real life, tangible manifestation. I had experienced the positive power of this miraculous phenomenon firsthand when God's spirit gently took over my body and painted His majestic expressions of art through me. But appreciating the Holy Spirit's occupancy wasn't enough; I also needed the wisdom to detect the idiosyncrasies of demonic enslavement. God began to expand my mind and educate me on the enigmatic experience because it was critical that I understood the aberration for what it truly was.

In spite of my flourishing relationship with the Almighty God and regardless of how outrageous the concept was, I had to be able to diagnose when and how I was under satanic control. For the first time in my life, I recognized what it felt like to be possessed by the forces of darkness.

In the tribulation view of the "Revelation," this abominable spectacle was characterized by the bloodthirsty beast annihilating the white, virtuous spirit.

God explained that when the maniacal spirits invaded my mind, their mission was to draw all the purity and goodness out of my soul and render me helpless and comatose. When the dark angels succeeded, I was essentially reduced to a vulnerable and acquiescent puppet. Silenced, inaudible demons were finally emancipated and thrilled to unleash their foul profanity using my subjugated mouth and vocal cords. The degenerate and very determined wraiths infused me with unequivocal malice and even dictated my decision making with complete ease.

As a result, there was suffering. David was the bull's eye.

For one extended weekend, I was determined to break off my relationship with David. I had had enough of him. I couldn't stand to be near him or hear the foul, disgusting lies that constantly spewed from his filthy lips. I was convinced that my frazzled life would be much better without him in it; getting rid of David would be liberating and therapeutic. No more sneaking around, no more lies. For the children's sake, I would stay with Phillip; I was determined to make our desperate situation work.

Staunchly, I believed that a very vulnerable David was constantly influenced by the devil's temptations and therefore, not worthy enough to fulfill God's destiny. How could such a weak-willed person be fit for such a monumental task?

When I finally brought myself to speak to David, I doused him with floods of intense aggression and indignation. I spewed out vicious, depraved language that I had never previously spoken. I would have sunk with utter embarrassment if my children or parents had heard just a fraction of the vulgar words that escaped from my mouth with such ease and eloquence, without an ounce of hesitation or thought. I told David that I didn't love him, that I never loved him. I declared that the filthy, lying dog was no good for me.

Just before the barbarity began, David witnessed an obvious change in my physical appearance. My eyes rolled and my expression transformed from loving benevolence to unadulterated evil. Deep down,

David knew that I didn't mean any of the despicable and unforgivable statements and assertions that vigorously emerged from my mouth, like an unforeseen, uncontrollable cyclone. Still, my calculated and menacing prose was cruel and painfully blistering. And although he knew that we shared a mutual love and preordained mission, David was still terribly hurt and wounded. Any human being would be.

David was stretched to his absolute limit and was torn between an undying, God-given love and a merciless, tenacious enemy that took stabs at his bruised and battered heart time and time again. On several occasions, David naturally retaliated with his own brutality, but for the most part he labored painstakingly to bring back the love that seemed to have suddenly and mysteriously vanished into thin air. Our love was rare and true, but it was extremely difficult for David to believe in its vivacity and endurance when nothing but razor-sharp acrimony was reciprocated. Even still, my resilient David diligently and tirelessly fought the invisible enemy with all of the unorthodox tools that God had provided him with.

As we coasted through the good and the bad seasons, I could never quite comprehend why my sentiments for David would radically shift from one extreme to another. For the most part, the malady began with a simple, rather innocuous trigger. But this weekend's episode was dramatically different; I was fully aware that this heated dispute was unlike any other that David and I had previously weathered.

On the third day of this grueling, long-lasting ordeal, God revealed an unsettling image of Satan in the "Revelation." His atrocious and sinister face could only be seen when the "Revelation" was turned upside down. Two conjoined horns protruded from his forehead; they resembled a small mountain range, typical of that which would be illustrated on a geographical map. The already exposed evil spirits that were zooming in my direction were embedded in and extended directly out of Satan's massive and monstrous countenance.

I was appalled by Satan's menacing and threatening appearance but even more perturbed by his iniquitous gaze. The intimidating behemoth was staring at the opposite end of the canvas, his eyes poised directly at my glowing white image!

The Holy Spirit stressed that Satan was ruthless and would never cease his assiduous efforts to conquer and reign over my soul. Before this exhausting event, the devil had relied exclusively on his underlings. But his battle with me had just escalated. Satan had stepped up his prowess. He would no longer find disappointment in his unfit minions; he would do the job himself. The enemy's sole objective was to pulverize me and subsequently thwart my God-given destiny.

During my educational conversation with the Lord, I reached enlightenment and came to the sudden realization that I wasn't fighting with David; I was at war with Satan himself!

I took several long, deep breaths and reflected on how I felt when I was consumed by anger and animosity. Suddenly, everything became clear. Satan had taken possession of my body and mind; I was slavishly imprisoned, hopeless and powerless. The real Cassandra was deep inside, locked up and heavily chained. Amidst the prevailing, evil forces dominating and governing me, somewhere deep inside of me, my desperate and feeble soul was silently crying for reprieve. I felt as though I was buried far enough inside of the earth that, no matter how loud I yelled or how vigilantly I fought, the distant world above could never hear my remote cries. Despite my desperate struggles, I could never be found or saved.

Although incredibly sequestered, the repressed Cassandra still felt the love and compassion that the devil was determined to crush and exterminate. I strove to overcome and break free from my bondage but I, alone, was too weak. Kind or loving words of affection were not allowed to escape from my lips; Satan completely manipulated and controlled my mouth and each and every word that came out of it.

At various times throughout my periods of subservience, I was shocked to find a single tear casually strolling down my cheeks. This was probably the only way that my sadness and agony could physically escape from the prison that I was caged in. It took a spoonful of God's love to release me from the devil's strangling grip and ultimately liberate me. The Lord typically used David to unshackle me from my heavy-duty chains.

When I finally broke free from Satan's incapacitating custody, I found myself mentally drained and exhausted. Physically, however, I felt completely normal. But my just captive mind felt as though it had just gone through a thousand cycles of high-heat tumble drying. There was usually a brief period of adjustment and reflection in which I became fully cognizant of the demonic confines from which I had just been released.

David was fully cognizant of my seizure and was always delighted when I finally escaped from my imprisonment. He was consumed by an unconditional love and devotion to me and Jeshua. With each heinous act of duplicity, David's love endured, and quite possibly magnified, as he frantically sought to rescue me from my ferocious captor. He fought tenaciously and prayed faithfully for my prompt recovery and return. And when I finally came to and savored the fragrant pleasure of release, David compassionately forgave me for the tremendous misery and torment that had been inflicted on him. He was fully aware that there was a savage puppet master behind the scenes pulling all of the strings.

When I revealed the new, revolting image of Satan to David, he was naturally vexed by the enemy's abominable appearance. But, in light of our iconic purpose, everything made perfect sense. The severity and stark reality of the malicious forces David and I were battling against was staring us right in the face! Fortunately for the two of us, the Lord had made everything incredibly clear in His miraculous masterpiece. There were no limits to the depths of God's elaborate and highly informative "Revelation."

The entire span of humanity would be impacted by the birth of our Son. Ultimately, Jeshua would overthrow Satan and end his monstrous reign on earth. Satan was aware of his eventual and inevitable demise. The enemy would wage war and battle viciously to prevent Jeshua's birth, but David and I had to fight even harder against our adversary's extensive armory. At all costs and in spite of ourselves, we could never back down. If we failed, the consequences would be disastrous.

As I meditated on this new, dreadful illustration, God gave me a very lucid and simple communication. He plainly stated that, despite Satan's daunting and horrendous presence, I must never lose sight of the fact that, in the "Revelation" and in my life, Jesus stood between me and the repugnant monster. Jesus was my protective force field and no harm would ever come to me.

But my mortal mind was still vulnerable and lacked the bolstering support of a suitable buttress; this is where Satan would infiltrate and strike. I needed to guard my mind perpetually or Satan would manipulate my thoughts and cunningly attempt to influence me. He would use his boundless bag of decoys and tactics to help me lose sight of my divine destiny and ultimately renounce God's plan. The sinister serpent would use his pervasive powers of mind control to deter me from my grand purpose. No matter the cost, the enemy would never stop launching his debaucheries or trickeries.

But the Creator of all things, the Lord God Almighty, was considerably stronger and greater than a wishful, soon to be defeated Satan. I needed to be mindful of this fact each and every time I was under the enemy's attack. This missile of truth would serve as my defense, but it was entirely up to me to deploy the annihilating ammunition.

God showed me Satan's revolting face, not to frighten me, but to embolden and bolster my position me by emphasizing the enemy's destructive undertaking. The Lord knew that this very vital intelligence would help me pay close attention to the devil's devious and

Machiavellian strategies and schemes. God kindly gave me the upper hand against my insidious enemy.

The spiritual war between God and Satan was evident throughout every phase of my life, but to see it all clearly manifested in the "Revelation" was absolutely staggering. The veil had finally been lifted and the dense fog had been cleared away. My God and my refuge had been preparing me for my destiny all along. Day by day and night by night, my Savior had been equipping me with all of the tools necessary for me to stay the course until the glorious day Satan would beg shamelessly for my Son's mercy.

CHAPTER TWENTY-THREE

The Birth of the King

Christmas was always a meaningful and special occasion, but this particular holiday season was extra special. The birth of baby Jesus and His meek and humble walk on earth held so much more significance after the Lord showcased the sacred secrets buried inside of the gripping "Revelation" and essentially seized my world. The course of my very existence was drastically changed from the very moment I saw the breathtaking image of Jesus on that glorious May 10th. On that very special day, after His unforgettable unveiling, He exquisitely captured my soul and consumed my every waking thought.

Though one day I would have the incredible honor of delivering Him into this dark and dismal world, He was, and had always been, the primary and fundamental source of my being.

Early Christmas morning, I recalled the colorfully animated dream of His birth and the beautiful life we shared together. He was such a loving and caring Son. I reflected deeply on the adorable pictures of Jeshua that God had permanently embedded in the "Revelation" and seared in my soul. I often looked to His bright and cheerful face for solace and comfort and sometimes just for a simple hello. I knew that His conquering smile was discreetly placed in the canvas just for me. Jeshua's penetrating love pierced through the oil-coated layers of the supernatural painting, from His heavenly realm, and shot straight through to my heart with each and every glance.

There couldn't have been a lovelier way to start the Christmas celebrations than to meditate on my beloved Son, Jeshua.

Phillip's family came to our home for our traditional Christmas dinner; the entire family was curious to see the legendary painting, up close and personal, for the very first time. Up until then, they had only seen the video that David and I had published on the Internet. The skeptics had natural suspicions, but the spirits of the faithful devout had already been convicted of His divine gift.

I, of course, was eager to showcase the astonishing transformation to our excited audience. I especially longed to observe the reactions of the cynics and watch keenly as their jaws dropped in complete amazement and wonder. My part in the unveiling was relatively simple; all I had to do was uncover God's dazzling gem and He would take care of the rest. The Holy Spirit would speak to the hearts and spirits of all who were present. Everyone would see and feel the ubiquitous presence of our Lord and Savior and all doubts would be eradicated.

The biggest nonbeliever in Phillip's family was a distant cousin named Sebastian. Surprisingly, he was the most determined to see the abstract supposedly transform before his very eyes. Even though he had already sat through the Internet video of the miraculous transformation, Sebastian claimed that he had to personally witness the inexplicable event for himself in order to believe it. Sebastian's heart was hardened; what was left of his faith was hanging on by a withering thread. I sensed great evil in his spirit, but I carried on innocently, without offense.

Interestingly enough, before we set up the painting for its viewing, Sebastian couldn't stop mentioning the "Revelation." Contrary to his stated reservations and doubts, he was overtly fascinated by the paranormal canvas and couldn't contain his exuberant stimulation.

But Sebastian's concentrations and curiosities weren't limited to God's mysterious "Revelation;" he had taken an ardent interest in the artist as well. He questioned my painting methods and asked me to describe the sensations I felt while overtaken by the Holy Spirit. Leisurely, he roamed through my home and examined the unpretentious collection of art that adorned my walls. He speculated as to whether any of my other pieces housed similar clandestine and celestial imagery that could have still remained dormant and concealed. Sebastian's fully absorbed eyes were filled with inquisitiveness and esteem.

And then, out of the blue, as he redirected his focus on me, Sebastian casually asked me whether or not I could make my head spin around at the drop of a dime. I immediately thought of "The Exorcist" and understood the repugnant and offensive implication. My heart plummeted with agony and despair. How could a member of my husband's family make such a hideous assertion? How could anyone, for even one moment, believe that the dynamic and illuminating testimony of Jesus Christ could have come from anyone other than the throne of the Almighty God? The insolent thought sickened me and my stomach began to turn.

God urged me not give into the discouraging bullets just fired at me. He told me that He would take care of Sebastian and for me not to be bothered by his spiteful comment. His harsh words came from the mischievous and merciless devil residing in Sebastian's spirit, attempting to bring me down. I was commanded not to give him the satisfaction of victory. God would show Sebastian His radiant glory in the "Revelation;" this was all that mattered.

It took a tremendous amount of effort and restraint but I did as I was told; I managed to conceal all indications of sadness or anger. I simply replied, "If you are the only one that doesn't see Jesus Christ in the painting, then I am going to have to ask you to leave my house." I was half sincere and half joking, but everyone at the dinner table was amused by my apparent comeback. A humbled and embarrassed Sebastian also joined in the frivolous laughter.

It was finally time for the much anticipated debut.

The viewing of the sudden and authoritative appearance of Jesus Christ and the extraordinary accompanying imagery brought joyful tears to some and tremors to others. Those standing in the presence of God's spiritually infused painting could not question or doubt the stunning metamorphosis. The nonbelievers were instantly injected with firm faith and admiration. Jesus spoke to their hearts, just like He said He would. The exhibition was incredibly emotive and inspirational.

By the end of the evening, those who had previously scoffed at me and His "Revelation" were gravely concerned with its security and preservation. But their obvious concern and focus began to transition from God's work to God's chosen one. Their scrutinizing looks were probing for answers that even I could not answer. Their inquisitive antennae were raised. But their thirst for knowledge was laced with unease and fright. They wondered why God had chosen me as the vessel for delivering His alarming message for humanity.

Why, in our day and age, did the Eternal God send the world His timeless masterpiece and why did He use my paltry, unpretentious paintbrush? Why didn't He use Van Gogh, Da Vinci or another renowned artist? Even still, why didn't He summon a prominent or well respected member of the religious sector?

I was asked if I had other "special" gifts or abilities. I heard the dreadful echo of fear intensify in the line of questioning, so instead of responding, I cleverly changed the subject. I wanted to enjoy the rest of the joyous holiday and redirect my focus back to the Savior and His momentous birth. I couldn't allow this sacred occasion to suffer any further form of contamination.

I carried on with the evening as best as I could, but the truth was that I was still troubled by the cruel and insensitive comment made earlier in the day. But my great Comforter reached out to me and covered me with a warm, enduring consolation.

The Holy Spirit informed me that those lacking faith or who had strayed far from God would have noticeable reservations and anxieties surrounding the truth of His consecrated "Revelation." Those influenced or controlled by darkness would find any way possible not to believe in God's supernatural powers. The demonic spirits abiding inside the bodies of unbelievers would shriek and gasp at the sight of the celestial painting. Though they knew the truth, these scheming spirits did not want the world to witness or believe in His glorious and magnanimous gift. They would do their best to renounce God's testimony and the validity of the "Revelation."

I would be ridiculed and my name would be slandered, but I was not to be distracted or deterred. My directive was clear and precise. My instruction was to persevere and continue delivering the testimony of Jesus Christ; this was His command.

As I reflected on my divine mandate, God kindly reminded me of Moses and Noah. They were both scorned and mocked for their outrageous beliefs; they faced hundreds of instances of opposition and discouragement. Friends and family attempted to dissuade and hinder their plans, but they each stood their ground and diligently followed through with God's instruction. Despite the many taunts and regardless of how insurmountable their tasks seemed, Moses and Noah persevered and savored the sweetness of success. The Holy Spirit encouraged me; He assured me that I would follow in their fruitful footsteps.

I was lifted by His compassionate words of reinforcement. The Lord always knew when my spirit was lacking or in need; He never failed to resurrect me.

The next morning, my soul was completely resuscitated and invigorated by His overriding presence. I was so enthralled by the penetrating power of the "Revelation" that I felt as though I had never before witnessed or experienced its grand magnificence. Just a few moments after waking and taking in His splendor, I was stimulated to take new photographs of the oil painting, only this time my directive was to capture a distinctive angle that David and I had not yet thought to examine. I was so transfixed that I couldn't leave the painting's vicinity for one minute, not even to go and retrieve my digital camera from the neighboring bedroom. I simply took the photos with my nearby cell phone.

Immediately after the photo-shoot, I went to a secluded area to survey the new additions to our ever mounting anthology of "Revelation" photos. I loved the thought of the sovereign God revealing more of Himself in the "Revelation." Each and every unique image carried a tremendous wealth of importance and weight. Every square inch and every dimension of His miraculous painting was meticulously designed and handcrafted. Whenever the Lord shared a new glimpse with me, it was as though I had just been offered a rare and priceless treasure from His everlasting kingdom.

This new set of divine imagery was manifested in an unexplored and entirely new realm of His masterpiece. The original "Revelation" view had basically vanished and was nowhere to be seen. As I sat and browsed through the additional pictures, God revealed a breathtaking and arresting illustration to me.

The first thing that caught my attention was a new but familiar face. It was strikingly similar to God's face in the dense clouds of the "Revelation" but instead of the profile view, the Lord had just revealed a captivating frontal appearance. Just above His Majesty was a magnificent white steed. The horse's rather large, imperial head was both opaque and translucent. God's noble face looked as though it flowed directly out of the mouth of the horse. The two silhouettes cascaded beautifully and gracefully and were obviously spiritual in nature.

The softly glowing stallion was located in the exact area where I resided in the traditional "Revelation" view, but from this new perspective my image was completely nonexistent.

God had just offered us another preview of Himself in His wondrous and dreamlike painting! I didn't know the exact connotation, but I knew that the stirring scene tied to the formidable premonitions of the book of Revelation; the distinguished, lordly white steed was unmistakably indicative of the looming end times.

As I further analyzed the surrounding area, I noticed another faint image in the far right corner of the canvas, a lone white figure standing tall and stately. Not clearly discernible, the luminous man blended into his surroundings. Although I couldn't make him out with great precision, my spirit informed me that this man was the conquering and triumphant Jesus.

My attention was then drawn back to the grand white horse. There was another animal embedded in the horse's face but its muddled and interwoven features were also difficult to detect.

That evening, I shared the spellbinding imagery with David. We were fascinated by God's pristine appearance as well as by the significance of His lustrous and loyal companion. The magnificent scene exuded purity and piety. It was an immaculate illustration of His glistening righteousness.

As David and I marveled in God's grandeur, David began to color enhance the photograph in hopes that the imagery would become clearer. He attempted several renditions and then came to an abrupt stop. The majority of the canvas turned into a dense, solid black while only two brilliantly illuminated small areas remained visible. The two white zones happened to be in the same lower right corner of the painting where David and I had just beheld God's royal image and chivalrous steed.

What we witnessed next was nothing short of a beautiful and intoxicating miracle!

The nebulous human figure that I could not previously make out became crystal clear. An imperial Jesus stood there, in what appeared to be a luxurious, thick white robe. His left hand gripped a long sword that extended down the left side of His body. The King's dignified stature was one of accomplishment and absolute supremacy.

The only other region of the captivating canvas that wasn't blacked out was located just above the new portrayal of Jesus Christ. This incandescent area highlighted a full-grown, intrepid and fearless lion. Unlike the other two lions of the "Revelation," this valiant lion had a full, plush mane and his presence conveyed great nobility and authority.

God's elaborate and multifaceted sensation was entirely hypnotic and surreal; I couldn't believe my mortal eyes! A portrait of a strapping lion and Jesus, the sovereign Lion of God, arrayed in His irreproachable robe of righteousness, were gleaming with a commanding intensity, while the rest of the painting was coated with darkness and obscurity! This was an exquisite representation of the victorious defeat of Satan and subsequent reign of Christ!

Stunned and mesmerized by each new astonishing unveiling of the "Revelation's" cosmic and enlightening contents, I couldn't imagine that there could be any more hidden treasures than what He had already revealed. On the other hand, I couldn't imagine that His generous outpouring of knowledge and insight could ever come to an end.

The extensiveness of God's consecrated creation was beyond our jurisdiction and human comprehension. How many undiscovered dimensions could have possibly been embedded in His mind-blowing piece of art? How many prophetic signs and previews did God camouflage in His intricately woven "Revelation"? It was highly likely that the world would never fully grasp the breadth and scope of His astounding phenomenon, just as His infinite vastness could never be fathomed.

I was certain that Jeshua would play a pivotal role in unmasking even more of the "Revelation's" transcendent substance and life. Although God's resplendent masterpiece shone with His blazing essence, I believed that the supernatural painting would somehow awaken to soaring, new heights upon Jeshua's highly anticipated arrival. The birth of the King would mark the beginning of an electrifying new era.

CHAPTER TWENTY-FOUR

Signs of His Coming Birth

The tremendous value of the breathtaking "Revelation" had already become glaringly evident to David and me. The soul saving, life giving testimony of Jesus Christ, that spanned the New Testament of the Bible, was dispersed throughout the entire area of the heaven-sent masterpiece. God's master stroke of pure genius and innovation was sent down to humanity as a final call to salvation and eternal life. All of mankind would witness the indisputable story of our Lord and Savior, Jesus Christ, from His crucifixion to His final triumphant return, portrayed in an oil painting that even the most modern technological advances could not come close to replicating!

Naturally, from our lowly perspective, God's marvelous creation was incredibly complex and expansive. But could we expect anything less from the Creator of all things? The same consummate hands that fashioned the cosmos had designed a miraculous painting filled with many exclusive dimensions that beautifully brought to life illustrations of both past and future biblical events! The extraordinary images morphed into entirely new designs in the blink of an eye! Some segments of His elaborate testimony could only be observed from distinctive angles. And still, some of His depictions and imagery were fundamentally awakened only by enhancing the brightness or contrast of an individual photograph.

David and I were passionate about and cleaved to the wondrous work of art painted by the God of the universe. But why wouldn't we be? He shared His astonishing creation with the two of us, explained its significance and tasked us with disseminating His powerful message to the ends of the earth. David and I witnessed the "Revelation" unfold and handsomely mature since its celebrated birth on May 10th and, as we grew more attached to it, we also evolved spiritually. With His stunning treasure at our center, we shared a remarkably rare and indestructible connection with God and each other.

But where David and I were fortunate, others were not.

The sheer vastness and mysterious nature of the paranormal painting instilled great fear among those who witnessed the telling video. Some of the apprehensions were instilled by demonic forces but some angst also stemmed from natural human predispositions. A transforming, multidimensional, supernatural painting was unheard of! It couldn't possibly exist! People were not accustomed to a spiritual manifestation of this astronomical proportion, certainly not in our time.

The universal mentality of the day was that God was a remote and detached God. He had only sent miraculous signs of this caliber in the very distant past, but those glory days were far behind us. It seemed to me as though most of humanity didn't fully appreciate the intrinsic nature of God's character. The God of wonders written of in the Holy Bible hadn't mysteriously morphed or retreated, just because the weak and easily influenced world had. The great I AM is the same yesterday, today and forever; He is the Everlasting God.

Mankind was not cognizant of the fact that the end of the world was imminent and God's inconceivable and incredible painting was a monumental token of His undying and ageless love for us all. The "Revelation" was fundamentally the sacred testimony of Jesus Christ in a contemporary, attention-grabbing medium! Our Father had graciously given His children another mechanism by which to physically witness His brilliant light. His phenomenal manifestation provided the world with another avenue for the lost to find Christ and accept His priceless gift of eternal salvation.

If God's numinous "Revelation" happened to instill fear upon our civilization, then that very well may have been one of His intentions. Maybe Bibles were getting too dusty for His liking. Were preachers all too often straying from the truth of His testament? Was manmade doctrine polluting and obscuring the purity and sanctity of His precious word? Perhaps a different approach was in order. Maybe it was necessary for people to "see" the graphic blow of Christ's blood stained face, experience the ghostliness of the lifelike angels and demons, embrace the finality of the grisly blood-stained sickle of the Harvest and dread the judgment and vengeance of God's Lion to permanently grasp the truth and severity of His resounding message!

The underlying and undeniable fact was that every single aspect of the astounding "Revelation" pointed to the Truth; Jesus Christ was the center of it all. Regrettably, as unmistakable and transparent as His admonition was, many hopeless and defiant souls would not come to embrace God's readily accessible beacon. Many would still reject His promise and remain imprisoned in the deceptive masquerades of darkness and despair; some would be bound for all eternity.

I could certainly recognize and appreciate how a mortal mind could have difficulties processing the overwhelming and mystifying concept of the immense and inexhaustible "Revelation." Even David and I had to come to acceptance in our own time. But, as His appointed witnesses, we were blessed and fortunate enough to have our Father gently holding our hands, with His unfailing love and illuminating wisdom, while ushering us through His cosmic canvas.

Our job, first and foremost, was to listen attentively and learn from the All-Knowing God and then work compassionately to enlighten the misled and disillusioned world. As daunting as this seemingly impossible task sounded, the Holy Spirit would help guide us through every step of the way.

David and I were well aware of our divine initiative, but somehow my gifted and perceptive children seemed to have had an indication of it as well. I was not at all surprised.

The spirits of both Alexandria and Allison were well educated on the magnitude of God's prodigious "Revelation." They spoke repeatedly of its grave importance and the prominent impact it would have on the whole of humanity. Both of my daughters joyfully proclaimed that my main assignment was to spread the word of God using His mind-blowing masterpiece as my main tool. Confidently and enthusiastically, they announced that our family was commissioned to do God's will and lead His efforts; this was the reason He gave us the miraculous painting and all the others that He created through me. In Alexandria's own words, we were the "protectors of the earth."

Allison believed that God, Jesus and His angels were perfect and that I was in training. She assured me that in her heart I was already perfect. With unshakable resoluteness, she declared that I was the best woman in the world and that one day I would raise the best man in the world! I was beside myself; I knew that my daughter's discerning spirit was referring to my future Son, Jeshua!

A few weeks later, Allison made another intriguing and bold commentary. She casually mentioned that I, her very own mother, was foretold of in the pages of the Holy Bible but she failed to elaborate or explain what she meant by her statement. I didn't pry; I knew exactly what her purely spiritual and unconscious declaration referred to! I imagined how Allison would react to the truth behind her outrageous statement. How would she handle the unimaginable reality of my divine destiny? Unlike most, my beautiful angel would not be surprised, she would rejoice in euphoria.

Time flew by as God sent us sign after wondrous sign. Before we knew it, an ephemeral year of submersion into the intricate and multifaceted "Revelation" had passed and another Mother's Day was quickly upon us. This one was also exceptionally notable and unforgettable.

Historically, I had never celebrated Mother's Day on May 10th; my family always celebrated on whichever Sunday the holiday fell on in the United States. But, out of the blue and in honor of Mexican Mother's Day, Allison handcrafted a very special card for me. Inside her card, she drew a massive heart that enveloped a union of me, Jesus and an angel. In an instant, I was reminded of Jesus and my guardian angel in the "Revelation."

For our traditional Mother's Day celebration, Allison gave me another handmade sketch; this one was a drawing of an isolated mountainside with a secluded woman sitting on top of a remote tree branch; loneliness and disenchantment were written all over her face. There was a loaf of bread and a single glass of wine placed directly in front of the woman. God was in the clouds looking intently upon the woman. Allison explained that the woman was me and that God had given me the wine and bread, representative of the blood and life of Jesus, to alleviate my grief. The solemn communion between Christ and I would guarantee that the rest of my life in the mountains would be filled with joy and peace.

I was mesmerized by Allison's stunning illustration! Was God utilizing art to prophesy through my daughter in the same manner He did with me? Did my daughter carry this amazing, supernatural gift as well? Allison had neither prior knowledge nor indication of the life God had designed for me, nor any idea that the book of Revelation prophesied my escape to the wilderness after my Son's consecrated birth. The time had not yet come to share my divine mandate with my children or family. The Lord would instruct me when the time was right.

Each of the children presented me with unique and visionary Mother's Day depictions that coincided with my preordained role as

Jeshua's mother. Their elated spirits must have been overflowing with zealous anticipation, though their physical beings were not at all cognizant.

Alexandria drew an angel that was in flight to the earth after being gone for thousands of years. She explained that the angel was prompted to return to our world for one singular purpose, a very significant global event that would drastically change the course of human history. The celestial creature headed gracefully towards an area in the ground that seemed to sprout out a cross. A heart was embedded in the center of the cross.

Was this the mighty angel that God introduced me to in my dream? Could this have been the very same angel soon to be sent to my world with the one sole purpose of protecting Jeshua?

Both Allison and Alexandria had created compelling and, quite possibly, prophetic sketches. But it was Alexander's engrossing sketch that cemented all three of my children's illustrations together in a most gripping and unforgettable way!

Alexander's focal point was a colossal cross that was strikingly similar to Alexandria's; the holy structure was rooted in the terrain and also housed a heart in its center. To the left of the cross stood a modern looking, lofty building labelled "Children's Hospital." A formation that resembled an oversized crown was situated on the top of the building. The towering skyscraper had many stories and corresponding windows, but one stood out like a sore thumb. The window on the far left of the top floor had a small cross etched in it.

The sedate sky was devoid of all lifeforms and, with the exception of one single, cottony cloud, completely vacant. Securely nestled on top of the cloud was a festively adorned castle. Lively Christmas trees lavishly groomed both the inside and outside of the castle. Four amicable angels cascaded down from either the cloud or the surrounding heavens.

I was entirely immersed by the implication and undertone of Alexander's drawing; I almost fell out of my chair when I asked him to describe the content to me! Alexander announced that his mother's day card symbolized the birth of a very special child; the angels would be sent down from heaven to watch over him so that no harm would ever come to him. My son indicated that the Christmas trees represented Christ's birthday. Brazenly, Alexander proclaimed that this child's birth was equally tantamount to the birth of Jesus!

Alexander was not conscious of the fact the he was actually prophesying his very brother's birth! It was breathtaking and surreal to find that each of my children's personal creations pointed to the second coming of Christ; they, completely unaware, affirmed the glorious news that God had just recently shared with me! The Lord God was cleverly using my children to emphasize and substantiate His magnificent word!

I cherished each of these priceless interludes with my insightful children. Their sharp awareness never ceased to astound me! God fed their hungry spirits directly; He propelled their excitement with classified, insider information that their minds could not even begin to fathom! As time passed, my children began to intoxicate me with His splendor on a more frequent basis.

Jesus Christ was in my dreams, visions, and paintings. His spirit filled David and my children. Everywhere I turned, I was entirely surrounded by manifestations of His supreme existence and signs of His imminent return! His inebriating presence paralyzed me with complete rapture.

And then, when I least expected it, the Holy Spirit revealed yet another stunning image of Jesus in the "Revelation." The Jesus of my dreams was real and living inside the miraculously interlaced oils of His inscrutable canvas!

This new portrayal of our Savior was the Jesus of my dreams, literally. The moment I saw His face I felt as though I was looking at a carbon copy of the adult Jesus of my animated, cartoon dream, a near exact replication of my adult Son when He reached the predestined time of announcing His true identity to the world. A familiar long, wavy beard groomed His serene countenance.

But it wasn't just the meticulous detail and impeccable similarity that caught my attention; the location and position of Jesus' free-floating face was especially distinctive and significant. This miniature portrait of Jesus was so tiny and inconspicuous that it could never have been discovered without God's explicit guidance. His sensational face was horizontally set inside of the Holy Spirit's nose, just at the starting point of the channel that surged to me from my three critical spiritual sources. This precise area of the "Revelation" was where the majority of the energy flow was most abundant and pronounced.

But, to my surprise, there was another figure suspended just behind the new image of Christ. However, this character was rather inauspicious and not at all welcoming. Staring at the back side of Jesus' head was a threatening and gruesome demonic entity! This highly disturbing, meager devil was strategically placed just on the outskirts of Satan's pointed nose and also appeared to be just inside the perimeter of my spiritual tributary.

I pondered on the symbolism and location of the dynamic duo. Jesus had been strategically placed inside the Holy Spirit's nose while the nearby demon dwelled just outside of Satan's. It didn't make any sense to me but I knew their close proximity and positioning in the painting was extremely significant. God didn't provide me with the level of insight that I had been accustomed to receiving, but I felt that He was preparing me for something momentous. But what on earth could all of this mean? Regardless of the answer, the two new extraordinary images proved to be a powerfully thought provoking combination.

I recalled a scripture in the Bible where Jesus spoke to Satan and commanded the enemy to get behind Him. Did this newly revealed union of good and evil in the "Revelation" represent Satan's unyielding desire to overtake God? Was this tactically placed arrangement symbolic of the fact that Jesus would always be the victor while the devil would always lag behind in defeat?

My thoughts eventually trailed to my dreams and visions and ultimately led me to reflect on my ordained purpose. The white stream that spanned the scope of the "Revelation" represented God's righteousness and spirituality flowing towards me. This new rendering of Jesus marked the origination of the spiritual flow that God used to infuse me with His goodness. A large part of me felt that this illustration signified the raw spirit or seed of Jesus flowing into me just before His return to live among us. I believed that this could have been another splendid portrayal of His coming birth.

But why was the malicious and sneaky devil there as well? Why was he always lurking in the neighboring shadows? God had explained that Satan would never give up or grow weary; like a slithering snake, he would wait patiently with the hopes of one day devouring my prized and precious Son.

But it wasn't the enemy's relentless taunts that haunted me. God would always protect my Son. Despite Satan and his loyal army of wraiths obstinately fighting against our cause, I accepted the Lord's protection as an absolute certainty.

What did disturb me, on a rather massive scale, was the fact that the devious devil appeared to be inside of the passageway that was headed straight for me! My thoughts went awry and I had to compose myself. Could this explicit depiction also serve as a sign of the Antichrist's imminent arrival? Did this astonishing imagery represent his birth as well?

Only once before did I have epic deliberations similar to the ones I felt on this day. I fought to control and contain the dreaded influences that crept into my mind; I had to stop the ominous whispers in their tracks before they violently sprang to life. Nothing in me wanted to acknowledge the atrocities that pervaded my consciousness, but the wretched, unspeakable thoughts plagued me like an uncontrollable disease. Could it be possible? I vowed to silence my outrageous notions and never speak of them to anyone, ever. I had to expel these appalling thoughts; I convinced myself that I had to be wrong!

CHAPTER TWENTY-FIVE

The Love of Christ

Fascinating features and dazzling dimensions were scattered and buried all throughout the intricately designed "Revelation" but the color scheme remained fairly subtle and consistent. The dozens of richly colored oil paints that were used and evident in the original abstract painting magically disappeared with the transformation; the covert and submerged "Revelation" was left with red, blue and white as the predominant colors.

The crimson red incisions and lacerations that decorated the crucified face of Jesus and His red and blue tunic were essentially the only bold and dramatic colored areas in the "Revelation" view. The obvious center and focal point of the piece was Jesus; at first sight, any audience would naturally be directed and drawn to our Savior.

There were only two bright and concentrated, almost glowing, white regions of His canvas, the rolling clouds that concealed the Father and Son and the area surrounding me and the accompanying prophetic imagery of His second coming. The passageway or spiritual stream that was headed in my direction was also white, but of a much softer caliber. The flow was not as lustrous as the other white zones and it was lacking in intensity. All of the other astonishing images of His exemplary work were predominantly gray or black and white by design.

David and I were very aware of the significance of the red and blue. We researched the meaning of the divine colors and were not at all surprised that God chose these two abundantly symbolic hues to exemplify the deity and humanity of Christ. The suggestive shades were perfectly fitting and would engage both believers and nonbelievers alike. The color scheme was astoundingly appropriate and gripping, but David and I never imagined that there could be more to it.

We were wrong.

After some excruciatingly painful skirmishes and battles with the inexorable enemy, David and I were blessed to have been given a day of incredible closeness and uncomplicated love. We shared a bond of togetherness that we had desperately been yearning for and fighting to maintain. Our already fortified union with God had elevated and intensified. We saw our beautiful, golden future with Jeshua on the near horizon. David and I were floating motionlessly in God's boundless ocean of love.

Hand in hand, David and I quietly sat reflecting on our unbelievable journey inspired by God through His prized masterpiece. David had recently hung an attractive 8-piece collage of the abstract's incredible transformation into the distinguished "Revelation." As I stared intently upon the raw purity and righteousness of Jesus Christ, I suddenly recognized that the tunic He wore took on the shape of a human heart; the resemblance was uncanny!

David and I examined the collection and noticed that, as the slant of the canvas increased or decreased, the heart appeared to pump just as a human heart would. With a greater degree, the heart grew wider and fuller and similarly, at a very narrow angle the heart appeared to deflate.

We reached far back into our memory banks and recalled the heart's role in the oxygenation process of blood. We vaguely remembered that the blood flowing into the heart was lacking oxygen and was actually blue instead of red. On the contrary, the blood that exited the heart was red due to the infusion of oxygen. David and I were intrigued and we rushed to investigate. We found that the red and blue sections that shielded Jesus' chest were almost identical to the placement of the right and left ventricles of the human heart! Filled with enthrall, we sat silently as we allowed His piercing message to fully penetrate and absorb our spirits.

Was the tunic that draped the body of Jesus in the "Revelation" also a depiction of His sacred, human heart? Could God have sent this convincing and graphic imagery as a literal symbol of His infinite love for His children? Was this bare and exposed blue and red heart meant to show the world the untainted, sacrificing and life-giving love that willingly carried all of our shameful sins on the cross through Jesus' bare and exposed body?

God's immeasurable love for humanity was a constant theme throughout the Bible. The most evident demonstration of His undying love was evidenced by the Crucifixion of Jesus Christ. Jesus freely laid down His life so that we could all be given the opportunity to be lifted up with Him in eternal rapture. The Crucifixion was a physical demonstration of God's pure, unadulterated and selfless love.

Did the rare love that David and I shared spring to life from the graphic heart that lie at the core of His tantalizing and arresting canvas? Was this the everlasting heart that loved the world so much that it sent down the testimony of Jesus Christ in a miraculous and supernatural painting for the entire world to behold?

Once again, I reflected on the millions of lost and desolate souls that dwelled upon and scavenged the earth. How could so many bamboozled not believe in the gift of eternal life through Jesus Christ? How could so many subdued victims have fallen prey to the manipulative and conniving devil?

The answer was really quite simple; Satan was the mastermind behind the hundreds of false religions and gods. Darkness had permeated and prevailed for so long that most of the easily impressionable world grew passively and naively into the comfortable confines of blindness; they could not see Satan's self-seeking motives and deadly traps. The duplicitous dragon had ensnared millions of negligent souls and each day was an opportunity for him to welcome more victims into his wretched and noxious kingdom.

But God's magnificent "Revelation" would help reverse the flow of souls by shining the spotlight on the one Truth, the only Way. David and I would help propel His blazing glory to the ends of the earth. Every ounce of our relationship and existence would be entirely focused and committed to Jeshua and the promise of His word! As His devout witnesses, we would broadcast His phenomenal painting to the masses. Our stubborn conviction would caution the world of the looming tribulation and Satan's horrific and appalling reign. But above all, we would adamantly proclaim the hope of redemption and salvation through Christ, the one Light at the end of the blackest and deadliest tunnel known to man.

David and I had fought many arduous battles, but we knew that the most grueling still lay ahead. As my relationship with Phillip came to its predictive dissolution, David and I geared up and aggressively braced for the war ahead of us - the war of souls, the war against the red dragon, the war to protect our prized and precious Son.

But we were not foolish; we clearly recognized that we could never fully prepare ourselves for the magnitude of what was to come. We didn't have any ounce of special training. We didn't raise our hands and volunteer for this elite militia. But for some mysterious reason, David and I were personally appointed by the highest ranking Officer, the Eternal and Living God. And as long as we had Him in our corner, we would fight and we would fight to the death!

A short and fleeting week had gone by when God marveled us yet again with another brilliant facet of his unending glory. This time, this incredible element of His continuing announcement came to us from the "Face of God" painting.

By this time, David and I were well aware of the unquestionable correlation between the "Face of God" and the "Revelation." The astounding "Revelation" captured the essence of Jesus Christ in a spectacularly timeless fashion. In one phenomenal painting, God had provided us with privileged glimpses and extraordinary imagery of Christ's crucifixion to His victorious return and everything in between. It was as though God had given us a rare and priceless snapshot of the manner in which He saw things, a view where time did not exist; a concept so foreign and abstruse that human beings couldn't come close to comprehending it. In fact, it would be easier for most to simply reject the profound idea than to give it any serious consideration.

On the other hand, based on everything the Holy Spirit had shared with me, I was under the strong impression that the intimidating "Face of God" focused on one specific period of time, the story of Armageddon or the end of world prophecies of the book of Revelation. In a sense, the "Face of God" encapsulated one sliver of the all-inclusive "Revelation," but both paintings were equally fascinating and critical to His overall admonition.

Using both intriguing "Revelation" and "Face of God" specimens, God had meticulously concealed and magnanimously unveiled a wealth of treasure and the priceless keys to some of His expansive knowledge. The sensational texts of the ancient prophets were confirmed and the unspeakable truths of His prophecies were awakened and brought to life with the delicate touch of His mighty hand.

God had done an immaculate job of acquainting me with the vital role I would play during the end times. Through His decisive words and the penetrating imagery of His *magnum opus*, the Lord had boldly proclaimed His will for my life. But still, David and I were shocked by what came next. Similar to His rendering of me in the "Revelation," God had incorporated a beautiful illustration of me inside the "Face of God" canvas as well!

One tranquil, mellow afternoon, I sat nonchalantly on my living room couch as I spoke to David on the telephone. Our conversation was quite typical and revolved around God's will and His galvanizing "Revelation." David and I rarely spoke without mentioning His preeminent glory and greatness and His tremendous impact on our lives. As our discussion carried on, I stared unconsciously at the "Face of God" canvas, which happened to be hanging on the living room wall directly in front of where I sat.

As I gazed deep into God's grand work of art, the Holy Spirit drew my attention to a splendid and glorious representation of Jesus Christ. With a full grown beard, Jesus' mesmerizing features looked strikingly familiar; the adult Jeshua of my dreams immediately came to mind. His placid demeanor brimmed with unsurpassed compassion and benevolence.

The riveting portrait of Jesus Christ bordered the top right side of the canvas and was located just to the right of the Antichrist's lifelike profile. And in the exact same manner as the Antichrist, Jesus also faced down towards the center of the canvas. Though one was much smaller than the other, it looked as though both faces were conjoined at the neck and their composition disconcertingly resembled that of Siamese twins.

Unlike the haunting Antichrist, Jesus carried an incredibly calm demeanor that brought about an inexplicable, supernatural serenity; I felt His divine peace radiate from His soft but prominent features. His soothing aura drew me in and magnetized me. I could almost hear the hypnotic whisper of His sweet summons.

The breathtaking details and imagery seamlessly revealed the meek and humble nature of our Lord, Jesus Christ. I immediately grabbed my camera and rushed to capture the new astonishing depiction of my venerable Savior.

The awe-inspiring photographs rendered David speechless. He was astounded by the incredibly realistic depiction of Christ that could have easily been mistaken for a Da Vinci or Michelangelo original.

I was completely transfixed and absorbed by the sudden manifestation of Jesus that I didn't notice anything other than His gentle, captivating face. On the contrary, the natural explorer in David quickly came back to me with some riveting and personally stirring discoveries.

David studied the remarkable imagery and found that, in this newfound domain, what was once the delineation of the antichrist, now from an entirely different viewpoint, had miraculously revolutionized into the worthy robe of Jesus Christ.

The plush garment gracefully draped the full length of Jesus' body; even the frayed and patterned hem was evident from this perspective! Jesus appeared to be kneeling or bending down, as was evidenced by the prominent curves and shadows of His robe.

His Majesty's refined features exuded supreme dignity and grace. How did I not notice the inspiring illustration of our precious Lord before?

But, what stirred my already engrossed soul, even more than witnessing a magnificent, head-to-toe image of the Son of the Living God, was the fact that someone was sleeping peacefully in His lap. It was David who had discovered this familiar face as he surveyed the photograph and delineated the robe of Christ.

David was very accustomed to watching over me as I slept. My preferred method of sleeping was on my side with half of my face resting on the pillow as my hair splayed gently behind me.

With His neck slightly bent down, Jesus' warm and consoling gaze was focused directly on me! His righteous robe and arm extended downward and came to a stop just above my head. David had easily recognized my image because half of my face was positioned on Jesus' lap as my hair sprawled behind my head and onto His leg, similar to the manner in which I slept each night. The likeness was uncanny!

David and I even made out what appeared to be a small and slender hand just above me. I couldn't believe my eyes; my Deliverer's comforting and healing touch sheltered me while I rested securely upon

Him! His elegant hand reminded me of the night I woke up to the glowing, ethereal hand hovering over me as I slept serenely. Exhilaration pumped through my veins! I was mesmerized by this stunning and intoxicating representation!

As the world around me rang with an echoing emptiness and nearly vanished into oblivion, a mysterious and concentrated tranquility encapsulated me like a heavy layer of dense fog. For one fraction of a second, I felt as though I could have been in limbo between the physical and spiritual domains; I nearly lost all sense of conscious awareness. Similar to the intimate portrayal just presented to me, I was completely alone with Jesus and His absolute and incomparable love.

In that moment, nothing else mattered. Words were meaningless, as were my surroundings. Nothing in this world could describe the torrent of love I felt flowing down from His throne. Nothing could compare to the accompanying, unparalleled sentiments I delivered up to Him.

The "Face of God" had quickly emerged with increased significance and magnification! In one realm of His multifaceted work, David and I clearly witnessed the defined profile of the antichrist and from another plane we experienced the splendid glory of Jesus Christ, in all of His grandeur and sanctity.

In the very center of the two adversaries, I slept peacefully and unperturbed. Why was I in between these two arch enemies? I was physically linked to them both, but why? What did all of this mean? My avid mind raced with questions and thirsted for answers.

Fascinated by the newly exhumed territories of this perplexing painting, I could hardly contain my zeal. In the midst of the chaotic discord between God, Jesus, Satan, the two beasts and the antichrist, I lie in a seemingly unruffled, harmonious slumber with His Majesty standing watch over me. Jesus Christ shielded me from all of the mayhem and evil influences; I was completely safe in His loving arms.

The pacifying scene was divinely resplendent. Could anything compare to this illustrious picture? This was as close to heaven as I had ever been. This was as close to Jesus as I had ever felt. I was accustomed to our Savior's radiant love erupting through His "Revelation," but now I could markedly see its proliferation flourishing out of the "Face of God" piece as well.

I knew that, as Jeshua's mother, I was up against the leader of the most abhorrent and brutal army in all of history, but this beastly brute didn't seem to ruffle my feathers anymore. I was prepared to smile in the face of Satan himself because I was certain that the Lion of God would be there right beside me, smiling with me. Even the thought of Satan slaying and terminating my earthly life didn't disturb me. He knew, as well as I, that, despite his diligent and concerted efforts, he could never conquer over my soul or, more importantly, my Son. In the end, Jeshua would annihilate the vile and vicious red dragon as I would applaud boisterously from heaven's throne.

Until then, I would carry on fulfilling God's consecrated plan.

The fundamental truth of my life's purpose, including my ultimate demise, was engrained deep inside of me, down to the very core of my spirit. My divine mandate pumped through my body like the blood that circulated through my veins. I had no doubt in my mind that, after my death, from the heavens above, I would observe my Son, Jeshua, defeat Satan in the earth's concluding and apocalyptic battle. But I never fathomed that this imperial illustration could be concealed meticulously in the enchanted fabric of the supernatural "Face of God" canvas!

He stood there, in all of His majesty and noble stature, staring confidently into the eyes of His once favored and subsequently fallen angel. Satan was mounted on a horse and faced Jesus head on. Thankfully, due to his direction and positioning, only a glimpse of his horrific profile was visible. But even just the side view of his ghastly face was enough to send chills down anyone's spine.

The epic, final confrontation between God and Satan was scrupulously buried in God's innovative and prophetic painting, in an area so obscure that no man could have ever discovered its covert location without His explicit instruction! I was enthralled by the depths of His masterpiece, by the unfathomable depths of the great I AM! Boundless and infinite, His phenomenal paintings captured this stunning facet of His character in such a sensational and compelling way.

I gazed into the Lord's victorious eyes and could feel His triumph as though I was there with Him. And I was! In the space just above Jesus' head, I was there in the painting, like an angelic presence, hovering over Him. God had already confirmed that, by the time of the final face-off, that David and I would have already been slain. This newly revealed scene was a vivid depiction of my spiritual form applauding my Son, Jeshua, in His ultimate victory over the enemy and every heinous activity he stood for.

Even in death, I loyally stood by my Son's side! I loved Him before He was born, I would love Him throughout my physical life on earth and I would continue to love Him for all of eternity.

I was engrossed by this personally captivating illustration and all that it signified. For obvious reasons, it meant the world to me, but this concluding act also represented so much more for all of humanity.

For most people, a world without evil or sin was an inconceivable notion, yet, that is precisely what Jesus Christ had offered each of us when He freely gave His life on the cross. Eternal salvation and freedom from Satan's rule were His generous gifts to everyone who would believe in Him. I was fully overtaken by this incredibly moving and spellbinding scene in the "Face of God;" I was completely transfixed by it. Jesus had poured out His blood for the whole of humanity and made a vow to return for His final triumph. Our gracious Father had given us a prophetic glimpse of this very moment in time. He gave us an exclusive preview of the decisive, end-all battle that would end the world as we knew it and ultimately deliver the faithful followers of Christ from out of Satan's reach and into the hands of God.

But there was something else that caught my attention and triggered my senses. There was an object, or multiple objects, in the space just between me and Jesus; the item was clearly detached from both of us and floated just in front of us as though it could have been guiding us. Its origin and importance weren't clear, but the structure immediately reminded me of a menorah or candelabra. I pondered over the bewildering artifact for about a week or so until God revealed its acclaimed significance to me.

As I snuggled up for bed one evening, the Holy Spirit encouraged me to read the scriptures. The Holy Spirit led me to John's prophetic writings; it was in the pages of these sacred texts where I heard His voice. The Almighty poured out a drop of His wisdom and illuminated me.

He guided me to His sacred texts, "I turned around to see the voice that was speaking to me. And when I turned I saw seven golden lampstands, and among the lampstands was someone like a son of man, dressed in a robe reaching down to his feet and with a golden sash around his chest" (Revelation 1:12-13, NIV).

How could it be? The mysterious, suspended articles that surrounded Jesus as He prepared for battle in the "Face of God" were the seven golden candlesticks of John's predictive scripts!

I shared my moment of enlightenment with David so he, too, could revel in God's unending magnificence. Overcome by astonishment and curiosity, David examined the symbolic object and, upon close inspection, found that there were exactly seven thin candlesticks hovering near Christ!

The distinguished depiction was incredibly moving! Submerged deep in the confines of the interwoven, multilayered threads of His immaculate and incomparable creation, the King of Kings, in all of His brilliance, stood in the midst of the seven candlesticks referred to in the gripping and prophetic book of Revelation!

The consecrated pages of His Holy Bible had come to life in His marvelous, innovative works of art! He sent miraculous signs and overwhelming wonders to a delinquent and rebellious world! He sent

His designated prophets and witnesses to testify to the Name above all other names! Despite His many selfless, but often neglected, attempts, our God continued to cry out to deaf ears. And He did so all in the name of love, His extraordinary and unfathomable love. In all of His altruism and magnanimity, His heart's desire was simply to save His disobedient and lost children from the abysmal pits of a perpetual hell filled with unrivaled torment.

In the midst of the severe iniquities of His beloved creations, despite all of the corruption, sexual immoralities, murders, rapes, betrayals, adulteries, deceits, selfishness and greed, false religions and gods, the Lord God Almighty remained faithful and dedicated to His wayward children. Though none of us could honorably proclaim that we were deserving of His unwavering devotion, the Lord never turned His back on us. Even for a civilization of unworthy sinners, the unconditional love of Christ remained absolute and beyond measure.

He had worked so hard and given so much of Himself. But what more did He have to do? What would it take to open the eyes of the blind and liberate the chained and imprisoned?

CHAPTER TWENTY-SIX

His Heavenly Skies

They shelter us from the scorching sun and shower us benevolently with vital sustenance. They surround us day and night. Our world relies heavily on the clouds that cascade through our expansive atmosphere, but just like the indispensable oxygen that we breathe, their presence is often taken for granted and casually disregarded. We see them every day and don't bother to think twice about their existence and purpose. We know what science and research has established, but that is the limited extent of our knowledge.

And, for most of mankind, that is sufficient. But, in the context of His word, there is much more to consider regarding these mysterious heavenly accumulations. Could we ever understand or even come close to gauging the metaphysical significance of the pillow-like formations that waltz through the skies just above our earth?

My curious soul thirsted for a greater understanding, not of the scientific, but of the enigmatic spiritual dimension that was shrouded underneath the obvious surface.

Although I had read through the Bible many times, I had never stopped to consider what clouds could possibly signify from God's superior perspective. I never gave any serious deliberation to the clouds that permanently draped the sweeping firmament until the day my

233

burgeoning appetite was awakened by the vast and eye-opening "Revelation."

The astonishing portrayal of both Father and Son in the white clouds of the "Revelation" was the first insignia that stirred my interest in these naturally occurring phenomena. The dense, downy area of the canvas showcased the first portrait of the Living God, the Father, revealed to us in His treasured work. The Holy Spirit confirmed that this small and specific segment of His exhaustive painting represented both the Ascension of Christ, as well as His second coming. Father and Son were immaculately concealed, and subsequently revealed, in this white, cloud infused area of God's gripping production. This lovely, snow white illustration symbolized a pledge of renewed faith and future hope.

But not all stories told by the clouds above represented a declaration of assurance and purity. At times, the bitter heavens howled with violent flashes of darkness and despair.

Well after God had educated me on Satan's deceptive and persuasive tactics, I, regrettably, fell victim to the enemy's influences. I was determined to end my relationship with David; as far as I was concerned we were on the brink of extinction. My polluted, unwavering mind could only see the end in sight; the death of our union was inevitable.

Once again, my relentless nemesis had taken full control over my consciousness. Fortunately, David saw right through the enemy's malicious maneuvers. He was fully conscious that the duplicitous devil had monopolized and contaminated my thinking. But my devoted David held on to the irrevocable commitment he had made to God.

Despite the severe atrocities that David endured, he could not and would not let me go, not without a fight anyway. His firm dedication would not allow him to withdraw and abandon the call of the Almighty God and the promise of a future with Jeshua.

During our intense and pivotal upheaval, David and I pulled over into a random, neutral parking lot as our heated quarrelling exasperated. Immediately, we noticed some peculiar activities in the skies directly overhead. The already gray clouds boiled with a furious rage as they grew darker and denser with each passing second. Sudden and swift turbulent swirls and motions, never before witnessed, exploded through the atmosphere like a first-rate fireworks display. The merciless and unbridled storm looked as though it was a computer generated, high speed rendering of a hurricane. It was unlike anything either of us had seen or experienced.

David and I were both fully aware that God was an integral character in this ghostly, paranormal atmospheric occurrence.

David was under the strong impression that God was ready to strike us down dead for my lack of strength and abrupt insurgence. With a loving and desperate heart, he tried frantically to disengage me from Satan's destructive stronghold but he failed with each vain attempt. The enemy's grip was unrelenting and David just did not have the wherewithal to set me free. My mind was completely overtaken and David's broken spirit was deflated. He grew noticeably weaker by the moment. Filled with desolation and hopelessness, David planted his frail body under a light pole, in the midst of a calamitous lightning display, and was prepared to die by the sovereign hand of the Almighty God rather than give up and walk away from His divine mandate.

In that moment, it really didn't matter to me if David lived or died.

I hopped inside my car and was ready to leave David for good. But the very moment I sat down, just seconds before starting my ignition, the Lord spoke to me. Though I was held captive by Satan's suffocating stronghold, I heard the faint voice of the everlasting I AM commanding me to go to David.

I struggled to break free from my confines but I, too, had suffered tremendously from our continuous quarrelling. In a very feeble state, I gave every attempt to resist my adversary but my efforts were unsuccessful. I was caught between the nearly inaudible whisper of God's voice and the malicious, manipulative and deafening echoes of

Satan's abysmal penitentiary. But God had graciously extended His hand to me and I was determined to find the strength to take hold of it.

As I wrestled to escape from my spiritual prison I found that the harder I fought, the louder God's voice became. "Go to him" was all He said. The psychological tug-of-war seemed to last an eternity, but in reality the vacillating episode couldn't have been more than a couple of minutes. With each passing second the enemy's powers over me were compromised and I sensed his reign over me was gradually relaxing. Finally, the enemy's campaign was vanquished and silenced and the Lord's thunderous voice was the only one I could hear. It was then that I realized that Satan's stronghold had been completely shattered and he had been expelled from my spirit.

I jumped out of my car and raced to David. We cried uncontrollably as we held each other in a tight, passionate embrace. In that exact moment, a radiant light broke through the thick layers of darkness and shone down on us from the heavens. David and I peered into the sky and noticed that the furious thunderstorm had instantly dissipated. The obscure, unrestrained clouds instantly calmed down and became stationary; not an ounce of turmoil or uproar remained. The prompt transition was a persuasive and compelling act of God, as was the storm itself.

As David and I dueled on this earth, I sensed that there was grave conflict in the heavens. My convicted spirit recognized that the seething and rumbling of the fuming clouds was a physical demonstration of a spiritual battle directly linked to David and me. I felt that God's army of angels was at war with Satan's militia of demons. Satan's goal was to foil God's destiny and prevent Jeshua's birth by extinguishing my relationship with David. But God's resilient powers would not accept defeat.

David and I surveyed the skies as the storm subdued in what was literally the blink of an eye. Rays of beautifully beaming light immediately followed the austere darkness and it became quite clear that

God's kingdom was pleased. I could almost hear the joyful sound of His angelic troops rejoicing in sweet victory.

David and I were convinced that the rare and mystical thunderstorm was divinely inspired and somehow connected to our union and God-given mission as His two witnesses. We were thunderstruck by His theatrical, aerial exhibition and every other consecrated manifestation He had bestowed upon us.

This tumultuous display was an indirect communication from His throne and though it was not captured or recorded, David and I could never forget its dramatic impact on our lives. This was only one of our Father's spectacular, attention grabbing-mechanisms, but there were still many others to come.

David and I were thoroughly acquainted with the priceless imagery hidden deep inside the supernatural walls of the "Revelation" and "Face of God" masterpieces. We were never surprised by the ensuing morsels of God's privileged insight or the remarkable imagery He would later reveal to us. In fact, we almost came to expect that there would always be more of the Divine to come, revealed through the paintings He created. But David and I were stunned to find that the Almighty had left us with another very authentic and physical imprint from His friendly skies; only this colossal keepsake wasn't enshrined in one of my paintings. This time, our gracious God had employed another avenue of communication.

I was very much accustomed to receiving celestial messages from my daughter, Allison. God had used His obedient emissary in so many unique and marvelous ways. She had written many letters counseling me on God's purpose for my life. Allison inspired me with her advanced and cultivated wisdom. She delivered many of His wide-ranging communications, but there was only one that specifically mentioned clouds. Allison simply claimed that God continuously dwelt in the clouds but even though we could not see Him, He could always see us. I recognized that my daughter's message was a preparation of some sort, but I didn't know exactly what was in store.

I reflected on Allison's acute perceptiveness and the depth of her penetrating statement. I recalled how difficult it was to see God and Jesus in the white clouds of the "Revelation;" both were flawlessly concealed but were there all the while.

I turned to His word, the sanctified pages of the Holy Bible, for further understanding. Several well-known references stood out on my journey for knowledge. During His life on earth, God spoke to Jesus from the clouds. Jesus ascended to the clouds after His resurrection. During the magnificent time of the Rapture, the faithful would be caught up in the clouds to dwell with Jesus for all of eternity.

My spirit was cognizant of the fact that an incredibly powerful correlation existed between God and the soft, billowing masses that danced and churned through the heavens. Although I was highly intrigued by this unchartered, foreign territory, I didn't expect to gain any special insight or wisdom during the course of my mortal life. But I was wrong.

One ordinary day God brilliantly confirmed Allison's innocent assertion; He gave us a mind-boggling taste of enlightenment that completely satisfied my fervent interest. But unlike the ferocious storm He allowed us to witness, this glimpse into His empire happened to be very palpable and enduring, unlike anything David and I had ever laid our eyes on!

David and I were in the middle of a romantic, candlelit dinner in David's cozy dining room; one of the walls had just recently been decorated with a collection of my photography. Though David and I enjoyed each other's company and conversation I found my mind wandering in another direction. Instead of focusing on David or the delicious meal, my attention had taken a sharp turn to the montage on the wall. I was distracted by the forceful prods of the Holy Spirit; He urgently nudged me in delightfully surprising manner. My concentration was drawn to and became fixed on one particular photograph.

Had I gone mad?

At first sight, I began to question my own sanity. I had seen so many unfathomable images of the Holy Trinity in the immeasurable "Revelation" that, for one fleeting moment, I believed that my mind could have been playing tricks on me. I was overtaken and consumed by the jolting power of the photograph just a few feet away from the dinner table. I couldn't take my eyes off of it, but my muddled mind couldn't quite figure out why I was caught in such a heavy trance. Then, in one instant, God lifted the curtain and activated His illuminating spotlight.

As soon as I distinguished the sacred figures, I was completely blown away and wondered whether or not I was dreaming. Or even more likely, I seriously considered the notion that I could have been receiving a vision from God.

I felt as though I could have been staring into one of the buried realms of the "Revelation." Was this photograph real? Of course it was real, I had taken it! But I needed some type of validation or confirmation, so I immediately stood up and shared with David what God had just revealed to me. Every ounce of doubt and uncertainty was eradicated as David also stood in complete astonishment and shock. He confirmed that I was not having a vision. The photograph hanging in David's dining room was another superior gift from heaven; our Father had sent us another exclusive and concrete manifestation of Himself!

But that wasn't all. There wasn't just one stunning image embedded in the photo, there were three exceptionally clear and sensational facets of God effectively protruding from the soft, amber clouds.

The most prominent of the three images was a near exact replica of God's immaculate face, as pictured in the thick, white clouds of the "Revelation." But, instead of gracing us with His left profile, this print captured the right side of God's profile as He looked to His left. The Father's small lips were on the cusp of a baby's forehead. The realistic, three-dimensional baby looked up lovingly towards the Father. The striking details of his left eye were incredibly defined; the white of his eye, iris and eyelid were impeccably clear. Just to the left of the infant, directly underneath the face of the Almighty, was a head on view of a young lion. The gallant lion looked as though he was about to jump out of the photo and into our world. The baby and lion appeared to have been connected or flowing from one another, very similar to the baby and lion depiction in the "Revelation."

The three divine images were positioned in a triangular fashion and nearly took up the entire glowing sky. The Almighty God was at the apex.

Each icon was beautifully and unmistakably connected to the miraculous "Revelation." This was another remarkable representation of the coming birth of Jeshua, my precious Son! But this time, God was there with Him in the heavenly clouds, affectionately kissing His forehead. This was another masterfully illustrated linkage of Father and Son.

David and I sat in quiet admiration and reverence as we absorbed God's presence and poignant message. We thanked our Father for the extraordinary and breathtaking photograph. We felt His saturating love and longed for Jeshua more than ever before.

The stunning photograph was another astounding indicator that the Lord was always there with us. David and I were well aware of His omnipresence but these priceless, tangible gifts were prized and lasting reminders for the two of us to cling to for the rest of our lives.

It became increasingly evident that God's desire for our lives was to be continually consumed by Him and Jeshua with no breaks, distractions, or interruptions. The swerving and rough road to fulfilling His sovereign future seemed to straighten out and widen as we beheld more of His royal and prodigious realm. My spiritual and physical senses were amplified; my conviction intensified.

The Bible prophesied that Jesus would return in the clouds. And God had given us a beautiful representation of this divination in a tangible and timeless photograph that I had innocuously taken. Jeshua was well on His journey down to us; I looked into my Son's blameless eyes and could hear His innocent cries and coos echoing through the photo.

During the early days of enlightenment and knowledge transfer, well before the life-changing news of Jeshua, the communication that impressed upon me most was the epiphany of the clouds in relation to Christ. The Holy Spirit explained that the white, clouded area of the "Revelation" represented both the Ascension of Christ and His highly anticipated second coming. This was His binding oath to all of humanity; at the end of days He would return and put an end to all of the suffering and sin by slaying the nefarious red dragon once and for all. Jesus would return and offer His faithful children a beautiful new heaven and earth, the immeasurable gift of an eternal life in His golden utopia.

I spent numerous hours gazing into the cottony clouds of the fascinating "Revelation," immersing myself in the presence of both Father and Son. Their extraordinary images could only be seen when the "Revelation" was turned upside down.

But could there be even more to this arcane area? I suspected that there were other clandestine messages in this exclusive region but none had yet been revealed.

God's calculated and flawless timing was an established practice of His grand design. It was only after He exposed His resplendent and prophetic photograph to David and me that He unmasked the shining star of His "Revelation."

Just to the left of Jesus' wounded, crucified face, in the incandescent clouds of the "Revelation," was the unblemished and irreproachable baby Jeshua. At exact eye level, the adorable baby Jeshua and crucified Jesus looked intently at one another.

Jeshua's right eye was wide open and its features were markedly delineated. Full lips and a button nose decorated His pudgy cheeks. But what stood out most about my beloved Son were not His familiar tell-tale features but a figure that sat in the distant shadows of His forehead. A small, perfectly crafted white horse was positioned just above His left eyebrow. This eloquent representation was a foretelling of the victorious white horse written of in the book of Revelation!

Jesus and Jeshua were one and the same, separated only by time. This new unveiling in the painting was a phenomenal and awe-inspiring illustration of His first death and His second birth, the crimson, blood stained face of His selfless sacrifice and the white, untainted promise of His imminent return! God's innocent, slain lamb and His mighty lion were the central theme and focus of the testimony of Jesus Christ graphically portrayed in His captivating "Revelation."

I stepped back in absolute amazement and embraced the clarity of both images. How could I not have seen this crystal clear ensemble before? The answer was rather simple; I was not ready. His mind-boggling messages were only revealed at His perfect pace and time.

This illumination was drastically different than all of the others; something magical stirred inside of my fervent spirit. My hands shook and goose bumps danced happily over my skin. I felt the indestructible, everlasting power of the Alpha and Omega penetrating throughout my entire body. His time was near.

As His influence over my life grew, His compelling signs multiplied.

On my way home from work one random and nondescript evening, I noticed that the heavens were overflowing with the Lord's splendor and brilliance. I sensed that there might have been a heavenly gala or some sort of glorious celebration that the angels must have been hosting and partaking in. The sun's prominent, but mostly sheltered rays, elegantly whispered their way through some of the distinctive cloud formations while the unoccupied skies resembled a tranquilizing blue ocean. For the most part, the face of the sun was hidden, but its golden radiance and warmth shone spectacularly in the epicenter of the celestial symphony.

I was inspired to take a photograph, just one single snapshot, of God's arresting demonstration. I was compelled to capture the majesty of the moment.

A week had passed and the magnificent photo was forgotten, but not for long. After a Saturday morning of continuous praise and worship, the Holy Spirit came over me quite abruptly. Throughout all of the morning's activities, my heart and soul were in a spellbinding state of elevation; I was completely focused on God's greatness and grandeur. In all I did, I exalted the Name above all names and found myself entirely intoxicated by His pervasive presence. Suddenly and rather unexpectedly, in the middle of my ardent devotion, I was urged to open up the photograph of the impressive skies. I didn't know why and I didn't ask. The only thing I was certain of was that this distinctive snapshot had to do with God's glory.

When He instructed me to examine the photo, I was overcome with emphatic interest. I surged with the zealous exhilaration of an impatient child on Christmas morning. The Lord's extraordinary gifts and manifestations were always fascinating and never failed to stupefy and immobilize me.

I was immediately drawn to the gleaming, glowing center of the illustrious display; it was here that I encountered and said hello to my miraculous bundle of joy. Jeshua's bright and transcendent presence was encapsulated within the margins of the concentrated and luminous intensity of the fiery sun.

Penetrating sentiments of elation and profuse love instantly seized and conquered over me. From His royal throne in heaven, God had sent me yet another personal manifestation of my mesmerizing Son, the triumphant Lion of God!

As I reflected on Jeshua's striking features and peered into His welcoming eyes, the Holy Spirit directed me to the upper left quadrant of the photograph. As I surveyed the isolated dark mass, my jaw dropped, my body tingled and my eyes watered as sheer reverence drowned my reality. There, before my very eyes, meticulously concealed in the bulging clouds, was the staggering image of our Lord and Savior, Jesus Christ!

Unlike the image of Jeshua, the effigy of Jesus did not materialize in a typical cloud formation where the likeness of someone or something could be misinterpreted or made out to be multiple things. Jesus' stunning facial features were solid and concrete, as though His physical being was suspended in mid-air, surrounded by and held in place by a delicate bed of virtuous clouds.

High cheek bones sat just below His deep set eyes. Jesus' nose was long and thin, similar to His slender, slightly elongated face. His lips could not be made out but appeared to be concealed by a layer of dark facial hair. This spectacular and life-like depiction of our Lord in the clouds was almost identical to the miniature illustration of the Jesus that resided in the spiritual passageway of the "Revelation."

This sublime illustration was the single-most significant and promising beacon that God had sent down for His people. This was the sign foretold of by John the prophet in his prophetic writings, "Behold, He is coming with clouds, and every eye will see Him, even they who pierced Him. And all the tribes of the earth will mourn because of Him. Even so, Amen. "I am the Alpha and the Omega, the Beginning and the End," says the Lord, "who is and who was and who is to come, the Almighty" (Revelation 1:7-8, NKJV).

This precious photograph was the sign that pointed to Christ's second coming and He magnanimously placed it in my hands! This priceless gift was beyond compare. As His unimaginable blessings poured out of His kingdom, all I could do was worship and give Him thanks.

As His witness, my job was to spread His monumental treasure to all of mankind, despite the accompanying obstacles and tribulations.

Witnessing His glory, His powerful presence gazing down upon us from the clouds above, could bring many nonbelievers to rethink their faith and turn their lives over to Christ. My deepest desire was for all of the civilizations of the earth to behold and embrace the meek and humble face of Jesus Christ abiding in the soft, insulating clouds of His majestic heavens. I vowed to share this miraculous manifestation with the world. Its impact would be monumental.

The return of Christ was exquisitely recorded in the heavenly skies. This stunning sign was a clear indicator that the Almighty would be with us much sooner than I could have possibly anticipated.

David and I zealously awaited the groundbreaking and historic arrival that would send titanic tremors to the ends of the earth. The greatest story ever told was about to repeat itself. We were primed for Jeshua's homecoming, but the fallen world would never be prepared for the Lion's decisive judgment and wrath.

CHAPTER TWENTY-SEVEN

The Awakening

Our journey was a dynamic and radical one. Our distinguished mission was revolutionary and eternally binding. From the initial May 10th encounter with Jesus Christ, our lives were revitalized and changed forever. Our earthly trajectory had been interrupted, redirected, dramatically and permanently shifted and elevated. There was no turning back.

As individuals and as a cohesive unit, David and I had systematically morphed and transformed. We had seen rare and majestic dimensions of God that our mortal minds could have never possibly fathomed or dreamed of witnessing. With the gentle stroke of His omnipotent, all-encompassing hand, He resuscitated our hearts and resurrected our spirits to soaring heights beyond this world's reach. The great I AM kindly granted us the privileged wisdom of His great prophets and presented us with the keys and secrets to the last days of humanity. We humbled ourselves before the Lord and took in all that He offered us with utmost thanksgiving. We hungered for more of His glory each and every day, though we were fully aware that our thirsting souls could never be completely quenched.

The Alpha and Omega, the First and the Last, had opened up His wondrous heavens and, with His commanding voice, called out to David and me in the most calamitous and foreboding age in all of history. We were given an explicit and authoritative directive and His supreme will would be done, as it always had been. The unforeseen and mind-boggling journey God had bestowed upon us on was well beyond our imaginations, but the imperative voyage we would soon embark upon would be even more extraordinary.

Jeshua's arrival would not only change our lives, it would change the world as we knew it.

About three years after the face of the Lord Jesus and my precious, almost blinding, Jeshua miraculously materialized in His resplendent and mysterious firmament, I gave birth to the promised One. By then, Phillip and I had already completed the process of an amicable divorce and the children and I were comfortably adjusting to our new life and home with David.

The glorious heavens shone with a never-before seen vivaciousness and intense richness on the day I found out I was pregnant with Jeshua. Deep down in my soul, I had always believed that the Father would notify me of this divine conception with an unforgettable epiphany or realization and He did so in a most magnificent manner. But, even before His splendid, telling signs at daybreak, the out-of-the-ordinary wake-up call was God's first and foremost communication.

The instant my six o'clock alarm went off, I woke to find myself surrounded by His overwhelming and prodigious presence. The Lord sat quietly at my bedside, patiently waiting for me to open my sluggish eyes from a deep and peaceful slumber. Within a couple of seconds of waking, He immediately directed me to a photo of His preeminent "Revelation."

Although filled with exhilaration and eager to behold His early morning surprise, my physical body and brain functions were still half asleep and operating in a semi-state of hazy confusion. My listless and languid eyes struggled to focus as they were urgently thrust into the brink of consciousness at the sound of His unassailable voice.

The moment I beheld the remarkable image that the Holy Spirit kindly led me to, my heart nearly melted. My darling baby Jeshua had just come to light.

His big, bold eyes and contagious smile shone just as brilliantly as His illuminated surroundings. His soft, squeezable cheeks and perfectly round head appeared to have been sheltered or covered; my Son looked as though He was comfortably snuggled inside His favorite warm and cozy blanket. A beaming and exuberant, lifelike depiction of Jeshua seemed to have popped up out of one of His secret hiding spots, as though He was in the middle of a friendly game of peek-a-boo.

In the early days of exploring the mysteries of our Lord's transcendent painting, God had communicated that the spiritual tributary spanning across the width of the canvas was essentially a symbolic stream that fueled me with God's goodness and righteousness. And, even before this inspiring announcement, the Holy Spirit had informed David that one of his critical tasks was to ensure that I had more of God's spirit in me; this was imperative for the success of our mission.

It was this same glowing, white flow in the "Revelation" that mysteriously gave David's friend, James, an intense and consuming sense of birth, even before David and I were given any indication of the joyous news that we would one day be blessed with an incredibly special child. Sometime later, when David and I were finally ready to receive the astounding news, my loving Father had announced that this distinctive and unique stream of righteousness represented the second coming of Christ via my Son, whom He named Jeshua.

And on that very special morning, that's exactly where He came out from hiding. Jeshua was perfectly concealed and securely nestled in the very center of the spiritual canal all along! But in all of God's grandeur and impeccable timing, He waited to reveal His Son to me until that very remarkable, treasured morning!

But the Lord didn't stop there.

The specific photograph the Lord guided me to was a color enhanced one; the stream, traditionally white, had been transformed to mixed shades of radiant and rich oranges and reds. The vibrant colors surrounding Jeshua were stuck in my mind as I prepared for the day ahead. When I stepped out of my house to take the children to school, I noticed something dramatically different in the atmospheric lighting. The colors from the photograph had made their way up to the heavens!

Each of my curious children gazed into the phenomenal morning sky and was immediately intoxicated by its captivating brilliance. They had never before seen a spectacular demonstration like the display broadcast directly above us. And up until about an hour prior, neither had I. The mesmerizing sky shone with the exact same orange and red intensities as those that meticulously cloaked baby Jeshua in the blazing "Revelation."

The awe-struck children shouted loudly with a fervent joy and hope. Filled with jubilation, they exclaimed that the hypnotic, celestial tapestry was directly tied to God's work and His imminent return to earth!

The marvelous wonders of that morning didn't end there. David had just arrived in town after being away on business. He had a compelling notion to surprise me on my way to the office with an invigorating cappuccino; he timed his visit perfectly and met me just after I dropped the kids off at school. Because of this unplanned rendezvous, David was also fortunate enough to have witnessed the glorious morning that God had decorated for us. David was also blown away by the rare and spectacular colors that paraded through the glowing heavens above. On the journey to meet me, he even stopped to take photographs of the spectacular exhibition, as did many other entranced parties. When I shared the new imagery of our Son Jeshua with David, he immediately understood why the sky exuded such liveliness and magnetizing fluorescence.

When David and I first heard the incredible news of the pregnancy, we rejoiced with thanksgiving and praise. We exalted God and made a promise to cherish and protect His beloved Son. David and I had relinquished our distant, former lives and faithfully dedicated our future to spreading the glorious news of the Lord's testimony to the ends of the earth.

But our zeal and excitement didn't end there and neither did the Lord's surprises. When we had our first ultrasound, David and I were shocked to see that there was another child sharing Jeshua's sacred womb. We later found that our treasured Son was going to have a twin sister!

How could this be? I wondered why we weren't given any indication of this confounding news beforehand. I thought of my grandmother. Was this the set of twins that she prophesied of before she passed away? I struggled with the startling announcement but quickly came to an acceptance.

David and I expressed identical conflicting sentiments; though we were both filled with elation our joy was lined with apprehension. We were naturally delighted that God had blessed us with another child but concerned about the amount of affection we would offer her. We recognized how special and prized Jeshua was; His care and protection was a critical component of God's grand assignment. The love David and I felt for Jeshua poured out from the very moment God revealed Him to us, before He was even conceived.

David and I vowed that, despite our advantageous knowledge and divine calling, we would do everything in our power to love and care for Jeshua and His sister equally. We would show no form of favoritism or bias. If the good Lord blessed us with another child, then she too would serve as an essential character in His intricate and immaculate design and blueprint. David and I would be the loving parents and devoted witnesses that God had appointed us to be.

Throughout the pregnancy, David and I were consumed with a dominant and controlling love for God and Jeshua that was desperate to be demonstrated by a life of commitment to His superior plan. Our humble lives, already changed, would undergo even more radical transformation. Our world, as well as Satan's wicked and corrupt domain, would be shaken; the reverberations would be eternal.

The joyous day had finally arrived. Jeshua was the first to greet us.

I cried softly as I gently kissed the smooth area of His forehead where His noble white horse had been mounted in the "Revelation." I passionately embraced the identical, living manifestation of the sanctified child that God had repeatedly shown me in my dreams and throughout each of His supernatural paintings and photographs.

This was the single most transformational and meaningful experience of our lives. David and I struggled to contain the extreme emotions and shock that accompanied this celebrated and miraculous event. After years of anticipation and longing, Jeshua, the Lion of God, had graced us with His hallowed presence.

As David and I attempted to regain our composure, the doctors hit us with an unexpected surprise; Jeshua's sister turned out to be His twin brother!

The shocking news rendered David and I completely speechless. We were expecting a girl and had spent months deciding on a beautiful name for our new daughter. We hadn't discussed or even contemplated another boy's name. Nonetheless, we were thrilled with the news; David had always longed for a son and God had now blessed him with two!

David and I briefly discussed the dilemma but we were short on time and our pensive minds were consumed with Jeshua's homecoming. The choice was relatively simple. We chose to name our second son after his father; we named him David Aaron Connor.

ABOUT THE AUTHOR

Cassandra Bohne is a freelance writer and poet and a member of the Author's Guild. She lives in the greater Houston metropolitan area where she has been cultivating her artistic creativity through divinely inspired oil paintings for nearly twenty years. To witness the remarkable transformation of the "Revelation" go to
https://www.youtube.com/watch?v=vWPjUjuScJw
(Testimony of Jesus unveiled in Miraculous Painting).

CPSIA information can be obtained
at www.ICGtesting.com
Printed in the USA
LVOW11s1638190117
521537LV00002B/393/P

9 780998 314006